Sarah

by TIMOTHY MCDONALD

ISBN 978-1-66780-959-5 (Print)

ISBN 978-1-66780-960-1 (eBook)

Introduction

"Sarah," like "Rebecca," is a novel haunted by a former wife. In Daphne du Maurier's novel, Rebecca casts a long dark shadow from the grave over Maxim de Winter's marriage to the unremarkable, unnamed, young woman he hopes will obliterate the specter of his late wife. There is more to Rebecca's haunting than her passing; it is the memory of her twisted, rapacious, carnal life that plagues de Winter. His new bride not so much reminds de Winter of the beautiful Rebecca, as she constitutes her complete opposite: quiet, unassuming, and lacking in confidence.

In Tim McDonald's quietly, moving, celebratory novel, widowed Henry Morrison is attracted to Sarah from a distance, not because she is the moral and physical opposite of his late wife Molly, but because she so strikingly resembles her. Henry has conceded to his lonely state of being, assuming, in his 60s, that he has had the love of his life and that all he will have to sustain him from now on are his memories. But the woman he meets, begins to know, and fall in love with, who so strongly evokes the charm, tenacity, and dignity of his late wife, are tenderly explored in the novel. Through his intense relationship with Sarah, which inspires revered memories of Molly, she assumes a stature and importance of her own.

She stirs Henry's heart, and their romance blossoms. What results is not gothic melodrama, which has its place if torment is the object, but a leisurely, patient, very human chronicle of how the human heart responds to grace and the offering of tenderness and communion. This is a lovely, quiet, calmly paced book as soothing, uplifting, and sustained in reverence as the experience of falling in love and continuing in love should be. It is haunting, yes, but in the best, never the meanest, of ways.

This book is dedicated to the real Sarah in my life.
The love of my life. Without whose love and support
this book would not have been completed.

"I swear I couldn't love you anymore than I do right now,
and yet I know I will tomorrow"

LEO CHRISTOPHER

Chapter 1

Help!

There we were: me, Jesse, and Brandon. The three of us were partners in a technology startup company. We were working over dinner and drinks at our favorite haunt, Drake's Pub. The place was busy for a Sunday evening.

We were seated at the front of the pub, near the busy street entrance. It was particularly warm for early March, so the huge front windows were open to the sidewalk and the street. On the downside, there was the noise from the road, but the upside there was a nice breeze. Between the alcohol, the breeze, and the food, it made for a nice working environment.

The three of us were preparing for a lunch meeting the next day with a valuable potential client. This deal was so important, it could literally launch our new company. If successful, it could make us a $60M company inside of two years. Jesse and I would handle the meeting, but we needed Brandon (our chief technology officer) to walk us through the more technical points to make.

It was also an evening of frustration and real lamentation. The previous Friday, we learned we were being sued for violating a non-compete clause in our employment contracts by our former employer, John. The three of us had been recruited by John to work for his tech startup last year. Jesse had brought logistics experience from his time in the Marine Corps., and Brandon, a theoretical mathematician, was the programmer. All these guys were 29 years old. I (Dr. Henry Morrison) was the "old man" of the group at 63. I had international sales, marketing, and licensing experience in the information industry. Essentially, the token mature person of experience. Because of my doctorate, I had also taken on the moniker of Doc, which my high school students had given to me.

Jesse had been sitting across from me and Brandon was sitting to my right. When seated, I had to be conscious of the seating arrangements to hear everyone. Two years ago, I had a tumor removed from my brain and the surgery left me permanently deaf in my left ear. So, in business and social settings, I had to arrange myself so that people were in front of me or to my right side.

We had been talking about the legal action from John, when Jesse leaned back in startled, covering his face with his hands. "Wait a minute, that girl looks like. No, it can't be. At the next table. But she's...... dead!" At the table next to us was a group of four young women. I hadn't really noticed them until Jesse leaned back for a second or two, then I saw her.

She wasn't looking at me and hadn't noticed me. For those brief seconds, I believed I'd seen an apparition, a ghost, a spirit from my past. Her look was so stunning it quite literally took my breath away. I hadn't seen that face and smile in nearly forty years. It was the face of my late wife Molly.

I tried to stay engaged in the conversation, but at best I was only halfway there. Memories were lighting up my brain like an electrical storm. Mostly good memories: our wedding day, flying kites together, long quiet walks, finding out we were pregnant, and the one horrible memory, her death. The whole flashback couldn't have lasted more than five seconds, but it must have been longer, as I saw Jesse staring at me as if I had just woken from a coma.

Chapter 2

Yesterday

read in a book once that "Like a good song, life has verses. Each verse has to be sung. It takes all of them to make a song." When you think about the song, it is always a favorite verse that makes you smile. For me, Molly will always be that verse. I can't help but smile when I hear someone say that name.

Molly and I met thirty years ago in Chicago. I had been transferred there from my company's New York office to take over the position as Regional Sales Manager for the 15 state Midwest territory. The company that I worked for was a pre-internet information-based company. Our clientele were librarians or information center managers, among other heavy duty consulting firms and Fortune 500 companies.

As my company centered around librarians, I was asked to be an adjunct professor at Dominican University in a suburb of Chicago. I was teaching a summer elective course in online information retrieval. That sounds antiquated in today's information world, but in the 1980s and 1990s, it was still a skill mainly reserved for librarians. Molly was taking the course along with about 17 other individuals working on their master's degree in library science.

It's funny now, but on the first day I called the roll, I got to her name, and looked up to find her voice. When I found her at the back of the classroom, I saw this stunning woman with shoulder-length, strawberry blonde hair, and the most dazzling green eyes. The other students had to notice that I stuttered a bit and looked as if I had the breath taken away from me for a moment. Molly later told me that she thinks she might have been attracted to me that first day, but the love part took a bit longer for her.

Since the course was in the evening three nights a week, I was taking the train out to the campus from work. I didn't really look the part of an unkempt college professor. I was 6'1 tall, a head of brown hair, which I lost many years ago now, blue eyes and I was always dressed in a suit and tie. She told me that she liked my professional look. It spoke success to her.

Molly Kniss had been a French teacher at an all-girl Catholic high school in Chicago and lived in a studio apartment near the campus in the suburb of Oak Park. She decided to make a career change to become a corporate librarian and began her studies at Dominican. Our first conversations, on breaks during the class, were kind of stilted as the air was filled with the static electricity of attraction and nervousness. Later we both said that we felt an immense attraction, but I had to maintain the proper student-teacher relationship. The tension between us was palpable.

During the lab portion of the class, I would walk behind the students and look over their shoulders as they researched their online assignments. I always lingered a bit longer over Molly's shoulder. She later told me how nervous she was when I did that and thought that other students could clearly see that she had a crush on me. Also, I had tried not to be so obvious that I favored her in class, but it was difficult not to call on her. I longed to have her attention and hear her soft voice.

Chapter 3

For No One

I snapped out of my gaze and tried to focus more on our business conversation, but it was exceedingly difficult to do. My mind kept going back to the girl at the next table and the woman in my classroom all those years ago. Re-engaging, we listed our options for a deal and tried to come up with reasons why the client may not want to work with us. We were a new company. We were still seeking to land our first client and there wasn't a company track record. We had each other's backgrounds and the hunger for a client where we could prove ourselves.

I couldn't but align my eyes as often as I could with the next table. I didn't want to be caught staring at this girl for fear of her thinking I was a "creeper." But it was damn near impossible. She had the looks of the woman I fell in love with thirty years ago. What a delight it was to sneak a glance and soak in, as much as I could, those happy memories. The conversation at our table brought me back again to reality, "Damn it!", I thought silently. We were now on the topic of the pending lawsuit against us.

How frustrating is it to have someone sue you and you haven't even landed your first contract? Just then, I received a text from our attorney asking when that Sunday evening we could be available for a phone conference. I texted back that we would call him in about twenty minutes.

Clearly, we could not do a speaker phone conference in the pub, but we could have one in my car.

We began to finish our drinks and make our way to the restroom and to my car. I flagged over our waiter and settled our account (at my age, I just happened to have a bit more money than my millennial partners). Our waiter was also the waiter for the now infamous table next to ours. I asked how much their tab was and he replied $62.50. I gave him $80 and told him to pay their tab and keep the change. I also said, if they asked why I paid their bill, he was to say because the one girl happily reminded him of his late wife and brought back many happy memories and this was his thank you.

I met the guys at my car, and they asked what took so long. I said that having drank a little too much, it took an old man a little while longer to get rid of it. We piled into my Jeep Cherokee, rolled down the windows, dialed Bart and put him on speaker. Bart picked up quickly. He asked if we all received the same letter. We did, indeed. Had we all signed the same non-compete agreement? We had. He began asking a series of questions regarding John's business and what we were doing to establish whether or not we were competing.

Bart said that John really didn't have a case against us and that he apparently was acting out in anger. We had three options for resolution. We could go to court, which would run up attorney hours and court fees which we could not afford. Another option would be binding arbitration with a retired judge or the cheapest non-binding arbitration. At the end of the conversation, we decided that Bart would call John's attorney and inform him that he was representing us. The three of us would have a face to face with Bart in the next week.

Chapter 4

Fool on the Hill

The waiter approached the table of four women with their check. When they tried to pay the bill, the waiter said there was no need, as their bill had been taken care of by the gentleman that had been seated at the table next to them. The four women were rightly puzzled as to why someone they didn't know paid their tab, especially without hitting on any of them.

The four were all professionals: a nurse, a public relations executive, an accountant, and a paralegal. Sarah, the public relations executive calmed the chaos and looked at the waiter and asked, "Why did they pay our tab?" The waiter clarified by saying, "Not they, but he paid your tab. The tall gray-haired man with the rimless glasses paid your tab." Michele, the nurse, asked, "Did you know who he was?" The waiter responded that he had never seen the man before this evening, but he was with two younger men, one of which tended bar at the pub part time. The waiter then turned and walked away.

Sitting there rather confused the women bantered back and forth about why someone would do that. Sarah said, "Usually in a bar there are ulterior motives or strings attached with buying a drink and certainly the whole tab." Janet (the accountant), suggested the next time the waiter came by, they needed to ask if the man had said why, he had paid the tab. "Yeah," said Jackie (the para legal), "There has to be a reason and hopefully it's not creepy."

A few minutes of discussion ensued when the waiter came back around the table again. This time Jackie stopped the waiter and motioned him to the table. The waiter had a look on his face like he wished he hadn't gotten roped into this and it might well have been a better decision to forego the generous tip, told the guy to go to the table himself, and pay the women's tab like any other guy would do. When the waiter approached the table, Jackie spoke up. "Did the man say why he wanted to pay our bill?" The waiter, Jason, took a deep breath knowing that his answer would probably lead to more questions and possibly an emotional response. He replied, "He said that one of you reminded him of his late wife. It brought back a lot of nice memories for him and because of that, he wanted to do something nice." Jason turned to leave, and Michele said, "Hey wait a minute, which one of us?" Jason looked and pointed at Sarah and said, "It was you."

Tears came to Sarah's eyes, as they did a tear or two to the other women. Sarah felt flushed, a bit lightheaded, and as if everyone in the pub were looking at her. A round of "That is so sweet," and "What a sweet man," was echoed around the table. Sarah asked the waiter if he knew the gentleman. Jason said, "I've never seen him in here before, but one of his partners (Brandon) tends the bar here part time." Sarah asked, "He's a partner in what, and tends the bar?" Jason said the three are partners in a technology startup.

Chapter 5

I Saw Her
Standing There

Throughout the rest of the summer session, Molly and I continued a dance of tension. We both felt a chemistry and were both nervous around each other. On the last day of the semester, one day after I had given an early final exam, I had thrown kind of a farewell party for the class with cake and ice cream. I had stayed up late the previous evening grading the final exams and recording the grades in Dominican's online system. I had announced this at the beginning of the last evening and had posted final grades.

Instead of a four-hour class that evening, the party was about a ninety-minute affair. I had announced to the students that after the party, I would be in my office for up to another two hours if anyone needed to discuss their grade on the final or the final semester grade. I had several students stop by my office, mostly to thank me for the course, and only one or two to challenge their grade.

I was still seated in my office and gathering my papers to leave, when someone else knocked on the door. The door was ajar, and I told the person to come in. It was Molly. She seemed not just a bit nervous as she entered my office, but almost struggling to get her words out. I asked what I could do for her. She said, "Dr. Morrison, I just wanted to tell you how much I enjoyed the course and your teaching style; how you weave humor in to make things memorable and understandable." There was just a hint of a quiver in her voice as she spoke. Sensing this I said, "Molly, is there something else on your mind?"

She said, "Grades are in, correct?" I said yes, everything has been finalized and submitted. "Well," she said, "I'd like to ask you to go out with me." I was thinking to myself, yes! There was an interest on her part and now the pressure is off me. I said, "When were you thinking"? She said she didn't know; she hadn't really thought about it and that it took everything for her to get to this point. I said, "Well, what are you doing right now?" I told her that it was getting close to dinner hour and that if she didn't have plans, we could hop in the car and head downtown.

What started at 6pm and ended at 2 am would be one of the best evenings of my life. We came into the city on the Eisenhower Expressway, parked in a garage on LaSalle Street and went for Chicago style pizza at a joint on East Wacker Drive and Michigan Avenue. We did a lot of walking that evening. It was a pleasant summer evening as we headed up Michigan Avenue to Lake Shore Drive and back down to East Wacker. Meandering into department stores, bookstores, specialty shops and talking all the way. We made comments about the crowds, found out a lot of our likes and dislikes throughout our walk on Michigan Avenue, Chicago's Magnificent Mile. It's called that because of all the upscale stores, but I call it that because of that magical evening.

Somewhere between Michigan Avenue and Grant Park, I began holding Molly's hand. We came to Buckingham Fountain in the center of the park and watched the colored light display in the fountain from a bench several yards away. We sat there saying absolutely nothing, listening to the water, feeling the cool summer evening, and the spray from the fountain. It was about midnight when we walked back to the car. Before we got up, I gently touched Molly's cheek, then pulled her close to me and tenderly kissed her.

We got back to her little studio apartment about one in the morning. She invited me in for a drink. We sat in her apartment by candlelight and drank white wine. I kissed her a few more times. I don't think I had felt that way since college. It felt as if everything I experience was brand new. I left at two, drove home (don't remember how I got there) and did not sleep all night.

Chapter 6

I Feel Fine

Sarah Swenson went home from Drake's Pub that night in sort of a melancholy state. She was in a sense, happy and light, that she had evoked such memories and pleasant thoughts in that gentleman. But there was also an element of sadness and wonder in her heart. This man was surely a sensitive and emotional soul. She hadn't met a man that approached that sensitivity or kindness. How sweet he was to pay their bill for a feeling of happiness.

However, the end of the evening made her curious about the man. What was his life like now? Was he married or "with" someone? What kind of work did he do? Someone that sensitive and in touch with his emotions must be an artist or a musician. She had trouble sleeping that night because her thoughts were consumed with thinking about HIM. Did she remember seeing what he looked like? She just remembered three men and one had gray hair. The other two were quite a bit younger. She remembered thinking it was maybe a Dad and two sons.

Sarah awoke early, with HIM on her mind. She dreamed of a mysterious older man who swept her off her feet. She thought to herself, she is being foolish and childlike, but she just couldn't get the man out of her mind.

Chapter 7

You Never Give Me Your Money

The weekend, as all weekends do, passed entirely too fast. I was still thinking about the apparition I saw at Drake's Pub. Man, that woman was the very image of Molly. It really set me back emotionally. I dreamt of Molly last night and when I awoke, she was on my mind as was the woman at the pub. I was forty years old when Molly was killed and for the last twenty-four years, I've lived as a bachelor. Maybe this episode at the bar was some sort of a sign or more likely, I'm a pathetic, lonely old man.

Today, Jesse and I had a luncheon meeting with our potential client Paul. We had been talking with Paul for eight weeks. He liked us as individuals, but as a new startup we did not have a company record to go on, only the experience of the individual members. Our individual experience base was good, he was interested in how or if we gelled as a team. While we more than understood his concerns, we were getting frustrated and anxious about winning his trust and his business. If we secured him as a client, the second, and third clients would become easier to come by, as would investment funds.

Jesse and I met at the restaurant about thirty minutes before our scheduled meeting was to begin. We discussed that we really wanted to move Paul to terms and a payment schedule. About ten minutes late, Paul walked in the door and spotted us. The waitress, Donna, took our drink orders with her deep southern, redneck accent. Paul and I were of the same age. We talked about the "old" days of the information industry, of 2400 Baud transmission rates, acoustic couplers, and "dumb terminals." Paul and I had entered the industry when personal computers were first being sold and the internet didn't exist yet.

Jesse just kind of stared at us, as if we were speaking a different language. Paul and I continued to make small talk; we both shared an interest in horse racing. Having amassed a small fortune, Paul was about to purchase his first racehorse. Being born and raised in Louisville, in the shadow of the Kentucky Derby, Paul loved horseracing and the backside of the track environment.

This meeting was the first face to face meeting we were having with Paul. He reached out to our company on the networking site, LinkedIn. He was interested in developing customized Human Resources software. Over the past six weeks, we traded a few phone calls and emails questioning features he wanted and our capabilities. Today we began discussing pricing, development costs, time frames, and benchmarks we were to hit along the way. Paul wanted a tentative release date of October for the product. We agreed in principle that we could meet that date if we reached a deal in the next two weeks. We could then commit our resources (Brandon and contractors he would oversee).

Chapter 8

You Really Got a Hold on Me

Friday morning came quickly, especially after getting in at two a.m. and getting up for work at 6 a.m. Henry decided to work only a half day today to try and rest and restore his energy from an exciting and blissful evening with Molly. No matter where he tried to focus his mind; the news, work, upcoming travel, Molly absolutely and completely took over his thoughts. A lightning strike is what it equated to. A sudden, white hot attraction, that had a positive effect on his outlook on everything.

Today he seemed to notice everything. The sound of birds, squirrels, and children laughing at the bus stop down the street. Henry lived in the city in a thirty-six-floor high rise on Ohio street near the Chicago River. He was just an eight-minute bus ride or a twenty-minute brisk walk from the office. On his walk he seemed to be noticed by people as if there were an unusual gait to his walk or the proverbial spring in his step. He couldn't remember whether he usually said hello to people he passed. He probably did; he was that sort of person, but today this pleasantry was more pronounced.

Meanwhile, on the west side of Chicago in Oak Park at the St. Cecilia School for Girls, Molly's French 101 class noticed something different about her. She looked tired but at the same time seemed to be happy and full of energy. Molly was a favorite among her students. She was the cross-country coach and ran with her girls. She earned the girl's credibility by running and finishing with good times as a marathoner. Molly was also a trusted teacher who did not judge them and was frequently sought out by the girls for advice.

When he arrived at the office, he was whistling a tune as he passed his secretary Betsy on the way to his office. This mood did not escape Betsy, as since the man arrived from the New York office earlier in the summer, she had become rather adept at reading the moods and habits of her new boss. He rarely missed a day of work. He was always in the office at 6 a.m. before anyone else and did not leave until 6 p.m. When she arrived to work at 8:30 and he wasn't there, she knew that something was amiss. He called her to tell her he would be in about 9:30 or 10:00. Fridays were a kind of catch-up day for the office. The account managers and trainers traveled to client sites usually Monday thru Thursday throughout the 15 states the office covered. There was also training in the classroom through the week in the attached classroom.

Henry called Betsy into his office. He said to her, "I've met someone. Someone really special." He told Betsy he wanted to send flowers to her at the St. Cecilia school in Oak Park. She said, "Roses?" Henry replied, no, that roses were going to appear too pushy. Tell the florist that I want multicolored spring flowers that say, "I really like you and you make me exceptionally happy, you know, in a happy sort of way." Also, regardless of the cost they need to be there by two as school ends at three. "Ah, now what to say on the card?" He thought for a long moment and said, "Betsy, how about this, I had a wonderful time, how about I cook dinner for us this evening?" Betsy pointed out that he didn't know how to cook. To which he replied, "I'll think of something." He told Betsy, to add the office number to the card.

Later that afternoon, as Molly was teaching a small class of senior girls in the advanced French class, someone from the office knocked on the classroom door. She told them to come in, and it was Sister Mary Phillipa carrying a bouquet of a beautiful colorful spring flowers. Of course, as high school girls are wanting to do, they all said (since they were in French class) ooo la la! Molly blushed as she read the note then smiled.

Chapter 9

The Night Before

Sarah went to work that Monday with the events of Sunday evening at the forefront of her mind. This MAN is becoming an obsession. She thought, "I really have to do something about it. Either I try to purge this out of my mind as one of those strange events that happen in life or I track him down." Just to make sure that she wasn't totally nuts, she decided to call one of her friends that was with her last night.

She called Michele; as a nurse Michele is steady, measured in her thought, and has a master's degree in marriage and family counseling, so that comes in handy at moments like this. Michele was coming off a seven p.m. to seven a.m. shift when the phone rang. It was Sarah. Michele asked what most people do when someone they know calls unexpectedly and at an odd time, "Sarah, is something wrong?" Sarah replied, "No, it's that man from last night that paid for our dinner, I just for the life of me can't get him out of my mind." Sarah said that she wanted Michele's opinion on what to do. She was so curious about this mystery man.

Michele said, "You know the old adage about how 'curiosity killed the cat.'" Sarah replied, yes, I do, and I remember also what my mother always said too "curiosity killed the cat, but satisfaction brought him back." Michele told Sarah that she didn't know anything about this man, and he could be a total creeper or worse. Sarah said, "I know, but what he did was so sweet and charming." "Sarah, they said the same thing about Ted Bundy." Michele advised caution and that Sarah needed to set boundaries if she was going to pursue this. Sarah said, "Look Michele, if I'm going to go through with this, I need a partner in crime. Would you help me with this?" Michele replied that she was just as curious but that if they do this, "We need to set boundaries."

Chapter 10

Run for Your Life

The lunch with Paul went very well. He asked us to type up a summary of the meeting and the decisions we made along with the issues that were still outstanding. Jesse and I were excited to finally get the ball in sight of the goal line so to speak. I think realistically, we are in field goal range at the thirty-five to forty-yard line. Still more work left to do, but we both feel confident that inside of a month, at roughly our three months mark we should be able to close a deal with our first significant client.

The partners could not just focus on the potential business and long-term relationship with Paul, as with a shark, they had to keep moving and looking for other sources of revenue to lift them off the ground. Henry had a contact in Bowling Green with whom he had set up an appointment with this week. His contact, to say the least, was more than mildly eccentric. Joshua Jacobs was a former oil man who had lost everything (a personal fortune of over $90M) when the recession of 2007 hit with a vengeance and oil price dropped to almost half of their normal trading price.

Joshua, within a short period of time had lost nearly everything. His business went bankrupt and his personal assets went to pay debt. Inside of six months after the recession, he was thirty-two years old, living on food stamps and public assistance and still owned tons of drilling equipment that he couldn't sell to offset his losses. Out of that desperate situation, he started another business while still on food stamps.

Joshua started a business of digital signage for retail advertising. You've probably seen his product in malls that have digital signs of restaurants advertising their menus and other similar businesses. Joshua once told Henry how he got his first client. He said, I don't lie, but I told one lie in business to get started. It seemed there was an election in the next county over from Joshua's for County Sheriff. He went to the candidate with mocked up ads for his campaign and a monitor ready to display the ads for the candidate. Almost immediately the candidate dismissed him. Joshua said, "Okay, but before I leave, under campaign law (making it up as he went along) I'm obligated to offer you the same deal as your opponent and he has already purchased my product." Then Joshua began to leave, and the candidate told him to come back. Well, the candidate bought his product. The next thing he did was go to the opposing candidate, only this time he told the truth, and the candidate bought the product.

Later that week, Henry went to see Joshua to discuss how the two companies might be able to work together. Joshua's digital business could utilize location tracking for their clients. As the two discussed possible arrangements, Henry realized that the profit margin would not be great but, if the deal with Paul fell through, the cash flow would certainly help. Additionally, Joshua like the business model of the company as Henry presented it and may be interested in helping the company raise funds.

Chapter 11

It's All Too Much

Molly went to the school's office after classes had dismissed for the day and called Henry's office. Betsy answered and then put Molly through to the extension in Henry's office. When he picked up the phone Molly's voice was there, his heart skipped a beat and then quickened its pace. On the other end of the line, a mere ten miles away at the Catholic girl's school, another heart mirrored his. Molly said, "Thanks so much for the flowers, their beautiful, and I'd love to come for dinner tonight." As he heard her voice a song was running in his head. It was an old song he'd heard as a boy in the early 60's. Jimmy Durante singing about being young at heart.

He recalled his favorite verse as he listened to that sweet, excited voice. The verse said something like life being exciting and love being on the way. He loved that song; mom had the record and when he could, he played it. That verse was his favorite and right now it was the one he focused on the most. It spoke to him in a way it never had before. As they talked, he told Molly he wasn't particularly a good cook, or a cook at all for that matter. They would dine tonight on a salad, pasta, and garlic bread. Molly was fine with that and said she would think about a movie to rent. He asked what type of wine she liked. She wasn't picky just a nice white or chardonnay would do.

Henry left the office early, again much to Betsy's surprise. He walked home from the office and stopped by the Treasure Island market a block away from his building. He picked up a bottle of Chardonnay and a Merlot along with a head of lettuce and a few other things for dinner this evening. He also grabbed a bouquet of fresh flowers from the floral section to place on the table.

It was going to be a clear and calm evening; perfect for a late-night walk along Lake Michigan and Navy Pier before he took Molly home tonight. Walking back, he heard for the first-time birds singing on Ohio Street. That couldn't be a first, surely not. No matter either way, he found himself loving it.

A few miles away, Molly got in her black Ford Festiva and drove home to her small studio apartment. She felt goofy after yesterday in Dr. Morrison's, um Henry's office. After this summer and the class, it would feel funny for a while calling him by his first name. She still couldn't come to terms with what it was that attracted her to him, but whatever it was, it was strong. As it was still warm, she would wear her blue sundress or perhaps a pair of jeans, tennis shoes and take a light cardigan in what she was hoping would be another walk in the evening. She wished last night wouldn't come to an end.

Molly would have to get her five-mile afternoon run in, shower, get dressed, and select just the right perfume for the evening. She thought back to last evening again, she kept going back there, it was a pleasant island to go to. "I'll keep last night in my mind; it'll help me run through any side stitches or cramps." Her run took her through Oak Park and on to the campus of Dominican University, and past the Frank Lloyd Wright house where she would make her turn and retrace her steps home.

Meanwhile back on Ohio street, Henry was just entering his build-ing saying hello to the doorman Larry and riding the elevator to the thirty-sixth floor. Just as he stepped through the door to his home, his flip-phone rang. It was his secretary Betsy calling to wish him luck and hoped he had a nice time. After all she said, "You really need to have a relationship with something other than work." They both laughed at that, said they're goodbyes and hung up. He had one last thing to do and that was to pick up a video for this evening. Living downtown was terrific if you could afford it, which he could, as everything was just a short walk away. The downtown life was great for shopping, going to restaurants, or just walking along the lake front.

There was a video rental place just a couple of blocks away from his condo, so he decided to stop by on the walk home from the office and pick something appropriate. When he got to the video store, it was almost empty of patrons since he took off work in midafternoon, as he was beating the rush for weekend movie selecting. He had several recent films to choose from including *Dead Poets Society, Batman, Indiana Jones and the Last Crusade, When Harry Met Sally, Parenthood, Major League, and Uncle Buck.* He picked a chick flick (*When Harry Met Sally*) and a neutral type of flick for himself (*Indiana Jones and the Last Crusade*) and let Molly choose.

Chapter 12

Nowhere Man

Sarah goes through her day-to-day life that week. Going to work at seven in the morning, seeing the same faces, meeting with new clients but with the same propositions. She doesn't rotate her lunch schedule much, so she often has the same spread of a ham sandwich on rye, a protein bar, and a variety of fruits all except raspberries. She never liked raspberries as a kid and that hasn't changed a bit. Once off work around five in the afternoon, she takes the same route back home to her one-bedroom apartment on the outskirts of the city. Occasionally, Sarah will make a stop at her local library and the closest Starbucks on her way home. She spends her time with novels, her beloved cat, Binx, and her single mother.

On that Friday, the curiosities of this man and his life still haven't passed, in fact they grew stronger every following day. Sarah decided to call Michele over for drinks and some girl time. Once Michele arrived, the two sat on the floor in front of Sarah's couch with wine in hand and the best of the nineties playing softly on her cell phone. Sarah exclaimed, "In most cases, normal people would feel the appreciation for that man paying for their tab, and then move on with their lives without a second thought. Something keeps pulling me towards him. I want to know about his life and his past. I just know there has to be an otherworldly force telling me I need to meet this man, officially." Michele replied, "It does seem a bit odd that you're so manifested in meeting him. I mean, he's a complete stranger and all he did was pay our tab. It is sweet but I don't know, do you think you are reading too much into it?" Sarah sat in silence just for a minute or so. She could hear Michele and understood where she was coming from, but nevertheless, it made her realize her decision was final. "Let's go to the pub Sunday night, I just want to see if I run into him again. If I do then it's fate, and if not, then whatever I'll drop it." Michele anxiously downed the last of the wine in her glass and agreed. She wasn't sure why it was Sarah asking to do something out of the box, but per usual, she's ready.

Sarah and Michele visit Drake's Pub the following Sunday night as last Sunday she had the encounter with the man. Her sights were hopeful in coincidently running into him again. The two girls walked through the entrance. Sarah scans every table and every face only to be left discouraged. There was no sight of the man. "Table for two please," Michele exclaims to the hostess. As Michele and Sarah are being escorted to their table for two near the bar, Michele can't help but notice Sarah's sense of awareness. It seems her flesh and bone are walking but her soul has distanced.

Chapter 13

Eight Days a Week

Since the guys didn't have an office space yet, they met either at Drake's or at Henry's house. The meeting this Sunday afternoon was at Henry's, which was a small but modern house on the Ohio River. Because the river would periodically flood, the Federal Emergency Management Administration (FEMA) required homeowners to build their houses with the living spaces fifteen feet above the ground so that essentially the first floor became the garage for these homes. Henry's house had a covered deck that was fairly sizeable with room for a table that seated six and on the other side of the deck an outside sofa and chairs to accommodate six in casual conversation.

The weather, this last week of March, was unseasonably warm, so the guys decided the meeting would also involve a barbecue. Brandon picked up some burgers and brats, Jesse brought drinks, and Henry bought some potato salad and macaroni and cheese from Kroger's. The meeting began on a light note, just really talking broadly about their plans for the company, but soon evolved to their prospect Paul. Paul had been on their radar for several weeks. This afternoon the main focus of the meeting would be a conference call with Paul at Paul's request.

Brandon was the grill master. Brandon lived in a small apartment in the east end of Louisville and loved any chance he had to barbecue. Henry took charge of getting the table set with the side dishes in place, while Jesse handled the drinks. Henry, because of being a bachelor for nearly thirty years, used heavy duty paper plates whenever possible to avoid dirty dishes. Sure, he used a dishwasher, but if he could avoid dishes of any sort he did and he liked a quick cleanup, especially today to prepare for the call.

Brandon, placed the brats and burgers on the table, Henry said a very quick Catholic grace and the guys dug in. A lot of Henry's role in the company was to mentor the two younger partners. Essentially, Henry raised the money from investors, handled coordinating with the lawyers, and provided quality control on the product development end. As CEO, Jesse set the goals and managed the daily operations, product coordination, client management, and finance. Brandon handled the programming of products and managing the contract programmers.

After dinner, Henry fired up one of his sacred Cuban cigars (he smoked sparingly), Brandon lit up a cigarette, while Jesse dialed Paul's number to begin the conference call. It was two in the afternoon and Henry's balcony afforded a view of the stylish East End Bridge, the river, and the shoreline of the East End of Louisville. A light breeze was blowing, it was 65 degrees, and the deck was a most enjoyable and comfortable place for the call.

After three rings, Paul came on the line. Jesse took charge of the call and introduced everyone on the call. Paul had met both Henry and Jesse but had never met or spoken with Brandon. Paul said that while feeling comfortable with Henry and Jesse, the new company, again really had no track record of its own. Their previous work at the past startup was their experience. While Henry had years of experience in the information industry, Brandon and Jesse were less experienced in the professional work force. Paul wanted the three of them to come to St. Augustine, Fl. to a conference he was attending. He wanted to set up a day of meetings with him, Scott his Chief Technology Officer, and Mike (his CEO designate). This would be the final phase in the vetting process.

Jesse looked at Henry and Brandon for approval and both nodded yes. With that, Paul said he would see us in St. Augustine in one week's time. The guys had to work out the logistics. The company only had $2000 in its account. On short notice, air fare for the three of them would be prohibitive. Jesse's grandfather lived in Jacksonville and would probably be willing to put the three of them up for a couple of nights. The plan would be for the three to pile in Jesse's three row SUV and drive the 12 hours straight through to Jacksonville, do the all-day meetings in St. Augustine, stay the night in Jacksonville, then drive straight back the next day.

Chapter 14

When I'm Sixty-Four

After the guys left, Doc put things away and went back out to the deck for another Cuban and another Bourbon. He really wasn't a smoker or drinker and limited himself to a couple drinks per week and usually just one cigar per week. He was one month from his 64th birthday. Whether it was the fact he was getting older or the physical challenges that made him feel older, he was becoming more reflective. A lot of men long for their "glory days", but that wasn't it for him, it was more an assessing where he'd been in life and pivotal events.

As he sat there, becoming more relaxed with each sip and puff, he recalled a line from the Beatles' song *When I'm Sixty-Four*. It talked about getting older, losing hair and wondering whether your love would still be sending you valentines. For most of the last thirty years, birthday greetings had come from his family and students. There were a few romances along the way to be sure, and no disrespect to the women, but nothing that would stick. It seemed now that this loneliness had always been with him. He could easily feel alone in a room full of family, friends, and animated conversation. His sister Kathleen, often told him he was a "tortured soul." Maybe he was a tortured soul, as he was very much alone except for his thirteen-year-old Golden Retriever Betty, who gave him companionship and lived for their long walks.

The catalyst for his reflectiveness today was most certainly the young woman at Drake's that looked like the identical twin of Molly. Molly represented happier times, not that she was the only happy time in his life, but certainly one of the most intense. It was a whirlwind romance with so many things packed into a short period of time. It seemed as if that time was over in a flash but remained the strongest memories in his mind.

As he sat there, events of his life ran like film clips through his mind. He had been through, accomplished, and survived a lot of things in sixty-three years. A lot of bizarre and somewhat unbelievable things that most people couldn't grasp happened to one person. In high school and college, he worked at a pharmacy where he went through two armed robberies in eight years. He had survived (so far) three heart attacks, including what cardiologists referred to as the "widow-maker." Once after college, he was with a girlfriend at Disneyworld where they were in a fire on the monorail. He'd been in a bad car accident and most recently a ten-hour brain surgery.

His education and work were also varied and full. He had been a private investigator, reporter, sales and marketing rep, journalist, international licensing manager, teacher, and adjunct professor of business. He earned four college degrees including his doctorate. He had traveled to thirty-four countries and five continents and lived in two foreign cities (London and Hong Kong). With all that, he still believed he really hadn't achieved anything. Maybe it was that he only had Betty to share these things. Molly was a touchstone, while most memories were happy, the fact that his child and wife were gone hit hard. He missed the joy of the birth of his daughter, raising her with Molly and thoughts of what life would have been had they not perished.

On the upside, his involvement with the two twenty-nine-year-old fellows and the startup was beginning to make him feel a bit younger. Being around young people had that effect on you. You felt a lift, you were more engaged, and these young men made him feel valued for his experiences, opinions, and insights. Yet, the young girl's image at Drake's kept taking him back to Molly.

Chapter 15

I'll Be Back

enry stepped through the door (held open by his door man Carlton) of his building on Ohio street feeling excited, and anxious, with a dash of failing self-confidence at the anticipation of his second evening with Molly. Ever since high school and college, Henry had suffered from anxiety about dating. He had dated a lot, but always with a state of nervousness about whether the date had a good time, liked him, or would go out with him again. His female friends told him he was smart and good looking and never understood his anxiety.

Mentally, he went through a checklist of things to do. A quick shower and shave, tidy up the flat, make sure he remembered to pick up flowers for the table and candles for his two candlesticks. He would be in a relaxed form tonight wearing jeans, and untucked button-down shirt (blue was the staple of his collection), no socks and a pair of Topsiders. He just thought with no socks, he better takes care to address his "funky feet." Don't want to frighten the poor girl.

Freshly showered and dressed, Henry set the table including the candles and candle sticks and organized the kitchen for when he returned with Molly. He left the flat, went to parking level three to retrieve his car. He had always been fascinated with cars and now drove a five-year-old 1985 Porsche 911 Carrera. He bought it when he was promoted to his position in Chicago. He had planned and saved his bonus checks and paid cash for his pride and joy. He primarily drove it on weekends, as one really doesn't need a car if living downtown. If it felt warm enough, he may even put the top down if Molly was game.

Meanwhile in Oak Park, Molly was putting on the finishing touches of her makeup. She was wearing a black lightweight pullover sweater (black highlighted her blonde hair and she was fond of black), blue jeans, and a pair of white Ked's tennis shoes. She put her shoulder length hair back into a ponytail since this was a casual evening. The last thing she had to do was make sure her black cat Bear was set for the evening with a clean litter box, food, and water.

Henry came out of the parking garage and navigated the city streets to the Eisenhower Expressway straight to Oak Park. He should be at Molly's door by 6pm. He had the top down, but Friday evening traffic pretty much precluded him from putting much speed on his Porsche. He thought maybe to make himself look like he was going faster he could double bend a stout hanger, slip it down the inside of the tie and while wearing it, have the tie going straight back.

Molly had a glass of wine to steady her. She was like a cat on a hot tin roof (no offense Bear). She wasn't nervous, she was extremely anxious to see Henry again. She was also anxious in thinking how he could top the night before. Molly was pacing back and forth in her small apartment. She was thinking if she continued to pace this much, she just may wear a hole in the hardwood and fall through to the neighbor's downstairs.

Henry was making good time through heavy traffic and was coming up on the Austin Boulevard in Oak Park. Now, he was only five minutes away from Molly's apartment and he felt his heart racing just about as quickly as the Porsche's engine. He thought to himself I've got to calm down and be cool. At last, he pulled into the parking area. Molly had told him to park in the side lot and walk up the outside steps to the kitchen entrance to her apartment.

Molly heard a car door and went to the kitchen window and saw Henry walking toward the stairs. Her heart quickened as she waited for the knock on her kitchen door and the excitement about what tonight may bring. She was thinking about what she was expecting, Henry seemed to be a gentleman and respectful of her.

Chapter 16

Hard Day's Night

The day had come for the guys to head south to Jacksonville to meet with Paul and his team. Doc had a previously scheduled physician appointment at 9am that Tuesday morning. As soon as he was finished with the appointment, the three would hit the road. At 9, Henry came out of his annual physical (with note towards heart disease, brain surgery repercussions) in generally good health. He made it home by 10:15, where Jesse and Brandon were waiting to go.

Henry threw his bag in the back, put his laptop and notebook in the middle row of seats with him and the three began their twelve-hour drive to Jacksonville. Driving straight through with only a quick stop to fuel and eat, they should be there by 11:00 or 11:30 pm with Jesse's grandfather waiting up for us. Talk was animated about doing twenty-four hours of driving in a seventy-two-hour period. It was crazy, but if this client wanted to get to know us to award us the business, well that was the price we had to pay. We had to land our first client to gain credibility and traction.

They were making good time and stopped for fuel and a late lunch in Chattanooga, Tennessee. The place where they stopped looked a bit sketchy and the surrounding neighborhood was a bit suss (suspect), but the gas station had a Wendy's attached to it. The entire stop took no more than thirty minutes, and they were back on the road. They headed south on

I-75 towards Atlanta, which would probably be the next fuel and food stop. They had packed a good bit of snacks and drinks in the car (Henry ended up gaining six pounds on this trip).

Unfortunately, their 10:30 am start put them in Atlanta at rush hour. They crept down I-75 through the center of Atlanta at a snail's pace. Just on the south side of Atlanta, the three stopped for fuel again, went through a Chick-fil-A drive through, pulled over in the lot and wolfed down their chicken sandwiches in the parking lot, then proceeded south towards I-10 and Jacksonville.

The sun had gone down, and traffic was thinning out the further south and away from Atlanta. Things were going smoothly, and the guys were making good time when suddenly, a very loud thump hit the bottom of the car. Henry said did you hit something? Jesse said he didn't see anything, none of us saw anything and we were all looking straight ahead. About a minute later, Henry said, "Do you guys smell gas?" Brandon said yes, I do. Henry said it's getting stronger and gas is spewing out the back of the cart. He dialed 911 as Jesse quickly got the car into the emergency lane. Safely in the emergency lane the guys quickly piled out of the car. Jesse looked underneath, and whatever they hit ripped a sizable gash in the fuel tank.

Within a few minutes, a county Sheriff's Deputy and a Georgia State Patrol officer were on the scene. Insurance company and a tow truck were called. The car would be hauled to a Chevy dealer and the insurance adjuster would arrive in the morning. The tow truck driver and his robust wife gave us a ride to the dealership, we emptied the car of our luggage and the tow truck driver drove us a block away to an all-night Waffle House. While we were happy that nothing sparked the leaking gas, which would have led to a fireball in which we all would have been toasted to a crisp, we were concerned about making the meeting in St. Augustine at 11 am the next day.

This was an important meeting not to miss. Rental car agencies were closed, and they needed to find a way to get to Jacksonville tonight. Jesse just informed the other two that while in the tow truck he called his grandfather in Jacksonville. He was driving the two and a half hours from

Jacksonville to Tifton to retrieve us. In the meantime, there we sat in the Waffle House. Over two and a half hours, they ate a late-night breakfast and got to know the two waitresses Kim and Tammy better that they wanted to.

Jesse's grandfather arrived at the Waffle House about 12:30 am. The guys threw their bags in the trunk and headed back to Jacksonville with "grandpa" still at the wheel arriving at his home at about 3am. They were anxious to get to bed as they had to be on the road to St. Augustine by 9:45 am. Grandpa showed them to their rooms, and they all went out quickly, well almost all of them.

Chapter 17
Come Together

Sarah doesn't see the man in the pub. She scanned every corner and every table. Feeling discouraged and relieved, Sarah didn't know where her mind was at this point.

She was trying to speak but didn't know what to say. Her thoughts were scattered, much like the laundry distributed across the floors of her apartment. Michele nods to Sarah in affirmation of reassurance that she is right there with her. The walk to their booth felt like twenty minutes rather than twenty seconds. Her mind was strictly concentrated on what her eyes were seeing, and her peripheral vision was blurred all around her. Time felt stopped. She manages to stub her foot on a passerby's chair, but she didn't carry a single bit of embarrassment following a few stares. Some things were more important. As Sarah and Michele take their seat in a tall booth in the back of the pub, Michele eagerly asks, "Do you see him?" To which Sarah replies, "No," with a silent intermission following. "Well, let's get something to eat and just wait to see if he walks in." Michele says.

As soon as she takes her seat, Sarah feels like everything around her unpauses. There are groups of friends laughing over drinks and enjoying the company they are with. There is a man, and a woman in the booth behind them celebrating their anniversary. Sarah can't help her heightened senses as she eavesdrops. All smiles and giggles as they cheer to their precious twenty years together. It made Sarah smile a bit to herself. She thought, how lucky they are to have that love. She reminisces for a moment on the love her parents had. Her father passed away at age sixty with cancer. She knew his passing left her and her mother with memories only, but beautiful memories they were. Her favorite memory of her parents together was her birthday parties. Her mom would make her a vanilla cake along with hand dipped vanilla ice cream. Yes, it was plain, but it was her favorite. Not to mention after so many birthday parties, it was tradition. Even after her father's passing, her mother still carries it on. She thought to herself, "I could never get bored of vanilla. It tastes like the memories."

It seems the restaurant is so lively. It was sort of refreshing, but also reminded her that she didn't fit in with them. Everyone in the building seemed comfortable and content from her perspective, except herself. Every other minute or so Sarah anxiously glances to the front of the pub at the double doors. She is anticipating for the man to walk in and at the same time she hopes he doesn't. "Do you know what you want?" Michelle asks intently. Sarah snaps out of her daze abruptly and tells Michele she is ready to order. After ordering their dinner for the night, the girls discuss their future with the man. Sarah can't help but think she is delusional for coming to a restaurant solely to run into a person she doesn't even know just to not speak to them.

She says to Michele, "We came to a restaurant on the same night and the same time as the last moment we encountered this person hoping it would be a coincidence we would bump into one another again. We are insane." Michele laughs in response. "Yeah, Em you might be right." After their meal had finished and left Sarah somewhat unsatisfied, the waitress brought Sarah and Michele their check. Michele grabbed it so fast that Sarah didn't even had the chance to look at it. "Thank you, you don't have to do that. I am the one that dragged you here." Michele replies, "Girl, you know it's my time to pay, regardless. It's not like you ate anything anyways! You really should have gotten a meal and not just fries. And technically you wouldn't have come without me!" Dissatisfied, Sarah says, "I know, I'm just not hungry. But thank you anyway," despite only eating half of her lunch that day, she thought. She feels disappointed the man hasn't shown up. But of course, what were the odds? Sarah says, "Okay, we can just go. He's definitely not going to show up now. It's almost eight o'clock. He's probably sleeping and carrying on with his life." Michele replies, "Alright babe. Are you sure? We can order drinks and hang out for a bit just in case." Sarah sighs discouraged. "No, it's fine. We both have to work in the morning anyhow. Let's head out."

As Michele and Sarah leave the pub, Michele expresses to Sarah, "Let's just get some ice cream. It makes everyone smile, right?" She nods with appreciation. "It's like you read my mind," Sarah says gleefully. The two finish their night off with two milkshakes from the ice cream shop down the road from Drake's Pub. Michelle with a cookie dough in hand, and Sarah with vanilla.

Chapter 18
Across the Universe

A s physically tired as he was, Doc could not go to sleep. His mind was actively thinking about the meeting in the morning, but it also kept going back to the young woman at Drake's. Somehow, he had to shut off the little gerbils turning the wheels powering his mind. Luckily, he brought along his iPad and his headphones to listen to music. He had created playlists to listen to for various moods. This evening he chose a playlist he had created of light classical music with selections from Mozart, Elgar, Dvorak, Beethoven, Handel, and John Williams.

He drifted off as Dvorak's "New World Symphony" (commonly known as "Going Home") played out. His mind entered a deep sleep full of dreams. He dreamt of a successful meeting with Paul the next day and he dreamt of the young woman at Drakes that had been invading his mind for the last several days. He woke up at 5am when he dreamt of the incident on the highway, but in the dream the car exploded.

Since he was up, he decided to make a pot of coffee, shave, and take a shower. After his shower, he dressed quickly. Henry was old school; business meetings usually meant a suit and tie. However, working with two young millennials in a tech startup, the dress code was different. Dress clothes for a millennial business meeting was an untucked shirt, jeans,

deck shoes, and if you really wanted to impress, a sport coat. He was starting to get used to it.

Grandpa was up, Henry made small talk thanking him for "rescu-
ing them" last night. Offered the morning paper, he took it just skimming
through. After a second cup of coffee and chit chat, he went back to his
room to prepare notes for the meeting. As he tried to concentrate, she
invaded his mind again. The thought of the young woman that looked so
much like Molly, that all those memories kept resurfacing that he thought
were so long ago filed away. The young woman could easily have been
Molly's identical twin. Ironically, Molly was an identical twin. Molly's twin
was Bridget and he recalled she was the most identical of twins he had
ever seen. It was a great time in his life, nothing ever like it or since. Both
Molly and Bridget were fun to be around. They both had a wicked sense of
humor and kind of a weird understanding of each other that twins often
had between them. They would very often finish each other's sentences,
seemingly read each other's minds. When the three of them were together,
Henry was most assuredly the third wheel.

The work with the startup and the young guys was fun, but nothing could replace what he lost nearly twenty-five years ago. He had to
shake the young woman from his mind and focus on the meeting today.
But he thought about taking some action to meet the young woman. He
wasn't a creeper, he was simply curious what she was like, what she did
for a living, were there similarities with Molly? His mind was racing with
these thoughts and memories of Molly. He was too old for this high school
thinking. Grow up man! Pull yourself together for Pete's sake. But the more
she was on his mind, the more he kept thinking of hatching a plan to meet
her and find out more about her. The question was how to do this without
coming off as an old "creeper."

Chapter 19
Act Naturally

Henry crossed the parking lot and bounded up the back stairs as Molly had directed. Nervously and anxiously, he knocked on the back door and moments later the door opened to reveal the most beautiful woman he believed he had seen, who every time he saw her, took his breath away. He told her how pretty she looked, and she blushed as her heart quickened. She thanked him shyly, went to get her cardigan and returned to Henry at the door, locked it and the two made their way to the parking lot.

As they got to Henry's Porsche, he asked Molly if she would prefer if the top was up. Molly had never actually ridden in a convertible of any type and was somewhat excited about the thought of the ride into town in this sports car. Gentlemanly Henry opened the door for her, placing his hand on her back to guide her into the seat. Molly's heart skipped a beat when she felt Henry's hand on her back. They made their way from the lot onto the street and then a couple of blocks to the Eisenhower eastbound freeway back into downtown Chicago.

Henry made a better time driving back into the city, he looked at Molly and she was smiling as they drove at a speed more appropriate for a Porsche. They made their way through the city to Ohio Street and into the building's parking garage. Henry put the top up, turned off the engine, then came around the car to open the door for Molly. He gave her his hand to help her out of the car. Once again, Henry placed his hand lightly on Molly's back to guide her through the door from the garage to the elevators to the upper floors.

Molly said, "From the look of the lobby and elevator, this looks like a very nice building you have here." Henry told her he almost felt guilty for living here and driving his five-year-old Porsche, but he had worked hard, had not accumulated debt, and had saved his bonus checks to be able to live here. He said, "Don't get too excited about dinner, it's only salad and pasta. I'm not much of a cook." Molly told Henry that soon she would have to cook dinner for him. Henry liked the thought of that; it meant at least she was thinking of another evening together.

He opened the door to his flat and Molly moved immediately to the far window, which basically encompassed the entire outside wall of the living room, dining room, and kitchen area. Glass from the ceiling down to about two and a half feet from the floor. The hardwood floors were a beautiful light-colored, red oak. The flat was an open concept type of flat. The living room had a Persian style rug, a coffee table, and two white sofas facing each other with a big screen television on the wall. The dining room table was already set with two place settings, wine glasses, and two candles on the table. Henry's flat faced the north towards Lincoln Park. He had a view of Lincoln Park, Oak Street Beach, Lake Shore Drive, and Lake Michigan. At this time of evening, the taillights of traffic heading north, and the lights of the other buildings made for a stunning view from thirty-six floors up.

"Molly, would you like a glass of wine?" She said, "That would be wonderful, and the view from here is terrific." He told her he never tired of looking out of the window and watching the world go by. The two talked over their glasses of chardonnay and made their way to the kitchen to prepare dinner. Molly worked on the salad while Henry chopped mushrooms and sautéed them for the pasta sauce. He also got out the oregano and chopped some basil to add to the sauce. He prepared the pasta sauce and boiled water for the pasta. Within fifteen minutes dinner was prepared and they moved the meal to the dining room table. Henry fetched matches to light the candles, he put on music from Puccini's *La Boehme* and began serving dinner to Molly and poured another glass of wine for the both of them. He went around to her side of the table, pulled her chair out for her, and then seated himself. As they ate their dinners, they filled each other in on their families, backgrounds, and careers. He discovered that Molly was an identical twin, and her parents were immigrants from Poland. Her father had worked in the steel mills in Gary, IN his whole life and passed away from cancer a few years ago.

Henry spoke of the love hate relationship with his mother. His parents were divorced when he was five and Henry's mother despised Henry's father for leaving her for another woman. They talked and ate for an hour and a half finding out more and more about each other. Henry told Molly that he felt as if he spent life on a treadmill never getting approval from his mother no matter what he did. He didn't know why he felt that approval was so important, but he still craved it. Molly felt sorry for him as he literally had an ache in his voice when he spoke about it.

They spoke of music and how they both loved classical, especially the heavyweight composers: Bach, Beethoven, Mozart, and Handel. Molly said she would love to take Henry to a Chicago Symphony concert sometime. They talked about different pieces of music they loved. Henry suggested they take a walk to let their dinner settle before watching a movie. They cleaned up the table, loaded the dishwasher and made their way to the elevator. As they made their way through the lobby, Lawrence the night doorman held the door for them.

Chapter 20

Anytime at All

The morning arrived too quickly for the guys. They had a one-hour drive ahead of them to meet Gary and the other members of his team. As they had no transportation after the ruptured gas tank last night, they had to borrow Jesse's grandfather's Lexus to get to St. Augustine. They all piled in with Jesse at the wheel, crossing their fingers they wouldn't hit anything in the road today.

The guys met Gary for lunch at 11:00 at the Beachcomber Bar on St. Augustine Beach. It was the first meeting for Brandon and Gary, so the lunch was a prep meeting for five to six hours of meetings with two other individuals from Gary's company after lunch. The discussion at lunch was lighthearted and proceeded as if a deal was just a matter of signing a few papers and passing muster with Gary's Chief Technology Officer.

While the lunch meeting with Gary was enjoyable, Jesse, Brandon, and Henry were wiped out from the events with the car the previous evening. Since none of the three got more than two or three hours of sleep, they had to be "on their game" for these meetings. While the lunch went well, they still had to get through the meetings this afternoon to close the deal and begin receiving payments from Gary.

The first meeting after lunch would be the most critical and that would be with Scott, Gary's Chief Technology Officer. While all three guys would participate in the discussion, it would be Brandon that would be evaluated most critically. The discussion covered features of the custom product that the company would build for Gary's company. Brandon was questioned by Scott on the languages he would use to program and why. Brandon acquitted himself well and kept a collegial attitude throughout.

Later in the afternoon Mike, who would be taking Gary's place as CEO met with the group. His questioning really was directed at sales and marketing efforts and positioning of the product along with pricing strategy. Henry and Jesse took the lead here in fashioning a discussion around creation of marketing materials and training of the one hundred plus sales staff of Gary's company to better leverage the product and assure a quick start.

All in all, the day's meeting went well, and the three "zombies" climbed into the Lexus to head back to Jacksonville for dinner and much needed rest. Before leaving the meetings, Gary had assured the guys that a letter of intent (LOI) would be forthcoming in a few days. The LOI would allow for the establishment of a line of credit to supplement the payments from Gary for development of the product.

Chapter 21

In My Life

It wasn't long after getting into the back seat of the car that Doc fell asleep. He entered a dream world that became a "movie" of sorts of his life. Once he read an article about why we dream certain things. In the article, the psychologist author wrote, "Dreams appear to be influenced by our waking lives in many ways. Theories about why we dream include those that suggest dreaming is a means by which the brain processes emotions, memories, and information that's been absorbed throughout the waking day."

Whatever the cause, his dreaming in the back seat of the car was strange in its combination. It started with the time when he was seventeen that he called his mother a "Bitch." Mom reacted with a strong slap across the face and replied, "Say it again." Henry did say it again and in fact a total of seven times resulting in a hard slap each time. It was stupid on his part, but it showed how stubborn each of them was. Henry ended up with a sore face after finally backing down, and in her mind, Mom had won another encounter.

It was strange really, ever since he was a small child, Henry was admonished to be better than his father, whatever that meant, Mom was never clear on that. But when he disobeyed or did something wrong, Mom never failed to call him by his father's name, Jim. In his college years and adult life, it was Henry that Mom reached out to for help or advice or to vent to.

He also dreamt of Molly, specifically of that time in London. It was just after they had lost their first pregnancy in a miscarriage. A couple of weeks after, they had been at the Field Museum in Chicago and had climbed the steps to the second floor. At the top of the steps was a month by month display of fetal development. They both broke into tears and held each other. He had suggested a vacation, "How about London?" Molly was astonished, "Really?" she had replied. He had a lot of airline miles saved up for two first class roundtrip tickets to London. And so, they went, not to forget their loss, but to ease the processing of it. They took a couple of day tours to Canterbury, Leeds, and Dover. But the loveliest moment was when he suggested to Molly that he rent a rowboat and row her in the Serpentine in Hyde Park. That day he had arranged with the concierge a picnic basket lunch for two with a bottle of wine and bottles of water. The quaint hotel where they stayed (The John Howard), even had an old-fashioned wicker basket for their lunch. He picked up the basket, tipped the concierge and hailed a London Black Cab for the short ride to the Serpentine. He rented the boat, helped Molly in and handed her the basket. On attempting to get in, clumsy as ever, he had lost his balance and fell into the Serpentine. The attendant helped fish him out and onto the dock.

As he rowed, they spoke of their grief. Molly was a devout Catholic and felt God may be punishing her for something by giving them this loss. He told her that God had a reason, that we may never know or be able to comprehend, but without a doubt, God was not punishing her. After a while, he had rowed the boat to an area of the Serpentine near the shore and underneath the shade of a tree. It was there, he told her just how much he loved and was in love with her. They toasted their love and a memory of a child they were never to know until united in heaven.

He also dreamt of the time when he worked in a pharmacy during high school and was held up. The robber put a gun to his head and said to the two pharmacists, "Don't try anything or I'll kill the kid." The elderly pharmacist who only heard the words but did not see what was happening (he was in the prescription shelves) and thought it was someone in the neighborhood joking replied, "Go ahead he hasn't done a damn thing all day." At that point in the dream and as a matter fact in real life, the robber cocked the hammer of the pistol and said, "I'm serious!"

He awoke in the back seat of the car with a startle as he dreamt, he was soaring off a cliff like a bird. The guys were laughing as before he snapped awake, he was singing the Beatles song, *"In My Life."* A song reminiscing on love, past loves, friends, and people one has known throughout their life but one special person being loved more.

Chapter 22

Dizzy Miss Lizzy

A s they exited his building, Molly and Henry turned towards Navy Pier and the Lakefront, but Henry stopped and said, "Let's walk down Michigan Avenue tonight." Molly said that was fine, so they walked the three blocks north from Henry's building to Michigan Avenue. He pointed out a Thai restaurant that he liked a lot and suggested it as a place for dinner one night. Somewhere between the Thai restaurant and Michigan Avenue, Henry took Molly's hand in his and instantly her hand was like turning on some sort of high frequency receiver. Everything around him seemed brighter, louder, and more intense and a sense of sheer joy washed over him and through him.

As they walked down Michigan Avenue, Molly couldn't stop thinking how happy she was to be with someone who was so thoughtful of her. They window shopped, they stopped for half an hour at the John Hancock building to take the elevator to the 95th floor observation deck to see the lakefront and the traffic on Lakeshore Drive (known as the LSD in Chicago). After an hour and a half of walking, they went back to the building and up to Henry's flat for a movie. As the door to the elevator closed, Henry gently pulled Molly to him and gave her a gentle kiss on the lips and then another on her cheek; the elevator rose at the same time and he said to her, I feel as if I am flying when I kiss you. She laughed and kept looking up at him while they went to the thirty-sixth floor.

As they entered the flat, he said, "Why don't you pick out a movie and I'll get together some cheeses and more white wine. She said, "Great." and retreated to the living room. In a few minutes Henry returned to the living room with wine and various cheeses on a platter. "Well, have you chosen a movie?" he asked. She said, "Yes, *Uncle Buck*!" He asked why she chose that movie and she said it was filmed in Chicago and she liked John Candy. He did too and went to put the DVD in the player. He sat down near the arm of the couch and Molly laid against Henry's chest. They settled in to watch the film and snuggle. For two hours they held each other during the film. Molly liked when Henry spoke to her. His deep voice vibrated his chest, and she could physically feel that vibration and felt, well, comforted by it.

By the time the film was over, it was just past midnight. Molly said, "I hate that you have to drive me home so late." Henry replied that he didn't mind the drive, but he had an idea if she didn't think he was too forward. He suggested that he sleep in the office (he had a pull-out sofa sleeper) and she could take the master suite. Put on my robe, throw your clothes in the wash, take a shower if you wish and I'll drive you home in the morning. After you're out of the shower, throw your clothes in the dryer and they'll be ready in the morning. I have plenty of shirts in my closet, choose one to use as your pajamas. Before you go to bed, we'll have a night cap to assure sweet dreams.

She said that would be fine with her. While Henry went back to the living room to give her some privacy, she went to the master bedroom, took off her clothes and picked out one of his shirts for "pajamas" and put it and his robe on. She liked his scent from his shirt enveloping her. She started her laundry and made her way to the living room and joined Henry for a drink. They chatted a bit more and she thanked him for letting her stay the night. She thought, not for the first time, what a gentleman Henry was, except for holding hands and kissing, he has not been forward at all.

She got up to put her clothes in the dryer. They talked a bit longer and finished their drinks.

He said, "Molly, I'll walk you home." He placed her close to him with his arm around her and they walked down the long hall to the master bedroom. He gave her a longer kiss and walked her to the bed. He said, "Just let me get a couple things from my bathroom and my clothes for tomorrow and I'll leave you to dreamland." As he was leaving the room, Molly called him to her as she was lying in the bed. She said, "Come here." When he did, she place her hands around his neck, pulled him to her and gave him a passionate kiss. Letting go she said, "You're a special man Henry."

He left the room on virtual cloud nine. He felt more alive than he could recall. He went to the guest bathroom and got ready for bed. He went into the office/spare bedroom, worked a bit, and then went to sleep.

Chapter 23

Tomorrow
Never Knows

arah remembered something her mother always told her when she was little.

"Courage doesn't always roar. Sometimes courage is the quiet voice at the end of the day saying, 'I will try again tomorrow.'" That quote got Sarah through the hardest days of her life. When her dad passed, she felt like a black hole, soulless and void. Getting through high school was the hardest part. All the "I'm sorries" and the well wishes. She wanted nothing but to have him back. She didn't want useless hugs or sympathy. She didn't want cards or flowers or special treatment. It was all so meaningless. She wanted her family back. It felt broken forever. For a few years following his passing, Sarah's strength was unaccounted for. Though, there will always be a fragment of her heart missing. She learned that she was lucky to experience a family at all. Most go their entire lives searching for what her mother and father had.

At the funeral, Sarah's mother, Anna, seemed like a zombie. Greet, hug, cry, give thanks, repeat. It was an endless cycle. Sarah watched her mother and knew that somehow this cycle would never end. It would always be a sympathy card from everyone she met. The hardest thing for Sarah was to see her mother without her love. She had never saw her mother cry of sadness before then. She is the strongest woman Sarah has ever known. Anna was always the woman everyone looked to for advice. Not only was she the shrink of the family, but of the street. Anna made friends everywhere she went, some she would keep forever and some just passing through.

Ever since she was a little girl, Sarah analyzed her mother. She used to sit on the floor in front of her bedroom vanity as she got ready for work and things. Her favorite time to watch her mother get ready was when her father proposed date nights. She sat looking in the mirror at her mother's reflection. She was so beautiful. Sarah noticed her makeup routine changed given the occasion. A bit of concealer, bronzer, mascara, and lip-gloss for work. For their date nights, Anna always added a few extra steps. First foundation, concealer, blush, and bright red lipstick. The red lipstick was always her father's favorite. Sarah hasn't seen her wear that color since he passed. It isn't the memories that make Sarah grieve, it is the mind-numbing fact that she will never again get to see the same glow in her mother's eyes as she prepares for a date night with her father.

Sarah and her mother's relationship had always been something out of a fairytale. Anna is like her fairy godmother. She has always been so strong willed and persevered through every bump in the road she's had to cross. Sarah was never grounded, or spanked, or yelled at for bad behavior. Not because she was an angel, but because her mother and father promoted kindness and love. If she did or said something distasteful or wrong, Anna would sit down with her and just talk about it. Because of the way Sarah was raised, she learned right from wrong quickly. She wasn't perfect, but she always trusted her intuition. Through past relationships, Sarah noticed red flags almost immediately, with her mother's advice of course. Sarah's parents had the most beautiful love, and she knew she wouldn't settle for any less than what they had.

Chapter 24

A Day in the Life

L ife is such a funny and mysterious thing. The stuff that happens in real life is often more unbelievable than something writers and screenwriters could make up for books or movies. Doc often liked to tell of his nine or ten encounters with death. He was a horribly sickly child. Before he was six years old, he stopped breathing on two occasions and was revived when the doctor came to the house (in the late 1950s doctors still made house calls) and revived him with shots of adrenaline. When he would get colds, many times he would go into pneumonia and double pneumonia.

During high school and college, like many kids, he had a job. Doc worked in a family-owned pharmacy. An elderly man and his son owned and ran the pharmacy. In thirty-five years of operation, the place had never been held up. It was the fall of 1972, and the 1970s were full of drug issues in society leftover from the hippies of the 1960s. Doc was walking to the front of the store when a young man came in with a .22 caliber blue steel revolver and pointed it at him, then walked him back to the prescription room. The young man had the gun on Doc (pointed at his head) and encountered the younger owner of the pharmacy and loudly announced, "This is a hold up, if you try anything, I'll kill the kid." From the back of the prescription room, not visible to the holdup man, a voice yelled back, "Go ahead, he hasn't done a damn thing all day." The younger owner yelled back, "Dad, this is the real thing." With that, the young man cocked the hammer of the pistol he was aiming at Doc's head.

The elderly owner was behind shelves of prescription medications and could not see what was happening. He had assumed since they had never been held up, it was a neighborhood prankster (of which there were a few) playing a joke. Luckily, no one was hurt, the young hold up man got the drugs he wanted, Doc passed out after seeing his dull and short life flash before his eyes. There were to be in the coming years three more hold ups, the last one also involved Doc. This time, the holdup man merely (out of desperation) had his finger in his jacket. You don't ask a hold up man to actually see the gun, it's risky for one thing and for another, it is a total breach of hold up etiquette.

In his mid-twenties, he and a girl he was dating went to Florida and spent two days at Disneyworld. While on the monorail going from the Magic Kingdom to the Epcot Center, the thing stopped, and smoke began coming through the air conditioning vents. It seemed that the rubber wheels underneath the last car on the train had locked and did not move when the train pulled out of the station. Friction took place and a fire ensued. Three hours later, the last of the cherry pickers from the fire department retrieved everyone from the train.

When he was in his early thirties, Doc was on business at a conference in Ohio when he was feeling flu like and having chest pains at the end of the day. In his early thirties, he didn't think anything of it. He went to the conference cocktail party thinking that would make him feel better. Afterwards he drove his rental car to the local "doc in the box" (immediate care center). The doctor checked him over, did an EKG and told him he was having a heart attack. He was sent by ambulance to the hospital. He told the paramedic on the way that he didn't have time for this as he had three account calls in the city the next day.

At age thirty-six, while working in Chicago, he was in a horrible car accident. His secretary was driving him to the airport when a hit and run driver sheered into the front of his secretary's car causing it to flip and roll. Doc suffered cuts to his hands, face, and scalp, and suffered a severe concussion.

Two decades had gone by without incident when at age fifty-six he suffered two heart attacks in a twenty-four-hour period. He was finishing the last night teaching a night class in an MBA program when he noticed a terrible ache and pressure in what he thought was coming from the site of two previous upper back surgeries. He drove home with pressure and pain in his back, arm, and chest. At home he could not lie down without pain, so he spent the night in a recliner. The next day, after work, still feeling tremendous pressure and pain he drove himself to the emergency room. The ER physician ran EKG, and blood tests. His blood enzymes indicated that he has suffered a significant heart attack the day before. He was placed in the CCU where at one the next morning he suffered another attack referred to as the "widow-maker."

Doc had two arteries that were clogged ninety five percent. The doctors said had he not been in the CCU already, the second heart attack would have killed him. He was released after a week and put on a heart healthy regimen, stayed off work for six weeks, and was sent to cardiac rehab. Six weeks of working on his health, diet, and exercise.

About four years later, when he was 60, he began to have trouble walking and driving. Severe dizziness and loss of balance occurring at unexpected times; behind the wheel of the car, at work, on walks. One weekend it was particularly bad, he could barely get dressed and walk for nearly four hours before things began to right themselves. One Sunday morning as he was dressing for church, the symptoms hit him again only more intense. He managed to get himself in the car and drive to the ER. He parked the car and literally staggered into the ER. An MRI was performed and identified a brain tumor on the vestibular nerve.

Remarkably, he survived all these "brushes with death" to keep going and live a very productive life. He often compared himself with Keith Richards of the Rolling Stones and cockroaches, as the three species would be the only thing left after a nuclear apocalypse. Keith Richards had done damn near every drug possible including injecting cocaine in his eyeball, falling out of a coconut tree, and suffering a brain hemorrhage. Richards even once admitted to treating his body as a human chemical laboratory. Cockroaches are virtually indestructible, and Doc had his nine brushes with death.

The only ill effect of these health issues on Doc, were migraines and balance issues from brain surgery. However, an overlying issue for Doc was questioning what his purpose was in life. He must be surviving all these things for a bigger purpose, he just wasn't seeing the purpose, and it bothered him.

Chapter 25
Flying

Back from Florida, the guys were feeling confident about winning the business from Gary. They had proposed a contract and Gary and his team would review and respond within a week.

This would be an important win as there would be development money from Gary's company monthly for six to eight months while Brandon and a team of contractors did the planning and programming. That money would allow Jesse and Doc the running room to develop other business for the new company.

A couple of months prior, Jesse and Doc had flown to Los Angeles for a couple of days to visit three former colleagues of Doc's to work on generating business. Mike Shaeffer and Doc had been friends for thirty-five years and had spent five years together at the same company selling information. Doc had worked in New York and Chicago and Mike had been based at corporate headquarters in Palo Alto. Mike now ran a lucrative consulting firm based in Los Angeles helping startup companies land their first big clients. Mike had agreed to help Jesse and Doc refine their strategies and make some introductions for them.

Their second meeting was with Jamal Absi another friend of Doc's from when he covered the Middle East in the mid to late 1990s. Jamal and Doc had known each other for twenty-six years and were like brothers in their relationship. They were remarkably close despite living two thousand miles apart and seeing each other maybe once per year. Jamal could also help the company in raising much needed funds through some of his wealthy contacts. Jamal had recently retired from a major Las Vegas hotel where he handled very wealthy Middle Eastern clients. Doc would make a deal with Jamal to leverage his contacts for a commission for any funds secured.

Jesse, Doc, and Jamal talked over a lengthy lunch at an Iranian restaurant, the oldest Iranian restaurant in Los Angeles. Jamal ordered for the table and Doc later paid the check. Jamal was an Egyptian Catholic fluent in three languages (English, Arabic, and French) and was well connected throughout the Middle East. It was an easy working lunch, no need to establish trust between two old friends. As far as Jamal was concerned, if his friend believed in the company, that was good enough for him and a deal was struck. To finish the deal, the two old friends and the one new one, celebrated over a bottle of Cabernet.

The third visit on the trip was with a former student of Doc's. Doc had spent two years in Hong Kong as principal of a U.S. based international school on the Kowloon Peninsula. Rajiv Kumar was a very wealthy young man from an extremely wealthy family. Rajiv had been a junior and senior in high school during the two years that Doc was principal at his school. After graduation, he went to California State University – Northridge studying physics and astronomy. Now with a PhD, he was both an astrophysicist and lecturer at Loyola Marymount University in Los Angeles. He was also an entrepreneur and a part time actor. Rajiv was devilishly good looking and had a charming personality and was very well connected.

They sat down to dinner at the hotel. Jesse and Doc explained to Rajiv the business model for the location product. Rajiv was involved with lots of charities especially dealing with stopping human trafficking. He had developed an "app" that was in use by the Philippine government. Jesse and Doc were hoping they could partner with Rajiv to develop his product more fully and integrate their product into his app. Rajiv agreed to provide Brandon access to the programming to see what needed to be done to integrate, and he would make introductions to his contacts in the Philippine government.

In just a couple of days, Jesse and Doc had leveraged Doc's contacts to expand their business and potentially raise investment cash. After the dinner with Rajiv was completed, they went back to their room (to cut expenses they had shared a room) to pack, check out, and head to the airport for the "red eye" through Chicago to Louisville. The next steps were to keep Gary focused and finalize a deal and deliver a Letter of Intent (LOI) which would allow Jesse to get a line of credit from their bank.

While most folks were sleeping on the red eye flight, Doc's mind floated back to the girl at Drake's. He had just about convinced himself to take himself to dinner this Sunday evening at Drake's on the off chance that the girl may show up with her friends again. He hoped this wasn't a pathetic attempt and he just wasn't going to embarrass himself as a silly old man.

No, it's not a pathetic attempt, a slight obsession maybe, but by God he was going to start showing up at Drake's every Sunday at 4:30 pm to see if the girl shows up. He would simply introduce himself, ask if he could have a conversation and tell his story that led up to him paying for her dinner. Yes, this Sunday he would be at Drake's.

Chapter 26

Got to Get You Into My Life

Henry woke up at 6:00 am as was his habit, even on the weekends. Molly was still asleep in his master bedroom. He would let her sleep and when she awoke, he would either fix her breakfast or take her to a breakfast bar down on McClurg. He went to the kitchen and made a pot of coffee, opened the door, and retrieved his morning Chicago Tribune and sat on the couch and began reading. He reflected on last evening and how while what he wanted and what he actually did were two distinctly different things. He was a man after all and going to bed with Molly was a normal feeling. However, he sensed this was something special and did not want to spoil it.

About 8:15, he heard stirrings from down the hall, and Molly shuffled into the living room. "Morning sunshine, did you sleep well," he asked. "I had a little trouble getting to sleep (she had been excited about the evening) but once I was out, I was out for the count," she said. He gave her the options for breakfast, and she suggested that she fix breakfast. He replied, "It's my house and I'll fix breakfast, when I am at your place you can have full command of the kitchen," he said. Henry told Molly he would get her coffee while she got dressed and they would go to the breakfast bar.

On weekends, Molly enjoyed ten miles runs in the woods of Park Forest with her twin Bridget. They did this on Saturday and Sunday afternoons on most weekends and the increased the mileage as the calendar neared October and the Chicago Marathon. They would usually meet at about one or two in the afternoon. After they left the breakfast bar, Henry and Molly walked back to get his car and drive back to Oak Park. They hopped in, put the top down, and headed through town to the Eisenhower expressway and the twenty-minute drive to Molly's apartment building. Saturday morning the traffic was noticeably light, and Henry got to put a little more speed to the Porsche. Periodically, he sneaked a look at Molly and thought to himself how lucky he was to be seeing someone as smart, witty, and beautiful. Then he thought to himself, as he always did when things were going well in his life, now just don't screw it up.

Molly was doing the same thing, sneaking looks and thinking. She had relationships in the past that started out too good to be true and in fact ended up too good to be true.

She thought it a good sign that while the past couple of days had been intense, Henry had not tried to pressure her physically and that was a good sign. She hoped he would ask to see her again and wondered whether she should be coy and slow down a bit or keep the intensity; maybe Bridget would have thoughts on their run this afternoon.

They arrived at Molly's Oak Park apartment building. Henry quickly moved around the car to open the door for Molly (no one did that any longer, not that she could remember) and walked her up the back steps to her door. After Molly unlocked the door, she turned towards him. He took her in his arms and gave her a long hug then bent down and gave her a long tender kiss, stroked her cheek with his hand and then said, "You're a good Catholic girl, how about going to Mass with me in the morning?" She said, "I'd love to." He said, "Great, I'll pick you up at 9:00."

Henry descended the steps to the parking lot and drove off slowly watching Molly in the rearview mirror as she entered her flat. As soon as Molly was inside, she called Bridget to confirm their run at two. Bridget could tell she was happy and excited by her voice and couldn't wait to see her and get the full scoop about this new man in her life.

Molly changed into her running clothes and shoes and packed a pair of jeans and a fresh top into a bag to change into at Bridget's place. It was now 12:30, she decided to call Bridget back and tell her she would meet her at her house instead of the running trail at the park. She would be there about 1:15, then they would go together to the park. She was too excited to start running without telling her about the last two days before their run.

Henry drove out of the lot, down the street and back onto the Eisenhower expressway towards the city. He turned on his favorite FM station and just caught the very beginning of a Beatles song *Got to Get You into My Life* and thought to himself, "Boy isn't that the truth." He was absolutely enamored with Molly. Was it love? Not sure but whatever it was it was intense and strong and felt incredibly good. Again, he said to himself "Don't screw it up."

Chapter 27
Ask Me Why?

Doc landed at Muhammad Ali International at 8:30 in the morning. He went to the long-term parking lot, retrieved his Jeep Cherokee, and drove to his brother Patrick's house to pick up Betsy. Betsy loved being with Patrick as Patrick loved to take very long walks every day, which is what Betsy lived for. It took only about twenty minutes to get to Patrick's. Betsy was excited to see Doc, tail wagging and jumping up and down. He said, "Hey girl, let's go for a nice long walk, how about that huh." Dogs are said to have a vocabulary of over two hundred fifty words, but at the top of the list is WALK or WALKIES.

Doc and Betsy bid goodbye to Patrick and headed to the park. On second thought, instead of going to the park, Doc drove a few miles further to a former monastery, Mt. St. Francis, where there were trails to be walked. He changed into running shoes he kept in the back of the car, grabbed his cane, and Betsy's leash. They were going to walk a three-mile trail through the woods. "Come on girl," he said. The two started down the winding path climbing up and down. Betsy was loving it and Doc was relishing the time to think. He thought about life's path that had brought him to this place and time.

He was sixty-four, walked with a cane, and a slightly frozen left side of his face. He felt a freak. This is really the first time he'd thought of his deficiencies since the surgery. It hadn't mattered to him till recently. Till that Sunday at Drake's and he saw that young lady. Well, young, being thirty-five. But to him, thirty-five is young with, a long future.

Yes, Sunday at Drake's had changed things. He was quite sure how, but things were different for him. He just wasn't sure how, but he felt different. He was distracted. He felt lighter in his step, but also confused. His last serious relationship was with Molly. There had been other women along the way, nice women, but he just couldn't find it within himself to make a commitment. He often thought of what his daughter Annie would have been like. Would he have been a good father? What would life had held for the three of them as a family. The past years had been filled with thoughts of what ifs. It was time to let things go, not forget, but after all these years to finally move on. He didn't realize it, but he had stopped walking and Betsy had been lying on the ground looking up at him as if to say, "Can we walk some more."

He got moving and Betsy was overjoyed. They walked the rest of the trail and got back in the car. He continued thinking on the drive home. A plan started coming to his mind. He would call Brandon and find out the name of the waiter at Drake's. He needed something, someone in his life besides Betsy. No offense dear puppy, but I have to have a life. That's it, call Brandon, get the waiter's name, and find out what he might know about the woman or that group of women.

Doc and Betsy arrived at their house on the river. Because the house is in a flood plain, the livable floor had to be built fifteen feet above ground making the first floor a garage. Doc also had an elevator installed which made it easier for the aging Betsy to get up and down. Once inside Doc got Betsy a treat, found himself a cigar, made a Bourbon and Amaretto and went out to the deck to enjoy the afternoon. The house was small, fourteen hundred square feet, three bedrooms (one served as an office) and a large deck overlooking the river. He took his drink and cigar to a zero-gravity recliner and Betsy followed and laid beside the chair.

Doc sipped his Bourbon and smoked his cigar, all the while wondering to himself, what he would do if he actually made a connection with the woman from Drake's. Was he too old for her? What really did he expect from a conversation? Was he going to date her, become a mentor, a friend? The more he thought about it the more an element of fear took hold. Go into it with no expectation other than a friendly conversation and to tell a story of why he bought the dinner. Try not to bore her but share some memories that her very appearance evoked in him.

Chapter 28

Carry That Weight

We all carry burdens in our lives. It was a wonder that Doc achieved at a high level, not because of a lack of intellect, but because of years of unintentional emotional abuse, an incident of physical abuse, and quite naturally low self-esteem and self-worth. Because his mother treated Doc harsher than his sister, his mistakes and frailties were always pounced upon as being reflective of his father's behavior. If he continued, he would become his father.

The relationship became a one of love-hate between them. He never felt comfortable in sharing anything with his mother. If he had a problem to share, he feared he would be assumed to be weak and compared to his father. In elementary school, he was molested by a male teacher and never told his mother or anyone. He finally at age forty told his mother, who quickly and shortly told him I'm sorry that happened to you and then quickly changed the subject.

He became a sensitive person in adulthood, but he also became a person who became easily hurt. His childhood affected his relationships with women. He was very thoughtful of women, caring, and nurturing toward them. However, when criticized by women, it felt just like it was mom. He always remembered that lyric of the song "Mother" by the Police, "Every girl I date becomes my mother in the end." Consequently, though throughout his life he would fall in love a few times, when women got too close, he would put up walls. He would not allow any woman to get too close. He would choose to end the relationship. The first casualty was his college sweetheart. It was a foregone conclusion that they would marry. Before he graduated (double major Secondary Education and Political Science) he was offered a teaching job at a rural high school. He turned it down reasoning that he would be teaching history to kids just four and five years younger than he was and what world experience did he have to offer? When he graduated from college instead of getting married, Doc broke off the relationship with Jean, moved to Dallas and worked for a prominent private investigator for the next two years.

He felt badly for Jean, but they never spoke again. His inability to separate criticism from a woman he loved from the memories and images of his mother when criticism came, left him frozen emotionally. His two years in Dallas were a wild ride. The man he worked for was manic depressive (today bipolar). It was a bit like working for a male version of his mother. However volatile, the two grew close. Doc was technically an investigator and researcher, but he became a personal assistant to this very wealthy man. He learned organizational skills from the man, how to manage business relationships and planning. He often planned trips and traveled with the man both domestically and internationally as he worked high profile cases.

Doc became good at his job and the man relied and depended upon him to organize and get things done, often on the fly. These skills would serve him well in his future career. He learned that what people say sometimes are vastly different from who they are inside. The traveling together with the man helped him to understand this anomaly. If Doc forgot a detail, the man would enter his office and say, "Henry I love you like a son, but God Damn it, pay more attention before you get things to me." Then he would proceed to give Doc a lesson on more organizational skills.

The man, Bob Davis, owned the investigative agency, a retail clothing store, a manufacturing company, his properties in Dallas, and two properties in Florida. Doc served as an intermediary for all these operations and their managers. His work involved prioritizing Bob's time, travel, paperwork going to his desk, and meetings. This wealthy man had a twenty-nine-acre estate within the Dallas city limits that Doc also was responsible for managing. His estate included a guest cottage where Doc could live, and he was also provided with a car with a two-way radio.

For a little over two years, Doc spent nearly 24/7 working for Bob Davis. It was intense, instructive, frustrating, and ultimately fulfilling in terms of maturing and learning. He was a twenty-two-year-old right out of college and by the time he left he was twenty-four and had an abundance of experience he never would have gotten had he stayed at home in southern Indiana. Bob is eighty-three now, but he and Doc still trade phone calls several times a year. One thing Doc learned from Bob, try not to burn bridges. That was easy for Doc throughout business and friendships, but certainly not in his love life. While he lived in Dallas, Doc dated two or three girls, only one (Carol) seriously, but broke up when he told her he was leaving.

After his experience working for Bob, Doc decided to move back to southern Indiana. He had saved up enough money (not having to pay rent living in the guest cottage) to put some in savings and to exist for up to six months without working while he looked for the right opportunity.

Chapter 29
Because

It's the Tuesday after Sarah and Michele went to the pub. On her way back home from work, Sarah's thoughts were scrambled. She realizes she needs a good sit down with her mom. She always knew exactly what to say. Sarah loved advice from her mother because she has always been brutally honest. Regardless of what Sarah wants to hear, Anna always tells her what she needs to hear. For the most part, Sarah is moderately independent. Throughout past relationships and friendships, rarely has she gone to her mother for advice. When she did, most of the time her mind was made, she just needed confirmation that she was on the right path. Sarah knew that Anna was the shrink of the family. Though without a doctorate or degree in psychiatry, Anna had been through so much trauma and hardship. She found her way through life by learning from those around her. Sarah administered that trait.

Once home from work, Sarah feeds Binx and plays with him for a bit. She decides to text her mom to see if she had plans for the night. Sarah can never guess her mother's schedule. One minute she is at a boxing class and the other minute on a spa trip. Anna loved to keep herself busy, but most importantly healthy. "Healthy body, healthy mind," she always said. Sarah believes that to be true as well. They do go to the gym together sometimes, but Sarah prefers the gym on the other side of town while Anna goes to the gym closest to her. Not to mention Sarah holds herself to more rigorous training. While Anna ages, she brings herself to the more straightforward means of exercise while in the gym. Boxing and Jiu-Jitsu are her more stringent forms of self-defense. Sarah took both boxing and Jiu-Jitsu when she was younger but doesn't consider doing it anymore. While Sarah's father was sick, he advised Anna to join a type of self-defense class. He wanted her to be confident with her abilities to protect herself, though she has always been a strong person. Sometimes it's satisfactory to just build confidence in yourself.

After a bit of chat, Anna is on her way to Sarah's for dinner. Once she arrives, Binx greets her at the door. "Hi, Binxie, how are you doing sweet boy?" Anna says to him. Meanwhile, Sarah was finishing the bit of tidying up. She wouldn't want her mother to think she lived in a barn. The two greet each other with hugs and sit down at the kitchen island to catch up on the past week or so since they've seen one another. Anna says to Sarah, "You know your birthday is exactly a month from today?! What do you want to do to celebrate?" Sarah was turning 25 on May 29th. She replies, "Yes mom I know, maybe you me and the girls can go out for dinner and go watch a movie at the theatre." "That sounds great to me," Anna exclaims "with vanilla cake and ice cream to finish the night off of course." Sarah giggles. "Duh, mom." Sarah began to ponder her thoughts while swirling the ice water in her wine glass. Her father's birthday is three days after hers. Since he passed, she likes to celebrate her father on her birthday as well. Though it's difficult to enjoy it fully like she did when he was there. "Are you alright honey?" Anna inquires. Sarah replies, "Yeah, I'm okay. Just have a lot on my mind." Of course, Anna went full mom mode. "Well, if it's important you know you can talk to me." Sarah says, "I know mom. It's nothing. I just miss dad is all." Anna says while leaning in for a hug, "Me too babe, me too."

The two spent their night with the chicken parmesan Anna made and the sweet snickerdoodle cookies Sarah baked for dessert. Sarah never found herself cooking other than basics, but she has always loved to bake treats. Her and her mother have such a good partnership in the kitchen. Though the two talked of many different topics, the man at Drake's never came up. Sarah thought about asking her mother's opinion, but what could she even say? The night wasn't over, so she thought maybe I'll just mention it. The two sat on the couch discussing Michele and her current boyfriend issues. Sarah says, "Speaking of Michele, me her and the girls were at Drake's the other Sunday. This older man paid for all of our dinners." Anna looks shocked, "Wow really? What for? Did you know him?" Sarah replies, "No, none of us did. He didn't speak to us. The waiter said it was because I reminded him of his late wife. It brought joy to him I suppose." Anna replies, "Wow, that is so sweet. What a sweet man. I wonder what happened to her. Did you get to tell him thank you?" Sarah says, "No, him and the men he was eating with left before we got to speak. It's kind of weird actually. Me and Michele went to Drake's this past Sunday just to see if we would run into him again. Just to say thank you and maybe speak to him for a while, but we didn't see him." Anna raises her eyebrows in response, "Oh really? Well maybe you'll run into him again. That's really kind of him to do that. I know you girls aren't cheap." She giggles, "I used to feed all four of you all the time!" Sarah smiles, "And you're a strong woman for that mom."

It was getting late, so Sarah escorts her mother to her car and says her goodbyes. On her walk back up the stairs to her apartment door, Sarah can't help but feel a weight lifted off her shoulders. She always feels so comforted when she gets time with her mother. Even with the simplest of conversations.

Chapter 30
I've Got a Feeling

Molly arrived at Bridget's house in Park Forest about 12:45pm well ahead of their 2 pm run through the park. Upon seeing her twin, Bridget said, "Well you better tell me everything about this guy, even the flaws." Molly told her that so far, he was terrific and hasn't seen any flaws. Heck she even stayed the night at his condo, and he didn't try anything. He even suggested she take the master suite and he slept in the guest bedroom/office. Bridget said, "What's wrong with this picture? He sounds too good to be true."

"He has been the perfect gentleman so far. By the way, I hit on him, not the other way around," Molly said. She told Bridget that she had a crush on Dr. Morrison from the first day of her class. "Geez, Molly, he was your teacher? Isn't that a fetish?" Bridget said. "I never thought of it that way Bridget," Molly said. "Okay Molly, let's get to it, tell me about him."

Molly described him as tall, slim build, dark hair (starting to lose a little in the back), had the bluest eyes I think I've ever seen, he's funny, and bright. Bridget said, "Is he gay? Is he close to his mom? Does he have a record? And he didn't try anything with you? Did he try to round third and try to slide into home?" "No, no, no, no, and NO!" Molly said. Molly told Bridget that Henry even asked her to go to Mass with him in the morning. "Oh, good lord girl, you've got to start your subtle interrogation," Bridget told her sister. Bridget suggested to Molly that she spend the night with her in Oak Park and go to Mass with them both in the morning. "Oh no you don't, Bridget. I can just see you asking provoking questions and blow any chance I might have with Henry," said Molly.

Bridget asked Molly where Henry went to Mass. Molly told her it was St. Peter's on Madison Street at the corner of Clark Street. "Does he live in the Loop?" asked Bridget. Molly told her that he lived in a condo building on Ohio Street near the new Sheraton Hotel on the Chicago River. The two chatted for a few minutes longer over a cup of dark roast coffee, then got in Bridget's car and headed to the park.

When they arrived at the park, they headed to the five-mile loop for their weekend two lap run. A ten-mile run allowed little opportunity for a conversation other than a few words here and there. They acknowledged the regular crowd of runners and friends along the trail. After their ten-mile run, they walked to Bridget's car and drove back to her house. Bridget asked the ultimate question, "Molly, when are going to take him to meet Mom?" "Have you told him anything about our family?" Bridget asked if Molly knew anything about Henry's family. Molly said that she knew that there was a bit of a tough relationship with his mother and was estranged somewhat from his father. Bridget didn't think that sounded good. They hugged each other, said they loved each other, and Molly drove back to her flat in Oak Park.

Molly had an uneventful evening, a dinner of pasta and two glasses of red wine settled her down a bit for the evening. She was happy about going to Mass in the morning with Henry. She wondered what he was thinking about the relationship but didn't really want to force the question. She wanted to enjoy every moment she spent with him and take each day as it came for now. The rest of her evening was spent with her cat Bear on her lap and listening to Mozart on the CD player. She went to bed about ten and set her alarm for seven in the morning.

Meanwhile, Henry spent his afternoon by going into the office to catch up on report writing and pick up his travel packet for the week that Betsy had left for him. He and Vice President of Sales for the Eastern Half of the United States, Mike Mackowiak, would be traveling to Palo Alto, California for a week of sales and product meetings. He would return on a Red Eye to Chicago arriving early Friday morning. About four o'clock while working at his desk, he fell into a daydream. His office on the ninth floor of the building looking down onto E. Wacker Drive and the Chicago River.

His phone at his desk rang jarring him out of his daydream about Molly. No woman had ever so captivated him like her. He picked up the phone and it was Betsy. She said, "I knew you would be at the office, so I didn't even try your home." Betsy was about the same age as Henry but had a mothering personality in general and specifically towards Henry even though she had only known him a short time. She asked if he had found his travel folder. He told her yes and thanked her for keeping him so organized. Betsy went on to ask how things were with him and Molly. He told Betsy, "I feel incredibly happy in general and I revel in every moment I spend with her and I find myself thinking of her constantly. I'm taking her to Mass with me at St. Peter's in the morning." Betsy said, "That's nice, I think you are getting serious in a very short time." "I am, but it feels good and right," he answered her.

After talking to Betsy for a few minutes he said goodbye and made his weekly phone call to his mother. It would be the same as every week. She would never ask Henry about his life; she would always jump into venting and bitching to Henry about his stepdad or his sister Kathleen. This week, she was bitching about Kathleen for some reason and Henry didn't pay too much attention any longer. The only time Mom would ever call Henry was if she needed his help. He was a sounding board and problem solver. It used to bother him, but it now was just the way things were.

After the thirty-minute phone call with his mother, he called Kathleen. She answered the phone and the first thing she said, "So who was on the chopping block this week? Me or Dad." He said, "It was you, but I honestly can't remember why, you know how she gets, I just let her ramble as usual." Kathleen asked what was new with him and he told her in depth about Molly. She told him it seemed awfully quick and, "You know your fear of relationships," she added. Kathleen reminded him that he had just come out of a relationship before you moved to Chicago and "I don't think you want another black eye," she said.

Before moving to Chicago a few months before, he had been in a three-year relationship with Madeline. They began as friends, good friends evolved to lovers and living together. They had lived together for about eighteen months and it is in living together that you really find out who people are. He had discovered that Madeline was essentially a functional alcoholic. One evening, not too long before he moved to Chicago, Madeline wanted to pick him up at the train station after work. It was his birthday and Madeline had planned to take Henry to dinner and to a comedy club to surprise him for his birthday. When Henry got off the train, he was thirty minutes late, it had been a busy bad day, and he had a pounding migraine headache.

They went to a nice dinner, but he did not really feel like going to the comedy club. Madeline had two to three drinks while Henry had one. Madeline persisted and drove them to the comedy club. When they got out of the car, Henry again said he really felt bad and would like to do this on another night. Madeline stormed around the car and hauled off and punched Henry in his left eye catching him off guard and knocking him to the ground. About a month later, he took the Chicago job. Surprisingly, despite the KO, they separated on good terms.

Kathleen told her brother that she sincerely hoped Molly would turn out to be a good relationship for him. She told him "Look, when you decide to take her down to meet Mom, make sure I'll be there to help run interference for you."

Chapter 31

Good Day Sunshine

Sunday morning broke sunny and clear. Beautiful blue skies, with just a few clouds. Molly started getting ready for church in happy anticipation of her church date. She put on a blue sundress and a pair of flats for comfort, and a white cardigan as cathedrals were notoriously cold. She took time to put on her makeup and brush her hair. She didn't want too much makeup, it was after all Mass, so she would be rather conservative. Her strawberry blonde hair fell softly onto her shoulders. She placed a black headband on to pull her hair gently off her face. By the time she was finished, Henry would be arriving within fifteen or twenty minutes.

Downtown, Henry was just putting on his navy-blue jacket on over a blue button-down shirt, khaki slacks, and a pair of loafers. He was ready for Mass, he always looked forward to Mass but today was special as it would be the first time in a long while that he would be taking a special woman with him. With a spring in his step, he went out the door to the elevators and pressed the button for the garage floor. He got off, went through the door to the garage and walked the one hundred yards to his parking space. He hopped in, started the engine, and put the top down.

Normally, he would walk to St. Peter's (which took about fifteen to twenty minutes), but what a special day this would be, and he hoped Molly would be up for the surprise he had in store for her. Before he knew it, he was on the westbound Eisenhower and coming up on the Oak Park Exits. His mind was on Molly, as she occupied most of his thoughts these days. He knew that after Mass she would go to Park Forest for another long run with Bridget, but he planned to ask them both for a relaxing picnic after their run. He had gone to Marshall Field's after he left work Saturday and bought one of those fancy wicker picnic baskets, he ordered a picnic lunch from the Marshall Field's deli and picked up a bottle of Chardonnay. The picnic basket had a checked tablecloth, flatware, and wine glasses for four. He would ask Molly if he could take her and Bridget on a picnic in Sauk Trail Woods after their run.

He was just pulling up to the parking lot to Molly's apartment building. He hopped out of the car and bounded up the stairs to the kitchen door of her apartment. She and her cat Bear were waiting on Henry. The cat was slowly growing fond of Henry. Molly invited him in then threw her arms around him and planted a passionate kiss on his lips. Henry said, "What was that for, not that I'm complaining." "I needed something for confession next week," she replied. "Well, all I've got to say to that is, um, keep on sinning!" he told her.

On the way to the car, he said to her, "Hey, by the way what are you doing after your run this afternoon?" She said, "Nothing really." "Then, why don't I take you and Bridget on a picnic in Sauk Trail Park?" he asked. She looked at him with a smile on her face and said, "Let me call Bridget really quick." He gave Molly his flip phone and said, "Give her a call on the way to Mass." As they got in the car Molly dialed Bridget, who was more than happy to go on a picnic. Molly said, "All set, she's anxious to meet you. Do I need to fix anything?" Henry looked over at her and said, "Nope all arranged and taken care of."

They were back on the Eisenhower Expressway headed into town. It was still early, and the heathens hadn't woken up yet, so traffic was exceptionally light. They got into town and Henry found his way to Madison and found a parking spot on the street just a half a block from St. Peter's. He put the top up, opened the door for Molly, locked the car and took her by the hand into St. Peter's. They were just a couple of minutes late and walked in behind the procession and Father McKenzie. They took seats in a nearly empty row near the back of the church. Henry always felt peaceful in the church. Today that peace was met with a feeling of bliss with Molly next to him. They sang together, they kneeled and prayed together, and took the holy Eucharist together. It was late August, and the gospel readings were from St. Luke and dealt with serving others.

On the way to the car, Molly said, "Why don't you drive me to Bridget's house, and you can wait there while we run. I'm sure she won't mind." Henry said, "Great, but I have to run back to my place and pick up the picnic basket and the food. It's all ready and I'll slip on a pair of jeans." While Molly changed into her running togs and shoes, Henry sat on the couch with Bear. Molly appeared a short while later in a tee shirt, running shorts, and her hair in a ponytail carrying a small bag with a change of clothes.

Fifteen minutes later, they pulled into the garage and made for the elevator to Henry's floor. When they got off the elevator there were a couple of suits and several shirts hanging on the doorknob with a note. The note was from Chris (the weekend doorman) "Mr. Morrison, the dry cleaner had this for you and added it to your bill, Chris." "Damn, that guy is good, he saved me again," said Henry. He told Molly he was leaving for San Francisco in the morning and had forgot to stop by the dry cleaner in the building. "I did tell you I was going to be out of town this week, didn't I?" Molly assured him he had. He told he would miss her while he was gone, and she said the same to him.

"Wow, you really prepared! A picnic basket with wine glasses, flatware, tablecloth," she said. He told her there was a bottle of Chardonnay in the fridge along with three plastic bags of goodies for the picnic, including a cherry pie for dessert. He told her he would be a couple of minutes and he changed into a pair of jeans, a Polo shirt, and a pair of Sperry deck shoes (no socks of course). They grabbed the supplies, and the picnic basket and headed to the garage. As soon as he came out of the garage he circled around to the front of the building and hopped out of the car and stepped quickly to the front desk. He found the doorman Chris and tipped him a five for saving him again and was just as quickly back in the car.

Since it was a nice day, Henry put the top down on the Porsche and took Lake Shore Drive (LSD) through Jackson Park to the Chicago Skyway and down to Park Forest. It was a fun drive in the Porsche driving along the lakefront on such a nice day. On the way to Park Forest, Molly told him about Bridget. They were identical twins; Bridget was the oldest by a couple of minutes and was the more serious and critical of the two. And yes, she told him, they did think alike, and many times finished each other's sentences. She said, "There is another big difference and that is Bridget is gay but really hasn't come to terms with it yet, more out of fear of our mother's reaction."

When they arrived at Bridget's house, Bridget was waiting at the door in her running garb. She welcomed Molly and Henry into the house for a few minutes of talk and coffee. Conversation was pleasant and Bridget told Henry to make himself at home while she and Molly were on their run. Henry had brought a book with him to read while the girls were running. Molly and Bridget left in Bridget's car for the five-minute drive to the running trails.

Chapter 32
Misery

It had been a surreal year for Doc. He had taken on two separate startup companies, done a consulting project for the county jail, retired from teaching, and was now facing a lawsuit. But perhaps the most surreal event had been the encounter with the young woman at Drake's. Sometimes, he wondered how he made it through the year.

A year ago, Doc retired from twenty years of public-school teaching. He had really not wanted to retire, he loved the kids and now dearly missed them, but it was the frustration with school administration that had driven him to his retirement. It was every day that he missed the students. He frequently ran into former students; several would stop by to visit and those were cherished moments for him.

Not long before he retired, he was asked by the county sheriff if he would take on an education consulting project at the county jail. He was to increase the level of education courses and opportunities for the inmates and education programs for corrections officers as well. His first task was to increase the number of opportunities for the female inmates. Throughout the year he introduced more GED courses for the women, brought in a Yoga instructor three times a week to aid in relieving female inmate stress, and began a culinary certification program for the women to help with careers when they were released. He also got the Center for Women and

Children involved to teach things like empowerment courses to help build self-confidence.

He had accomplished positive things at the county jail. He had put his doctoral work in emotional intelligence to work in the selection process for classes. He screened applicants for the courses with a short emotional intelligence (EI) survey to determine those inmates with higher self-awareness and self-management skills. This led to a higher success rate in the courses among the inmates. At the end of the year, he turned the program over to the sheriff's staff to hire a full-time person to carry on and manage the programs.

Of course, there was the frustrating experience of working with John and the first startup company where he and Jesse and Brandon had met. John was continuing to be a problem that would not go away. We had a phone conference with our attorney Bart just the other day. He informed us that John had instructed his attorney to notify us that he was going to file an injunction with the court to shut our business down, as we were stealing business from him and decreasing his revenue.

First, he needed to have revenue to decrease. John could not focus long enough on one product to allow for sales of it. He had a million ideas and sent his developers galloping off in three and four different directions. John had not generated in the year and a half the company had been in operation. In Bart's legal opinion, John really did not have a case for an injunction, furthermore, all the judges in the county were loath to award an injunction against a company. Bart told the guys to relax, that more than likely the case would be dismissed by the time it got to court.

The company was moving forward with Gary's project and four other proposals in the pipeline. Things were looking particularly good for the new company and Doc turned 64 this week. With a cigar in his mouth, he was beginning to look a lot like Churchill only not drinking nearly as much. Birthdays are a melancholy time for Doc. He reflects on his life and depresses himself thinking about the things he hasn't accomplished. But the one thing that hangs over him the most is that question about his legacy.

Men tend to think about their careers and family legacy. Doc did not have any children and had not married after Molly's death. So, what will his legacy be? Over the years of teaching, he had encountered over one thousand students at the rural school, the Catholic school in Louisville where he was principal, and the school in Hong Kong where he was principal. Many still stayed in touch with him over the years and in fact today, his birthday, he had already received over fifty birthday wishes from former students on Twitter. That warmed his heart, but it felt like there was a void, an emptiness that was children. His students meant a lot to him, but it wasn't really the same. Had Molly and his unborn daughter lived, his daughter, Olivia, would have been twenty-six years old this year. He couldn't help but wonder what Olivia would have looked like, what her personality would have been, and what she would have done with her life. And the big question, would he have been a good father?

It was all this reflecting that influenced him to call Jesse to meet him for dinner at Drake's, his treat. Jesse was still driving for Uber to pay the bills until the company began bringing in enough income to pay the three of them. Two hours later, he met Jesse at the bar and got a table near the front where they met the last time they were here. It was a Sunday night, just like the time before, and he was hoping the women, or the one woman would be there again. Drake's was the kind of place that had its regular customers.

Doc and Jesse began talking about the lawsuit and the project for Gary. It was clear to Jesse that Doc's attention wasn't all on their conversation. Jesse said, "Doc, where are you tonight?" Doc apologized and told Jesse what had happened the last time they sat here at Drake's. Jesse remembered that Doc had seemed distracted that night as well. Jesse said, "Why don't you just ask the waiter if she has been in lately, he always works on Sundays so he would know." Jesse called the waiter, Jason, over to their table, and Doc asked, "Do you remember the last time we were here a couple of weeks ago?" "Yeah, I remember, you paid the bill of a group of women seated over there (he pointed to the table near them)," said Jason. Doc asked Jason if the one woman had been back. "Yes, just last Sunday afternoon late," Jason said. Jason added that it seemed the woman was looking around quite a bit. Doc said, "Jason, here is twenty bucks for you (pulling a twenty out of his wallet) and my business card with my number and email. If she is in again, please pass it on to her, that I would like to have a dinner and conversation with her." Jason said, "Sure and thanks and I'll give you a call if that happens." "Great," said Doc. Jesse asked, "Do you know what you're doing Doc?" "No," answered Doc. "But I'm getting too old to start questioning my instincts," he added.

Chapter 33
I Want to Tell You

The girls finished their run and came through Bridget's front door giggling. Henry asked what was so funny? Both Bridget and Molly answered together "Girl stuff!" They disappeared upstairs to get a shower and change clothes while Henry waited. About thirty minutes later, they both bounded down the stairs. Molly was in jeans, a black tee shirt, and her running shoes. Bridget was in jeans, running shoes, and a white tee shirt. They looked like the twins they were, white and black, yin and yang look. Except that Bridget had severely short hair and Molly's laid on her shoulders. Since Henry's car was a two-seater, they took Bridget's car back to the park.

Bridget had a four door Ford Granada. Henry let the girls have the front seat while he and the picnic basket and supplies took the back seat. They arrived at the park and walked to a spot on a hill under a nice shady tree. Henry took the checked tablecloth out of the basket and spread it out on the ground. Henry asked if the girls minded if he said a prayer before they ate. Neither objected so he began. Henry gave thanks for the beautiful day and for placing Molly and Bridget in his life. Molly took the plates and flatware out and spread out the cheeses, fruit, cold cuts, bread, and condiments. It seemed that Henry had planned for everything. Henry said wait, I did not bring a flower, so he jumped up and traipsed off into the forest to find some wildflowers. Bridget said to Molly when Henry left "He seems very sweet and thoughtful." Molly replied, "He is and that is what I find most attractive about him."

The three ate, drank wine, and talked for better than an hour and a half over the picnic lunch. Henry discovered that both girls were fans of classical music and classic rock and that Bridget was a non-profit fund raiser, which involved a lot of party throwing, direct mail campaigns, and an annual black-tie banquet. He also discovered that the two were in an ongoing "twin's study" at the Indiana University Medical school. They would go to the medical school campus in Indianapolis to participate in a different experiment about twice per year. They received mileage expense, overnight accommodations, and a small stipend.

This past year the twin study required one twin to drink until they were inebriated and the other to remain sober. They both would have to perform various tasks and the drunk twin would have to do the tasks in various stages of drunkenness. Bridget asked about working in New York as Henry had for five years. Henry told the girls that he had worked in the Pan Am building which sat on Park Ave above Grand Central Terminal. He was one of three men in an office of fourteen. On Friday nights after work he, Alvin Tostig (the gay receptionist in the office) would go down to the Tropica bar for cigarettes and Martinis and dish the dirt for the week. Henry wasn't a smoker except on Friday nights with the girls.

He shared an office with a tall, slender, fortyish blond, ex-Marine named Beth. He told how when Beth was out on an account visit one of the other women would come sort of snooping sheepishly around her desk, which faced Henry's. He would look up and say, "They're in the top left drawer." The woman would respond, "What?" Then he would say, "The Tampons, they're in the top left drawer." The woman (whoever it was) would open the drawer, take what she needed, then slip back out of the office. Henry's best friend in the office was an attractive brunette named Diane. He pronounced her name like the character on the TV show pronounced the lead character Diane, and in turn Diane always referred to and called him Cliffy. The two shared a wicked sense of humor and held court at the Tropica on Friday nights.

Bridget had gotten her degree from the Pratt Institute in Brooklyn and loved to talk to people from New York City or folks who worked there. After a couple of hours or so, it was getting time for Henry to get back to the city and pack for his California trip. He told the girls that business would take up Monday through Wednesday, then Wednesday evening he would drive to Sacramento to stay a couple of days with his half-brother Jack, and then the two would drive to the foothills of the Sierra's to spend a day or two with their father. Henry explained that he had been estranged from his father when he was growing up, but once he was about twenty-five and began traveling the United States on business, he would make time to visit his father, who lived in a small town called Plymouth a few miles east of Sacramento near Sutter's Mill.

The three gathered up the picnic basket and the leftovers and piled into the car for the short drive back to Bridget's house. They had finished the bottle of wine but there were cold cuts, fruit, and cheese left over. Henry told Bridget to keep the leftovers as he would be gone until early next Sunday. The girls went into the kitchen to put away the leftovers, while Henry waited in the living room. When Molly returned, she had a smile on her face and a slight giggle. Henry gave Bridget a brief hug, she wished him a safe trip, and then Molly and Henry got into the Porsche and headed for the thirty-minute drive back to the city.

On the way, Molly said, "How about I take you and pick you up from the airport?" Henry replied that he used a car service that was the same cost as a cab, but the driver always had the morning Wall Street Journal and a cup of coffee waiting in the car. Molly then said, "Why don't I come down Sunday when you get back and fix you a nice dinner?" He replied, "That was a deal he could not refuse." He then asked Molly if she knew how to drive a stick. She replied that she learned to drive on a manual transmission car. He suggested that she keep his car for the week and use it, then she could come down Saturday and stay the weekend. He would be arriving at

O'Hare on a red eye flight from San Francisco and the car service would have him at his building at about 8:30 on Sunday morning. She looked at him and said, "You trust me with your Porsche?" "Of course, I do," he replied. But just for safety, why don't we find a parking lot where you can get used to the gearbox since you'll be driving it home tonight."

They took the Chicago Skyway into Jackson Park and got on LSD (Lake Shore Drive), they pulled into the empty parking lot at Soldier Field and switched seats. After a bit of practice Henry said, "Why don't you drive us to my building?" Molly drove the rest of the way and did fine with the high-performance car. She even remembered the parking garage entrance and where the parking space was.

Molly helped Henry pack, he said to her, "I need one suit, two dress shirts, and two ties. You pick those out and I'll get my casual wear together." Molly picked out a white button-down shirt and a blue button-down shirt, one rep stripe tie, and one paisley tie for the white shirt. She also looked in the closet and picked out a navy-blue, soft pin, stripe suit." Henry complimented he on her choices. He grabbed his black Tumi garment bag and hung the items in it. He packed a nice pair of loafers for the suit and his Sperry Top Siders for casual. He also packed a couple of Polo shirts and a couple of pair of jeans.

Henry went to the fridge and hit the tap on the "wine in a box" in the fridge and poured two glasses of Chardonnay. The two of them went to the couch in the living room and sat close to each other. Henry took a sip of wine, then put the glass on the coffee table, and put his arm around Molly pulling her close to him. He began kissing her neck, then her cheek, then placing his other arm across her he kissed her tenderly then passionately on the lips. Molly reciprocated and their kisses moved into some heavy petting. After several minutes, he took her hand in his and gave her a light kiss. He said to her, "It's not that I don't want to go further, it's that I think this is something special and I want you to know that I am interested in you, and believe I am falling in love with you." Molly blushed and said she felt the same way too. After a few minutes, Henry said, "It's getting late, I have an early flight and I want to make sure you get home safe." She said, "You're just worried about your car!" They both laughed, then slowly got up. "I'll walk you down to the car, but let's go to the lobby first, I want to make sure the doorman knows you."

They went to the lobby and Larry was on duty. Henry introduced Molly and Larry said he would alert the other doormen. Henry then took Molly up to the garage space. When they arrived at the car, he gave Molly a spare key chain with the car key and the condo key on it. "If you want to stay the week, that's fine with me. Stay as much or as little as you want. He pulled her to him and gave her a tender kiss and said, "I love you Molly." She blushed and said, "I love you Henry." He told her to drive safely and to call when she got home, then she got in the car, put the top up, and drove off. About twenty minutes later she called to say she had arrived safely and was locked up for the night and before she hung up, she said, "I do love you." He said, "I know, and I love you. This is the beginning of something wonderful, I think. Good night sweetheart." She said, "Good night Henry."

Chapter 34

Good Morning, Good Morning

Henry was up early Monday morning. The flight was at seven a.m. and James (African American) the owner of the car service would be picking Henry up at five a.m. for the twenty-minute ride to O'Hare. "Mr. Morrison, how are you this morning sir?" said James. "I am livin' the dream my friend, livin' the dream," Henry replied. They exchanged pleasantries, James handed him a Starbucks coffee (cream and two sugars) and Henry slid into the back seat and picked up the morning's *Wall Street Journal*.

James proceeded through the early morning light traffic on the expressway to O'Hare. Henry would meet Mike at the gate and hope for an upgrade to first class. Traveling with Mike Mackowiak was always a laugh. He was always lighthearted no matter the situation. Mike Mackowiak was Polish and a son of first-generation immigrants. The meeting they were heading to a manager's meeting preparing for the annual sales meeting in two months' time in mid-October. Mike was Vice President of Sales for the Eastern United States for the company and was Henry's immediate boss. Mike had six region managers reporting to him.

After clearing through security, he made his way to United Gate C 19 for the four-hour flight to San Francisco. He checked in at the gate and inquired of the gate agent how it looked for an upgrade to first class. The gate agent said it was a light flight today and checked Henry's name on the upgrade list. As she was checking his status, Mike walked up next to him and asked if she would check his status as well. Both men were Premium fliers. The gate agent said they were both in luck and were upgraded to first class. God how Henry hated to fly coach.

In a few minutes Time, the flight boarded, the plane backed away from the gate and taxied out. They were ninth in line for takeoff, a typical Monday morning at O'Hare. After twenty minutes of waiting their turn, they lined up for takeoff and were rolling down the runway. Four hours later they landed at San Francisco International, rented a car and made the drive to company headquarters in Palo Alto, about forty-five minutes south of the airport.

It was going to be a day of meetings with the President of the company, the VP of Sales, and an assortment of product managers presenting new databases that were in development or about to launch. Marketing managers would be telling how to position the company and its database products against the competition. Tuesday would be the day when district sales managers would meet with product departments to tell requests from customers and how customers perceive the company against their competitors. Wednesday would be a half day of working out the schedule of presentations, dinners, special events for the three-day sales meeting in October.

At the end of the day Monday, Mike, Henry, and a couple of other managers went out to dinner at a pub called Gordon Biersch, a microbrewery and restaurant not far off El Camino Real, the main road running from Stanford University through Palo Alto into the heart of Silicon Valley. Before Henry went to the table, he made a call to Molly to say he arrived safely and to say good night. He was realizing as he listened to her voice, just how deeply in love with her he was. He told her good night, that he loved her, and would call her the next evening. After hanging up the phone he made his way to the table. The men ate their dinner, talked about business, and stories about customers and competitors. At about ten, they finally broke to go back to their rooms at the Palo Alto Hyatt. Henry went to his room, got ready for bed, took a book out of his briefcase, and read for a few minutes. Thirty minutes later, he put the book down and went to sleep.

The next two days dragged on with product presentations. One lady from the patents and technical database development area went to the overhead projector with a three-inch stack of framed overhead transparencies with yellow sticky notes hanging off them. An audible groan could be heard from the sales managers with a sure nap to follow sometime in the next hour. By Wednesday afternoon with the last meeting, Mike and Henry went to lunch at a little place called Hobie's on El Camino not far from. Hobie's was a little dive breakfast and lunch place, popular with the company's employees.

After lunch, Henry drove Mike to the airport, telling him he would meet with him on Monday when he came back to the office. He said, "Tell Betsy if she needs me the next two days, not to hesitate to call, and fly safe my friend." "Will do," said Mike. Henry then headed out of the airport departures terminal to Highway 101 to I 5 North for the approximate two-hour drive to Sacramento. He would be staying with Jim tonight and Thursday before driving to the Sierras to spend a couple of days with his father. It was an interesting situation spending time with Jim if he thought too much about it. They shared a father. But it was that father who was having an affair with Jim's mom all those years ago. He just tried not to think too much about it.

As he got closer to Sacramento, he called Jim to tell him roughly where he was. Jim answered and said, "Tom and Susan will be meeting us at the Rubicon. Why don't you just pick me up at my house when you get to Sac, I'll leave work a bit early." The Rubicon was a microbrewery on Capitol Avenue in downtown Sacramento and it is where Henry and Jim usually got together when he came to town.

Meanwhile, back in Chicago, Molly was finishing her day teaching. One of her students said, "Miss, did you get a new car? It sure is cool." Molly said, "No, it belongs to my...... um my new friend." The girl, Cindy, said, "I'd like to have a friend like that." "Yes," said Molly, "He is a special friend." "Oooooh, a boyfriend!" said Cindy. A couple of other girls joined in. "Yes, I think so," said Molly, and then she began to blush. The teenaged girls gathered around her saying they were happy for her. After school was out, Molly gathered her things and walked to the parking lot. She unlocked the car, got in and put the top down. She started up the engine and noticed the car phone near the gear stick.

She picked up the car phone and dialed Henry's cell number. After three rings he answered. He said, "Why hello honey, I was just thinking of you." She asked how he knew it was her. He told her he recognized the number as his car phone. She told him about the girls in the classroom at the end of the day and she was a bit embarrassed, not ashamed, just caught off guard, but finally told the girls she had a boyfriend. She said, "I really miss you Henry. I was with you four days in a row and without you for two, and I really miss you." "I miss you too sweetheart," he said. He told her he was in the car on the way from San Francisco to Sacramento to stay with his half-brother and then spend two days with his father. He said, "I'll remind myself about the time change and call before you go to bed." She asked, "Do you mind if I go on to your condo tonight and stay until you get home?" He told her to go right ahead that it was fine with him. She said, "One more thing, can I sleep in one of your shirts?" He told her to pick any one out of the closet she liked and that he couldn't wait to see her.

After they hung up the call, they both silently smiled to themselves. Henry was just about thirty minutes from Jim's house near the California state capitol. Molly immediately drove home, sat with Bear for a while, changed the litter box and made sure Bear had enough food for a day. She gathered schoolwork, changes of clothing, and a few other things and got back in the Porsche for the drive downtown. It only took about twenty minutes or so to reach the building.

Within forty minutes of hanging up with Molly, Henry was pulling up to the small house downtown to find Jim waiting on the porch. It was 4:30 and Jim suggested they go onto the Rubicon and spend an hour or so catching up. Tom and Susan would be along about 5:30 and would be leaving early, as they had to drive the state road back to the foothills of the Sierra near where Henry's father lived. Jim and Henry arrive at the Rubicon about ten minutes before five, immediately got a table and began to look over the beer selections. Jim ordered the Amber Ale and Henry ordered an Angry Angus.

As their drinks arrived Jim asked Henry, "Are you still driving that old piece of junk Jaguar you've had for years. It must be close to twenty years old; it was ten when you bought it. And I bet you have more money in repair bills than you payed for it." "To answer your questions; no, yes, and yes." He told Jim that he was now driving a five-year-old Porsche Carrera that was in excellent shape as certified by an independent mechanic. "Boy, Dad will flip when he finds out you've bought a souped-up Volkswagen," said Jim. "I'm sure he wouldn't refuse driving it if I had it here." The two laughed over that. Neither one of the boys inherited their father's mechanical aptitude. Their father could almost take apart an engine and rebuild it blindfolded.

Chapter 35
Day Tripper

E veryone has a routine, or at least most people do. Doc would arise at
5:30, take Betsy out, then shower, and shave (if it were a weekday),
and have breakfast with the morning paper and a cup of coffee. For his
second cup of coffee, he would pick up whatever book he was reading, and
read until the sun rose. He would dress, grab his cane, put the leash on
Betsy, and then begin his morning walk through the village out to a main
road, then turn around and come back. The route was about four miles and
would take him about an hour and ten minutes to do a brisk walk.

At about 8:30 or 9:00, he would sit down and turn on a news channel.
Rarely, he would watch the local news, but he would find the BBC channel
to get a world perspective. The local news depressed him. It was always
shootings overnight, and what he perceived to be a collection of fluff filled
pieces that did not interest him. Around 11:30, he would have a salad, soup,
and half a sandwich of something and prepare to go to the office and work
with the boys from about 12:30 pm until 4:30 pm, Monday through Friday,
unless there was a meeting outside of those times.

In the evenings, Doc would take another long walk (evenings or
mornings only for Betsy) before dinner. Three nights a week he would go
out to eat, sometimes alone, sometimes with a friend and sometimes take-
out. Other nights would be pasta, or salads. It was a boring existence after

traveling the world and living in bigger cities. Sometimes he would go to a concert (rock or classical), a film etc. but mostly he preferred to watch a film or documentary on Netflix or read his books.

Now his routine would involve (at least for a while) late Sunday afternoon and evenings at the Drake's in St. Matthews. He just had to find someone to go with him each week. This was starting to feel a bit like a surveillance mission. And, really, what would he say if he ever saw the young lady. "Excuse me, I'd like to introduce myself. I'm the creeper who paid for your meal a few weeks ago." Not the best of introductions. He'd have to work on that. He was anxious about meeting the woman but excited at the same time. He would approach the opportunity with no expectations of any kind, other than at most making a possible friend.

He also had a routine at the end of the day. What hardly anyone knew outside of his family was how much pain he is in on a daily basis. That pain has become routine. Doc has eight inches of metal on each side of his cervical discs, and nearly every one of his remaining discs T12 to S1 is bulging and degenerating. Part of his daily routine is to lay on ice packs a couple of times per day to numb and ease that pain. This ice routine was part and parcel of his life as were periodic epidural injections into his back.

The phone rang and it was his friend Chuck White. Chuck and Doc had been friends for almost forty-five years, since college. Chuck was a retired high school assistant principal who had worked in a rural district rife with nepotism. He spent fourteen years of his career in that district trying always to do the right thing for students but being blocked by the nepotism and narrow mindedness of small district thinking. Chuck said, "How are things today with Dr. Morrison?" Doc replied, "Just about right old friend. What's up with you?" Chuck was suggesting that the two of them write a book on education. "Okay, I know how this will go, just like when I helped you with your master's thesis. I'll help with research. You will pace back and forth pontificating and dictating, while I type and disentangle your ramblings," said Doc. Chuck laughed and said, "Maybe so, but I think we can write something good." Doc said check with Victoria and see which night she can cut you loose, I'll buy your dinner and we can come back to my house and begin drafting an outline if you are serious." Chuck said he would call the next day to confirm a night.

Just as he hung up the phone, it rang again. Doc answered and heard, "Hey Doc it's me Mason Hutchinson. You had me in class two years ago." Doc replied, "Oh yes, Mason Jar, how are you my friend." "I'm fine, remember how I told you I was going to become a Marine? Well, I just graduated from boot camp and am now Private First-Class Hutchinson." Doc congratulated the boy and asked about his trade in the Marines. The boy told Doc that he was going to be in the Military Police. Doc said, "Are you going to work on your degree while in the Marines?" "Yes sir," replied Mason. They talked for a few minutes, Doc wished him luck and said he was proud of the boy and told him to keep in touch and Mason promised he would. After dinner, Doc picked up a book and read for a couple of hours, then took Betsy out and settled down to get ready for bed and a repeat of the routine tomorrow.

Chapter 36

She's a Woman

O thers had their routine. For Sarah, it also began early with a five-mile run through her neighborhood in the Highlands neighborhood of Louisville. On weekends, that run would go through the flats and hills of Cherokee Park. Sarah hadn't always been a runner. It started in college at Northwestern University, just north of Chicago. Several friends were runners and worked on her to start joining them. They ran along the lakefront of the campus in the mornings and sometimes in the evenings. The lakefront of the campus was a beautiful place to run. The breezes off Lake Michigan made even the toughest run, an enjoyable run.

Sarah majored in journalism. Northwestern was famous for its school of journalism; Sarah was a talented writer and had excellent possibilities. She wasn't sure in college if she were going to be a reporter or work public relations. Eventually, she opted for public relations after a short stint as a city reporter for a metropolitan daily. Writing about council meetings, and the police beat was not what she wanted to do with the rest of her life. She returned home to Louisville and went to work for a public relations firm. She enjoyed the work of forging images. She was lucky in that she worked for a firm that had ethical standards for the clients, corporate and individual, that they would sign on.

More recently, Sarah had been assigned to a group that dealt with crisis management, helping prominent figures and companies manage through critical times. For example, if a company individual embezzled, or did something illegal, Sarah's team would work behind the scenes at the company to guide the management through the crisis and move forward. She had managed situations from white collar crime to manufacturing plant explosions and also worked with a police department where an officer was involved in inappropriate behavior with several other officers.

Sarah had done well for herself. She followed the advice of her late father "Do not live beyond your means and avoid debt other than a mortgage." She had built a respectable career, bought a small home in the highlands, and financed it for fifteen years instead of the traditional thirty-year mortgage, and contributed heavily to her 401K, which the company matched. The only debt Sarah had was her home, which she had ten more years till she could burn the deed and she had stayed away from credit cards and the urge to finance a new car. She drove a ten-year-old Volvo station wagon.

Her experience was vast at this point in her career. She had a great circle of friends, a wonderful mom, a supportive family, but there was something missing. She loved her work and career, but she was beginning to yearn for a relationship, and yes, even a child. She was facing that choice that so many women face; a rocketing career versus relationship and family and was there any way to manage both without any of them suffering. She did want a family, but her relationships so far haven't been so great. The men were either immature, self-involved, irresponsible, or totally focused on their own careers. Maybe she needed to date above her age bracket. She needed someone that was confident in where they were in life, willing to be part of a true partnership. Does that person exist?

She began thinking again about the man at Drake's. She was interested in his story, what had his wife been like. How had he moved on, what was his career? She did not feel strange about pursuing a meeting just out of curiosity and see what happened. She needed someone to go with her to Drake's again. Would Michele go with her again or does she think she is crazy? No matter, she would get one of the girls or more to meet again at Drake's this Sunday.

Sarah had an assignment working for a healthcare client facing an unfounded but potentially damaging discrimination claim. The firm was in Los Angeles, so she would be flying out this afternoon and spending two or three days with the management team advising them on what to say, to whom, and when. Keeping management calm and not over reacting was a major part of crisis management work. Before she left, she would have to call her mom and make sure she could come by the next couple of days and take care of Binx.

She had packed her bag the night before so she could go straight to the airport from the office. She took a late lunch and, on a lark, drove to Drake's in St. Matthews just fifteen minutes from her office downtown. She went into the restaurant and sat at the table at the front of the restaurant where she sat the Sunday that the man bought her dinner. A young woman waited on her and took her drink order. A few minutes later, she felt a tap on her shoulder, it was the waiter Josh that waited on her group that night. He said to Sarah, "I have something for you from the man that bought your dinner. He was here last Sunday, "He said to give you his card and if you wish to send him an email. He would be happy to meet you here and buy your dinner." She said, "Thank you Josh." As she thanked Josh, she felt herself blush with slight embarrassment. For the next forty minutes as she ate her lunch, she felt more than slightly dazed. Now what would she do. She saw no other choice now but to send the man an email. His card said Dr. Henry Morrison and his company name, phone, and email address.

Chapter 37

Don't Let Me Down

Dinner at the Rubicon with his half-sister Susan and her husband Tom and half-brother Jim was cordial and pleasant. Henry didn't have much in common with Tom and Susan, they were (no offense intended) a bit redneck and country. Jim and Henry followed politics, although Jim's views were a good bit more liberal than Henry's, yet they found a way to get along and not let political views get in the way.

Susan and Tom left early as they had a one-hour drive to get home. Henry shook Tom's hand and gave Susan a hug and kiss on the cheek and promised to stay in touch. After Tom and Susan left, Henry asked Jim "What does Dad have planned for the next two days?" Jim replied, "You're not going to like it, I don't." Jim told Henry that their Dad wanted to take them to Reno for a couple days of gambling and a couple of shows including, ugggggh Charo.

The brothers left the restaurant and headed to Jim's house for the evening. First thing in the morning after a cup of coffee and a bowl of cereal, the two began their drive to the Sierra foothills and the town of Plymouth. When they arrived, their Dad was in the garage working on another project. It was hard for Henry to relate to his Dad. Too many years had passed, and they didn't have anything in common really except for genes.

James welcomed his sons, came to them, and place his arms around the both of them, albeit quickly. James Edwin Morrison was not a touchy-feely guy. Thirty years in the navy made him rather tough. Henry said, "Dad what are you working on in the garage?" "It's a sprint race car and I'm rebuilding the engine for the race team," he said. Jim got in some teasing about the Porsche that Henry owned as his Dad was a fierce American car proponent. They spent the morning talking, went out to lunch in the small town and grilled steaks for dinner. That is when their father said they were going to leave for Reno in the morning for some gambling and a show. Henry was not a gambler and really didn't look forward to a day and a half in casinos.

Remarkably, the time went quickly and the three of them had a good time. On Saturday morning, the three were sitting at a breakfast bar when Henry leaned over to his Dad and said, "How's it feels to have kids this old." His father replied, "You know, I never really wanted kids." Jim and Henry looked at each other with the thought, did he just say that. Henry said, "Well Dad, I don't know if you realize this, but you've fathered four kids and I think you know how to control that thing."

Saturday afternoon, they drove back to Plymouth where they had a late lunch. After lunch, Henry and Jim got into Henry's rental car for the drive to Sacramento and then for Henry, on to San Francisco for his red eye flight from San Francisco back to Chicago. He arrived in San Francisco, where he checked into the airport Marriott Hotel to try and get a few hours of sleep before his 11:30pm flight. He reflected on his time with his Dad. Dad had his own world of engines, racing, and the volunteer fire department. Family members on his mother's side say that he emotionally abused his mom and may have physically abused her. Henry had been too little when his Dad left when he was five. The more time he spent with his Dad, he realized that Dad was a sad, shell of a man, with minimal personality. He never seemed very happy.

Henry managed to get four or five hours sleep before he checked out of the hotel, returned the rental car, and went through security to his gate. Luckily, he got another upgrade to first class which allowed him to get some sleep on the overnight back to Chicago. He quickly fell asleep as the plane rumbled down the runway. He dreamt about his childhood and the man that had a huge impact on him, his maternal grandfather Harry Sandman. Harry grew up poor, had to drop out of school in the seventh grade to help support his mother and five siblings when his father died. Despite Harry's lack of extended formal education, Harry was smart, wise, and a good influence on Henry, as a buffer to his mother's anger and bitterness. He remembered sitting on Harry's lap as a child and being sung to. The song that Harry sang often was *Far Away Places*. It was a song that to this day when Henry thought about it or heard it, he would tear up remembering his grandfather. The song spoke to a wanderlust and a longing to travel. It's ironic that Henry had jobs throughout his life that involved a lot of traveling.

Whatever goodness that existed in Henry, came from his grandfather.

Chapter 38

Baby You're a Rich Man

I t was a Monday night after dinner (take out Chinese), Henry was relaxing on his deck, with Betsy at his feet. He was just watching the river and the barges go by. The river has a calming effect on people. The sound of the water and the breeze blowing put him in a deeply reflective state. He looked back over his life of the last few years.

Henry had been a "traveling man" since the mid-eighties. He had traveled to thirty-five countries, five continents, and lived in two countries outside of the United States. He put aside his business career at the turn of the century and began a career in education that he had abandoned right after college. He turned down a teaching job just after graduation. It was a good opportunity and there he would have been for forty years until retirement. The more he had thought about the job, the less enticing it sounded. At some point, he would come back to teaching, but not until he had seen a bit of the world.

The business world had been good to him. He had made good money, collected good bonuses and commissions through the years and invested well and lived within his means. He owned his house, he had $1.3 million in retirement savings, two pensions, and his only extravagance was travel and automobiles. He finally got rid of his Porsche when it reached the twenty-year mark and bought a new Audi TT, which was now ten years old but was driven mainly on weekends and warm weather. He owned a Jeep Grand Cherokee for daily use but was about to sell it and buy a Land Rover. He had a net retirement income of over $100,000 per year. There was also his small salary from the startup and his stock in it. During the great recession of 2008, he purchased a small condominium in Naples, Florida. Henry was in good shape, but he was missing something. He had been lonely for a lot of years. Almost, as if on cue, Betsy sighed and looked up at him. Was it too late to find someone? Sixty-four wasn't that old, if he was serious about it, did he think he was too old for a child? He thought about it, he would be eighty-two when the kid graduated from high school! It was still the "man question" about leaving a legacy; your name carrying on once you are gone, somebody who would remember you.

Doc's legacy was his work, he was thinking about some of his accomplishments in education. The one he was most proud of was serving as principal of a Catholic K-8 school in the west end of Louisville. He was contacted by a board member of the school (a friend) who appealed to Doc to take over the principalship of the foundering school. The neighborhood had been solid blue-collar working class in the 1950s and 1960s, but the last few decades the working class moved out and poverty moved into the neighborhood.

The enrollment of the school had declined to only one hundred and twenty-five students; only a third of which could afford to pay tuition. In the 50's, the enrollment had been well over 600 kids. The school now, was called a "mission school" by the Archdiocese. It could not support itself, but the Archdiocese wanted to do the outreach to the community. The building had fallen into disrepair, some windows broken and the heating and air system in bad shape. His job was twofold; first a lot of fund raising to pay for tuitions, and repairs to the building. His second job was to convince the frustrated faculty to stay for the next school year.

The job did not pay much, but once he walked through the building, he knew he had to take on the position. The two years he spent as principal there were probably the two years of his entire working career of which he was most proud. Henry made calls to prominent citizens who had attended the school in its heyday in the 50s and 60s, and who could help raise funds from other prominent citizens and organizations. He convinced the faculty to stay by gathering them together to hear their needs. He then met one on one with each teacher to hear their concerns in private. Within a week he gathered the faculty together and reviewed each one of their concerns. He grouped them into what he could definitely do, what was possible, and those things that he would not be able to do. He only lost one faculty member and set about keeping to resolving concerns.

The main concern of the faculty was the janitor and the appearance of the building. The janitor, according to the faculty was lazy and a perv. He met with the janitor, developed an agreed upon list of things to accomplish in one month's time. One month later, he met with the janitor and not even half of the tasks had been completed. He fired the janitor on the spot and told him to expect two week's severance, plus any accumulated unused vacation time.

He also hired a PhD psychologist to serve as school counselor. He could not afford her but found a donor to match her salary paid by the Archdiocese. Along with the psychologist, they evaluated each child before school started in the fall. They also administered the WISC

test to determine intelligent quotient and cognitive ability. The previous principal was disorganized, and the files of the students were not uniform.

During his time at the Catholic school, he practically lived there working ninety hours per week. He even got new windows donated, paint donated, and seventy-six GE employees from a Six Sigma group to donate a day of their time to paint hallways, classrooms, and the outside foundation of the building. All Doc had to do was provide lunch. The building looked good, the enrollment was going up slightly, the faculty remained, and the janitor was gone. All that was accomplished in the three months before the fall semester started. Just then, he was jolted back to reality by a ding from his phone.

Doc looked down at his phone and saw an email from a name he did not recognize, an ESwenson. Using his phone, he opened the email, it read:

Dear Dr. Morrison,

I got your business card from the waiter at Drake's. I was hoping somehow, we could meet. I will be out of town this week, but how about Drake's at 5:30 on Sunday?

Sarah Swenson

Chapter 39
And I Love Her

Molly could hardly sleep. It was five in the morning and she has been up half the night anxious for Henry to come home. She knew he was going to be tired, but she was anxious to see him. After the whirlwind of the previous week, a week without him has been exasperating. It was hard to focus on teaching this week and her students sensed her tension. Even Bear could sense her tension. She was in one of Henry's dress shirts that she was using for pajamas, sleeping in his bed, and letting her thoughts run wild to visions of him lying next to her.

The captain announced "We are beginning our initial descent into Chicago. We should be on the ground and at the gate in thirty-five minutes." Henry awoke and looked at his watch, it was seven a.m., and he was looking forward to seeing Molly even though he was dog tired. About forty minutes later he was getting off the plane and walking to baggage claim where James would be waiting to take him home. He grabbed his bag from the carousel, James handed him a cup of coffee and they walked to the short-term parking.

Molly knew Henry was on the way from the airport judging by the time his plane was to land. Now she was wondering should she put on some jeans, just leave the shirt on, or go back to bed and wait for him to come to her. "Would that be manipulative? Probably, but would he expect me to be waiting for him or sleeping?"

Henry got out of the Lincoln Town Car that James drove and went into his building. Lawrence was on duty and opened the door for him and called the elevator. Reaching inside the elevator, Lawrence pressed the floor number for Henry and wished him a good day. Henry watched the numbers above click by until it arrived at thirty-six. The doors opened and he fished in his pocket for the key. He reminded himself to be quiet in case Molly was still asleep. He came in the door quietly, dropped his bag and briefcase by the door, and walked to the kitchen to finish the coffee James gave him at the airport. He threw the cup away and walked down the hall to his bedroom. He cracked the door and saw that Molly was asleep. He crept over to her and kissed her gently on the forehead. He rose, turned and was nearly to the bedroom door when he heard, "I'm so glad you're home," said Molly. He turned around and Molly, in one of his shirts, came to him and wrapped her arms tightly around him. She looked up and gave him a sweet gentle kiss and hugged him even closer. He told her how much he had missed her and thought about her every day.

She said, "Do you want to have some coffee and tell me about your trip?" He told her I'm pretty tired and if you don't mind, I'd like to nap a couple of hours and then tell you all about the trip. "If I'm not too forward, you can lie down with me and we can set an alarm for lunch time and we'll get a bite to eat."

The two of them walked back towards the master bedroom. Henry took his shoes off and got in bed, still wearing his jeans and polo shirt. Molly got in next to him and as she did, Henry pulled her close to him with her head against his shoulder. They talked for just a few minutes before Henry was out like a light. Molly thought to herself how nice this was, lying against Henry as he slept, until......the snoring began. Henry was in a very deep sleep, snoring and mumbling to himself. She wondered if he was dreaming about her; "Well that was a bit of a conceited thought, wasn't it?" she asked herself.

Henry rolled over and as he did, Molly spooned him, and she loved it. She had totally fallen in love with this man in such a short period of time. She closed her eyes and thought about their times together, smiled to herself and within twenty minutes drifted off to sleep. When they awoke, it was about 11:30 a.m. Henry said, "I want to take a quick shower; I feel yucky after being on a plane all night. I won't be long." She said she would take a shower in the spare bathroom. When Molly finished, she assumed Henry had finished before her and headed back to the master bedroom, in a mirror she saw his reflection standing in the bathroom in his underwear and shaving. He wasn't well built, but built nicely all the same, and no gut yet. He had a pair of gray boxer briefs that hugged his legs tightly and he had nice legs she thought to herself. She retreated back to the living room. A few minutes later, Henry appeared in the living room in a pair of khaki pants, blue button-down shirt untucked and sleeves rolled up and wearing his Sperry topsiders. He said, "How about we take a walk to Michigan Avenue and try the Bandera Bar and Grill?" She replied "Great!"

Before they left his home, he put his arm around her and said, "Molly, have I told you today how much I love you?" She replied that she didn't think so. He said, "Molly I have fallen head over heels in love with you, and I DO love you very much!" Molly got a lump in her throat when he said that to her and a tear in her eye. He went on to say, "I really want a deep meaningful relationship with you." She looked up and said, "I love you Henry." She then gave him a sweet tender kiss. They took the elevator to the lobby. Lawrence was there to open the door for them Henry said, "How's it going Lawrence?" Lawrence replied, "Very well thank you and you look a lot better than when you came in this morning". Henry replied, "Yes I am better in oh so many ways."

They walked hand in hand to Michigan Avenue and to the Bandera Bar and Grill restaurant. It was on Michigan Avenue on the second floor, the front wall was all glass and looked over the Michigan Avenue sidewalk. Henry liked to sit there, and people watch as he ate. Luckily, they got a seat looking over the street. Molly had given up her long run today in anticipation of Henry coming home, so there was no time pressure on their lunch. They people watched and made comments about the folks as they walked by or made-up stories about them, which caused several laughs. Molly asked about the time he spent with his father. He said, "You know I've been going out to California once a year to visit with him. It's difficult, he left my mother for another woman all those years ago, so it is kind of tough to connect with him. Also, we have nothing in common and he has a bland personality. But I want this connection with a father and for whatever reason I have found it unfulfilling. It would take a therapist to help me figure that out."

On the walk back to Henry's building he said, "Are you up for a serious talk when we get back?" Molly replied, "Well that sounds kind of ominous." "No, I wouldn't say ominous. I love you, and I want to be transparent with my feelings, who I am, and my flaws so that if you are feeling serious, you know what you're getting into." "Okay, in that spirit, I'll do the same for you." Molly thought to herself that in all her relationships, there hasn't been a man that has been willing to put himself out there so early. She thought I hope there is nothing dark in his past, but he does still seem special to me.

When they got back home Henry asked, "For this discussion, do you want wine or coffee." Molly replied, "Wine I think." He went to the fridge and tapped the "box-o-wine" and poured two glasses. He walked to the sofa and handed Molly her glass. "I guess the best way for me to start is to say that I am an overly sensitive person. Sensitive in the good ways and unfortunately some not so good ways." He proceeded to tell her about being raised in a critical manner by his mother and grandmother, always criticism and never praise. "Please don't misunderstand me, I love my mother and I know she loved me. She was bitter and angry with my father and anything that reminded her of him, including his male child." He went on to tell Molly that his mother was obsessed with what people thought of her and her children. When his sister Kathleen was in middle and high school, she battled a weight problem and became bulimic trying to please their mother.

For two hours he talked as Molly listened intently. He told her of the special relationship he had with his grandfather; how much he missed him, what a good, decent, and sensitive man he was. When he spoke of his grandfather, he got tears in his eyes. Molly drew closer to him and held him. When he finished his life history, leaving nothing out, he began to tell her why he told her all of this. He said, "Molly, I love you. I felt drawn to you the first week I had you in my class. The times we have spent together, although a short time, have been intense and special to me. I want to have a serious relationship." He went on to tell her that if they were to become serious, "It's only fair to let you know that all that stuff with mom has had an effect on me." The entire two hours Henry had been talking, Molly had thought to herself that no man she had seriously fell for had ever opened up to her so completely.

Henry told Molly that when criticized by a woman with whom he was serious, his defenses would go up, walls would go up, and his sensitivity would lead to defensiveness. It was "the old tapes from childhood that would begin to play," he said. He told her that if she wanted what he wanted that he promised to go to a therapist to try and work through those issues. He concluded by saying "Okay, I've put myself out there and made myself very vulnerable now, I guess the ball is in your court whether you want to take our relationship further." He told her he did not want to waste her time or emotions.

By this time, Molly had tears in her eyes. She was touched deeply by Henry's vulnerability and truthfulness. She could tell that it caused some amount of pain for him to relive parts of his life. Her first words to him were "Thank you." She said, "I do feel something between us, and I do want a serious relationship. Your vulnerability confirmed it for me that I want to be with you."

Chapter 40
Golden Slumbers

S arah sat down on her window seat on the plane. She got lucky enough to not have anyone in the seat next to her. She felt anxious, but not distressed. It was almost an excited feeling. She felt as if her life were about to change right before her eyes. Her flight to LA was a little over four hours. Her plan was to read for a fraction of the flight until she got tired. Though, her thoughts were cluttered and out of control. Sarah found herself incapable of focusing on her book, so she slipped on her headphones and listened to music. After a while, Sarah fell asleep with her head leaning against the window of the plane.

While waiting to board, she had already searched Dr. Henry Morrison on all social media platforms. There was practically nothing. She did find a few newspaper columns he had written in a local newspaper; she found a scholarship that he had co-founded with another man for a fallen law enforcement officer, and his dissertation on emotional intelligence. The few men she found with a social presence under that name were younger and weren't him. She felt so silly trying to find him on social media before she was to meet with him.

She had already called Michele to tell her a bartender gave her the man's business card. Michele eeked over the phone. "You have to call him! Or email him or something! This was supposed to happen!" she exclaims.

While Sarah stayed silent, she agreed. Her first instinct was to email him. She sent the email before boarding without thinking twice. Now she sits wondering if she should have. Clearly, he wanted to speak to her if he went as far as to get his business card to her. Michele said she would come with Sarah on Sunday to meet Henry. For some reason Sarah was so much more comfortable with this situation than she figured she would be. The only thing running through her mind is saying the right things. She thought, "Do I ask him about his late wife? I don't want to trigger bad memories for him or hurt his feelings." Overthinking was Sarah's specialty.

Though accustomed to it, Sarah's mother hates when Sarah goes on business trips. Anna has always had a fear of flying. She checks in with Sarah consistently when she knows she will be flying. Once she got checked into her hotel, she called her mother to check in on Binx and give her peace of mind. She decided not to mention emailing the man to her mother just yet. Sarah thought she would just tell her once she got back.

Sarah arose early the next morning to get organized before her meeting with the senior staff of the company, she was there to advise on how to deal with the discrimination claim that a disgruntled employee had made. An hour later, she grabbed her briefcase and went to the lot and got into the rental car. Traffic in Los Angeles was always heavy and while she enjoyed the city and had made some friends here, she hated the driving. After forty minutes, she arrived at the company headquarters and was quickly ushered to a fourth-floor conference room. Within a few minutes, the CEO and three senior executives came into the meeting, then the public relations person, human resources executive, and the chief financial officer. Over the course of the two-hour meeting, Sarah laid out her plan. First, between public relations and human resources, the company needed to compile a statistical hiring list of the last few years broken out by gender, race, age, national origin etc. to make sure that any discrimination claims are unfounded. Secondly, begin drafting a training program to create an awareness of discrimination including interviewing techniques. Third, begin making drafts of press releases covering both sides of the claim, if in fact there was discrimination and one release that covered if the claim was totally unfounded. Lastly, work up the financials of a possible settlement with the individual if the claim is true.

Sarah would stay for the next two days to evaluate findings of the HR research, meet with the claimant if necessary and finalize a press release. She would also be meeting with the individual manager that the claim named. She would also check with HR for the background and corporate career history of the individual manager and hopefully there was no previous incidents with the manager.

Hopefully, she would be able to leave on Thursday with a problem solved and a plan for the future put in place. Late in the afternoon, she called her boss Dave Irvine to give an update including her advice, which he agreed with. He said to her, "Be sure to call me when the rough drafts of the press release are done, email them to me, and I will review for you if you wish, but it sounds like you have things well in hand. Good job." With that comment, Sarah smiled to herself knowing that she did good work and laid out a solid plan. If only she felt more confident about her next meeting on Sunday with Dr. Morrison.

She was thinking about how to start the conversation. Maybe she could ask about his career or his dissertation. Maybe, ask why he wanted to meet or what he does now, his career, or broach the subject of his late wife. She thought to herself "Stop stressing and just let things happen!"

The rest of the week revealed what normally happens in crisis cases. They are never black and white, but rather variant shades of gray. The hiring manager apparently used language that would make a person believe that they may be being discriminated against. That wasn't the intent of the manager. To resolve the issue Sarah recommended a fair settlement, the candidate be offered a position, and training of managers be implemented. All of this would be issued in a press statement with the company admitting training issues, but also revealing a sterling hiring record. Had they not addressed the problem, it would have smoldered for weeks or months and revealed itself to be a bigger and uglier problem, possibly going to court and a larger settlement and unwanted press coverage.

Thursday afternoon, Sarah left Los Angeles and flew back to Louisville. She arrived in the evening, called her mother to tell her she had landed and would pick up Binx the next day. When she got home, she fixed a snack, turned on the television just for background noise and finished her snack. She went to bed with a book and quickly fell asleep. Sarah had a peaceful deep sleep and dreamt of her meeting on Sunday with Dr. Morrison. It was a pleasant dream where the two agreed to meet again and she found Dr. Morrison to be a delightful and charming man.

Chapter 41
Drive My Car

Kathleen called Doc on Tuesday morning. "Hey, I haven't heard from you in a couple of days, you are doing okay?" He reassured her he was fine, and today he was going to buy a new car. He asked her "Which of my lovely nieces needs a car the most?" "You're giving your Audi away?" "I don't think so," said Doc defiantly. He told her he was going to buy a new or newer SUV for his daily use and would give his Jeep Cherokee to the niece who needed a car the most. Kathleen had two daughter, Sara and Susan. Susan was a CPA and divorced with two daughters of her own. She made a good income and had reliable transportation. Kathleen said, "Sara could really use a car." Sara was married with one child, but she and her husband had incomes far less than Susan. Doc said, "Why don't you go with me today and if I do buy a new vehicle you can drive the Jeep home and surprise Sara with it? Besides, I have something I want to talk to you about."

Doc drove the thirty minutes to Kathleen's house in rural Southern Indiana. Kathleen was waiting for him and came out of the front door and got in the car. They drove the fifty minutes to the Land Rover dealer in Louisville. On the way, Kathleen asked "So what do you want to talk about." Doc told her about the young woman he bought the dinner for and the process of attempting to meet her and the email he received. Kathleen said, "Well you sort of started this thing, so it's up to you to follow through.

You've already put yourself out there." He asked her about expectations, the age difference, the propriety of an older man and younger woman. Kathleen replied, "You've been alone for an awfully long time and I don't think you've been happy since Molly's death. You're more than overdue for happiness and companionship. I mean really, Betsy can only give you so much and she's no spring chicken, no offense." Doc agreed with Kathleen, he hadn't been happy for an awfully long time. He had his career successes but personally he was adrift, a bit of a tortured soul. He told Kathleen, that he would be meeting the girl for dinner at Drake's this coming Sunday.

Kathleen advised her brother to just let things take their course, friendship, relationship, wherever it may go. "By the way," she said, "how are things going with the startup company, how is my money being spent." He told his sister that her money was being spent well. Doc said, "I love working with these two guys. They are bright and talented, and they take a judicious approach to being good stewards of investor's money." He told Kathleen that the guys made him feel young again, kind of like teaching and being around young people. Kathleen and Doc had fought like cats and dogs when they were in high school, but through the years they had grown close and they learned to trust each other's judgment.

As they got closer to the Land Rover dealership Kathleen said, "You're really going to buy an expensive vehicle like a Land Rover on a lark?" He told her that "He had been planning the purchase for quite a while." As they were approaching the dealership, Doc kept an eye out for the branch of his bank that was near the dealership, and he spotted it just about a block from the dealership. Not long after he got out of the Jeep, Doc was swooped down on by a sales lady. He told her he wanted a good deal on a new Land Rover, a demonstrator, or a two-year-old model and he would be paying cash. After about an hour on the lot and test driving, he found a demonstrator model with 9,000 miles on the odometer and all the premium features. List price was $92,000, Doc agreed to $68,000. He went down the street to the branch of his bank, got a cashier's check made out to the dealership and came back to retrieve the new vehicle.

He gave Kathleen the two key fobs to the Jeep and said he would follow her to Sara's house to deliver the Jeep and surprise her. They drove to his niece's home. Doc said I have a surprise for you. They walked out to the driveway and Doc handed her the key fobs to the Jeep and told he was giving it to her. He said the car is in incredibly good shape, maintenance record, engine recently rebuilt, and the maintenance record is in the glovebox. "Thanks, so much Uncle Henry, we really needed a better car," said Sara. Doc said, "You are very welcome."

Doc and Kathleen got back in the Range Rover and headed to Kathleen's house. On the way Kathleen said, "You didn't have to do that you know." "I know, but your girls are good kids, and I am happy to help. If Susan needs help with cars for her twins when they get to be driving age, I'd be happy to help them," said Doc. They arrived at Kathleen's house, Kathleen said, "Do you want to come in?" Doc told her not this time that he needed to get back to register the new car, walk Betsy, and get dinner.

He loved the feel and the handling of the Range Rover. With his bad back, it was easy to get into and out of. He didn't know how much longer he would be able to drive his beloved Audi TT; it was easy to get into, but tougher to get out of. He completed his registration within an hour and headed for home. Over the next couple of hours, he took Betsy for her walk, gave her a couple of treats, and then drove to get Chinese take-out, again.

Doc finished his dinner and then went out to the deck for a cigar and a bourbon. This is always the time of day that he spent for reflection. Tonight, his thoughts were on the young woman Sarah. He wasn't sure if he expected a contact for the girl or not, but now a meeting was certain and Kathleen was right, just be friendly, ask a lot about her, and let things take their natural course and forget about age and age difference.

Before he turned in for the night, he received a call from Jamal in Los Angeles. Doc and Jamal had been working on raising funds for the company, to get some running room to finish development of the product for Gary. Jamal told Doc that he had a group of Arab-American businessmen interested in hearing a presentation and could he come to Los Angeles the following week. Doc assured Jamal that he would be available for meetings Tuesday through Saturday the next week. Jamal said he would try to lock down a date and time in the next day or two.

Chapter 42
Getting Better

Molly said, "Well I guess it's my turn to be vulnerable." She told Henry how she was from a strict Catholic family from northwest Indiana. Her father had worked in the steel mills his entire life and was near time for retirement before he died of cancer. She did not elaborate. Molly of course had her twin sister, they had an older brother, Bob. Bob was the CEO of a small manufacturing company, was divorced and had a teenage boy and girl.

Molly said, "I told you that Bridgett is gay, well Bob is different too, and it is what destroyed his marriage." Molly went on to tell Henry that Bob was successful, bright, and was on the surface a man's man, who hunted, played golf and........... liked to dress in drag and go out to bars. The look on Henry's face must have been priceless. Molly was looking at him waiting for a reaction. Henry said, "Well...everybody has to have a hobby, don't they?" They both laughed and Henry said, "If you think I'm judging you or him, think again, I'm in love with you and your family is part of the package."

"So, my dysfunctional family doesn't concern you?" asked Molly. Henry replied, "Every family is dysfunctional, it's just a matter of degrees. Your brother isn't some kind of black widow, is he? Now that would be a concern," said Henry. Molly said, "May I ask you a question?" Henry said, "Sure, I'm an open book and I want to make this relationship work." "I would like to start seeing a therapist with you. You have captured my heart and I want us to grow into this relationship and help each other. I'm sure there are things that I need to work on as well and we might as well start off on the right foot," said Molly.

Henry told her that he was touched that she would be willing to do that for him, for them and said he would research a good therapist. They hugged each other and kissed tenderly. Henry said, "It's 4:00 o'clock and Mass is at 5 at St. Peter's, do you want to go?" They hopped in the Porsche and drove to St. Peter's. They both went through the motions of the ritual, but neither could remember the liturgy or Father McKenzie's Homily. On the way out, Henry asked Molly if she could tell him what the Homily was about. When she said no, he told her "We are both going to burn in hell. My mind was on you sweetheart." Molly blushed and put her head down, then looked up and told Henry she loved him.

It was a short drive to Oak Park. When they arrived, Henry helped Molly grab her things and helped her carry them to her flat. She looked at Henry and said, "I hope you don't mind that I brought with me one of your shirts that I was sleeping in." He said, "No, that's fine with me. By the way, when are we seeing each other again? Do you have plans for next weekend? It's Labor Day Weekend, if you want, you could spend the weekend downtown with me, dinners, the airshow on Sunday." Molly replied, I'd love to do that. I'll take Bear to Mom's on Thursday night." Henry headed for the door, turned around, and Molly came up to him and hugged him tightly, then they kissed a long passionate kiss. Molly said, "Call me before you go to bed tonight." He replied, "I will."

The Eisenhower had pretty light traffic Sunday evening and Henry was able to put a bit of speed on the Porsche going back into town. Admittedly, the relationship was going quickly, but everything seemed right and he had to take great care to do everything he could not to screw it up. He thought, "Imagine that. She is willing to go to therapy with me, most women would have been frightened off by what I said about relationships. I am awfully lucky."

Molly was thinking some of the same thoughts. How unique it was that a man would make himself that vulnerable to a woman he was trying to woo. "There was no wooing to it, I've been wooed and captured by him," she said out loud to herself. Molly was standing in her kitchen with her heart beating quickly. Already, she was looking forward to spending all next weekend with Henry. She thought to herself "Would that mean sleeping, going to bed with him?" She had spent more time with Henry in a short time than she had spent with other men over two months.

On Monday, she was teaching her French classes feeling as light as a cloud and once again, her students noticed it. One girl asked "Miss, where is your Porsche today?" Molly blushed and responded, "Time and place Sally, time and place." The girls in the class giggled at Molly.

Henry arrived at 7:30 am at the office, but of course his secretary Betsy was already at her desk. She asked Henry how his week was. Henry responded, "Absolutely wonderful. The visit with Dad was as boring as ever, but Sunday with Molly was terrific!" "Oh really," said Betsy. She proceeded to try to exact more information from him, and Henry was only too glad to oblige her interest. "Betsy, my friend, I am head over heels in love with this beautiful woman. And when I marry her, I want you to stand up with us as a witness, and I will marry her!" he said.

"Betsy, send a beautiful arrangement of flowers to Molly's school in Oak Park. No roses, but a beautiful arrangement of different flowers including…yes, some daisies and other like flowers," said Henry. He told her what to put on the card and to make sure they made their way to her classroom before school was out today. Betsy said, "I've only known you a little while, but you are absolutely giddy over this young woman." "I most definitely am," he said.

Later that day at Molly's school, a student aid from the office knocked on her classroom door. It was her last class of the day, her senior girls in French IV. Molly told the girl to come in, when she did, she presented Molly with a beautiful bouquet of flowers of several types and colorful.

Molly blushed, the girls said a collective "Aww how sweet". Molly opened the envelope that contained the card it read:

My dearest Molly,

How can I tell you how much you have come to mean to me in such a short period of time. I am giving you my heart to break. It is in your posses-sion. I will always be here for you no matter what. You nearly made me cry when you volunteered to go to therapy with me. I am glad, ever so happy that you have chosen to go further with our relationship. I love you with all my heart and soul.

Je t'aime

Your Henry

"Oh my gosh, that is the loveliest note I have ever read," said a senior student named Melanie who had been looking over Molly's shoulder without her noticing it. Molly did not reprimand the girl, as she was over-whelmed with happiness, a rush of emotions, and gratefulness to God for the man he brought to her. The girls in the class became quiet, some got tears in their eyes as they saw how overwhelmed their beloved teacher had become. There was just fifteen minutes left in the school day and Molly just let the girls have free time for those last few minutes.

Chapter 43

The Long and Winding Road

Doc went into the office on Friday to meet with Jesse and Brandon regarding the Los Angeles trip on Monday. To save money in the corporate account, Doc would pay for the expenses for the trip and hold to be repaid later. They discussed the individuals that he expected to meet with as Jamal had put the meeting together. Doc would make the presentation at the hotel conference room near the airport. Jamal would make the introductions and assist with interpreting duties for the foreign speakers. The goal for the trip was to gain financial investment commitments of $100,000 to $250,000.

Jesse told Doc that at a bare minimum, he needed to come back with $50,000 to keep the development process going for the next three months. It would take a total of four to five months to deliver the product for Gary and for his sales staff to begin selling. Once Doc secured the financial backing, he would then begin work on the training materials for Gary's one-hundred-person sales force. Once the sales force was engaged, they could expect revenue coming in within thirty to sixty days. But for now, the product was only half completed.

Brandon, said that If more funding were secured, the quicker he could get the product to beta testing phase. The funding would be used to hire contract programmers so that all the work did not fall to him. That was understandable. Doc and Jesse were searching for companies to partner with in developing a secondary product in the hopes of bringing in much needed revenue. Raising funds is not a fun job, but Doc had a lot of contacts on the west coast, as did Jamal. Between the two of them they should be able to raise at least the $50,000 to $100,000.

Brandon asked "Hey did anything ever happen with that girl at Drake's. Doc said, "As a matter of fact I'm meeting her there on Sunday evening. I gave my card to Josh last week to give to the girl if he saw her come into Drake's. He saw her, gave it to her, and she emailed me." He went on to say he would talk with the girl and see where things go from there in terms of the type of relationship that develops. "My sister Kathleen says I shouldn't let age get in the way of my happiness," Doc added.

The talk returned to business with Doc adding that he may head north to the San Francisco Bay area to potentially investigate another finance source. We'll see how it goes but I am confident of coming back with something. Jamal has set up a good group for our meeting and I am working on one more contact in Los Angeles, possibly two, while I am there. I know how important it is to bring in some money to take the load off Brandon.

After work, Doc returned home, put a leash on Betsy and took a long walk through the village and back. This usually tired old Betsy out for the evening, but she loved the "walkies." After a soup and sandwich for dinner, Doc read for a while. He was re-reading Malcolm Gladwell's book "Talking to Strangers," which was a collection of case studies regarding how humans have a default to truth when listening to other people speak. Humans have a genetic default to believing rather than disbelieving. There were case studies from the CIA, police agencies, judges, etc. It was a fascinating read as were all of Gladwell's works.

Before bed he poured a shot of Basil Hayden's bourbon and went into his office just to organize his papers and presentation folders for the trip to LA. He opened his laptop and sent a quick message to Ms. Swenson:

Dear Ms. Swenson:

I am very much looking forward to our dinner on Sunday. I think we will have much to talk about; our careers are a good place to start as I am at the end of mine and you are at the height of yours.

Best wishes,

Henry

Just then his phone rang, and it was his sister Kathleen. She said, "Henry, Sarah is overjoyed with the car, I can't thank you enough for being so generous." He told her he was glad she was so happy with the car and he would pay the registration fees if she needed the money. Doc was generous with his two nieces and three great nieces. Except for Kathleen and his brother Patrick, they were his family. Kathleen told him that Sarah wanted to do something for him to thank him for the car. Doc said, "Nothing is required, but maybe a thank you card if she wants to send one. I was glad to do it." Kathleen said she would tell her.

After they hung up, he called his brother Patrick and asked if he could stay at the house Monday night through Friday to take care of Betsy. Patrick lived alone in an apartment and loved to take care of Betsy and quickly agreed.

Chapter 44
I Should Have
Known Better

I t was early on Sunday afternoon and Sarah was thinking about her meeting with Dr. Morrison in just a couple more hours. She wondered what he was like. Was he a scholarly nerd because of the PhD? Was he an "old man" in his thinking and actions? She wasn't sure she would like to spend a dinner with a man who acted "old", although going out with men her own age had left her unsatisfied to say the least. Mom had given her the best advice; "Sarah, just be yourself and let things take a natural course. At the very least you may have met an interesting person, maybe a mentor, maybe someone you might like to date."

That last comment from her mom had her thinking, maybe someone I would like to date? She seemed to get along with older people better than people and especially men her own age or near to her age. Older men seemed obviously more mature, settled in their careers with a lot or experience of life to draw upon. Would she want to "date" an older man? Wait, wait, she was getting ahead of herself. Her more immediate concern was how to appear this evening. Drake's was a casual place so that would dictate the overall "theme" of her appearance.

She began to get ready later in the afternoon. She chose a nice light blue blouse, a pair of jeans, and high heels. To add to the ensemble, she put on vanilla perfume, subtle but not overwhelming. High heels were a risk as she was going to walk the four blocks from her house to Drake's, but she thought she could do it okay. She called Michele to talk and burn off a bit of her nervousness before she walked to Drake's. She planned to be there a bit early to wait for him rather than make a fashionably late entrance.

Michele was trying to calm her nerves and to pump her up with confidence. Just view it initially as a visit with one of her accounts. Start off slightly professional and see where Dr. Morrison led the conversation. Michele said, "I am so excited for you girl, and you better call me the very minute that you get home tonight!" "I will, I will," Sarah replied. Either this will be a one-night curiosity fulfillment or there might be another "date." Michele said, "Did you say date? Is that where your mind has taken you? To a relationship with an older man before you've ever met him or seen what he is about?" Sarah told Michele that she was "reading an awful lot into one word." "That word is mighty telling," said Michele.

"I plan to be on good behavior, no flirting, just listening to him, and asking a few questions here and there," Sarah offered. Sarah added that, "With a PhD and a full career, he, at the very least should be an interesting man." Michele said, "Are you going to ask about his ex-wife?" "No," answered Sarah.

Chapter 45
I Call Your Name

Sunday afternoon and Doc was as nervous as a schoolboy. He fret-ted over what to wear to meet Ms. Swenson. He settled on jeans, his Sperry's, a blue button down and a navy-blue jacket. He slapped on some cologne and tried to decide whether to take a small bouquet of flowers as a thank you for meeting with him. He decided yes, but not from a florist that would look pushy and presumptuous.

With a lighter than normal step, he bent over and petted Betsy and as he walked down the steps to the garage, he passed by the hook where he kept his cane. Should he use his cane or not? He really only needed it for long walks or crowded situations, so he decided against it. Doc got into his new Kelly-green Range Rover. He really loved this car, with its tan leather interior and all the high-tech features. He decided to drive by the nearby Kroger's grocery and stop by the floral shop. He chose an eight-dollar bou-quet of simple flowers.

It was just a fifteen-minute drive to Drake's, but it only seemed like a couple of minutes as his anxiety seemed to make time fly, plus his nervous-ness. When he arrived at the restaurant, he noticed he was a few minutes early so he sat in the car until it was time to go in. Finally, he got out of the car and walked towards the entrance. When he entered the restaurant, he was in luck, the waiter Josh was working today. He pulled him aside and asked if the young lady was there, he said yes and directed him to the table.

Doc walked up to the table and tapped the young woman on the shoulder and said, "Ms. Swenson I presume?" She said, "Yes and please call me Sarah, and you must be Dr. Morrison?" Doc answered, "Yes and you can call me Henry or Doc." He gave her the flowers and said, "These are for you, for your kindness in meeting with me." "Oh, that is so sweet of you Henry, thank you," Sarah said. She urged him to have a seat. Josh appeared and said, "Can I get either of you a drink?" Doc said, "I will have a bourbon on the rocks, and the lady will have?" Sarah told Josh she would have a glass of Pinot Grigio.

"Well, here we are then," said Doc. "Yes, here we are," Sarah replied. Doc asked, "I suppose you're wondering why I wanted to talk to you, and we'll talk about the elephant in the room, you reminded me of my late wife. You could be her twin as a matter of fact. I guess I just wanted to find out about your life if you don't mind? I'm not a creeper, but when I saw you, I thought I had seen a ghost!"

"I didn't mean to frighten you, and I don't think you are a creeper. Right now, I think you are a sweet man who mourns deeply for someone he loved, which I think is very dear of you," said Sarah. "Tell me about you first," Sarah asked. "That can be a very long story, I suggest we order our dinner first and then I'll give you the ugly story," Doc suggested.

Josh took their diner orders and Sarah said, "Okay, let me hear early the ugly truth." He told Sarah about being raised by a single mom, living with his grandparents, his wild freshman year at Indiana University, the robberies at the drug store, and the beginning of his career in Dallas with the private investigator. She learned about the first serious relationship with Jeanne that he broke off, his fear of intimacy. Doc quickly got to what got them to meeting each other. He said, "When I saw you, I thought I had seen a ghost. You looked just like Molly. I had fallen in love with her quickly, and we were married within three months or so. She was beautiful like you and was very loving and patient with me." Doc didn't say any more about Molly, he would save that for later, but he took her all the way up through working in London and traveling three weeks a month for three years covering the Middle East and Latin America.

Their dinner arrived which resulted in a short break in the conversation. "Now where was I," said Doc. Sarah reminded him that he had just gotten to 2002 and moving to Hong Kong to be Principal of American International High School. "The Hong Kong experience was perhaps the most interesting, surreal, and bizarre two years of my life," Doc explained. "But I've been talking too much, tell me a bit about you before I go any further," Doc said. Sarah said she grew up in a loving household with a father and mother she adored. She graduated from college and began a career as a reporter, but after a while she decided that public relations was a career path that she wanted to pursue. She did get an MBA from the University of Louisville to help propel her career. She had risen quickly through the ranks of Williams & Clark Public Relations and was now leading a crisis management team. Relationships of any meaning had been few and far between. The men her age have been either immature or on the make for their own careers, or simply "on the make", or a combination of all of those and she found that to be incredibly frustrating. She was now at a point in her career that she was facing life choices. She was interested in starting her own firm, but she also was feeling the draw to start a family which was leaving her particularly confused.

"Wow, crisis management. I had a friend who started a crisis management firm in Louisville in the early nineties and was quite successful with it. Matter of fact, he sold it for a pretty fair profit and the acquiring company moved it out west, so there is an opportunity in this area for another firm," Doc told her. "That's interesting. Could be an opportunity for me," Sarah said. "From my limited knowledge of you, you have the smarts to do it, you just need the financial capital to do it," suggested Doc. The two continued to talk business for a while until they had finished their dinner.

Sarah said, "Tell me more about Hong Kong. You said it was surreal, give me an example." "Well, I had a high school counselor that reported to me. She had been in Hong Kong for eight years and hated the Chinese, except for the students. She also hated the Chinese owners of the school. One day she came out of the owner's office and straight to mine and asked me; is there a secret file on me, well is there? I replied I don't know Elaine as it would be, you know, secret. She yelled at me, you're one of them, aren't you? She left my office and slammed the door," Doc said with a laugh. "You're joking, a secret file?" asked Sarah. She told her it was a true story, that Elaine was just this side of crazy, that Elaine often told anyone who would listen that her husband was a recovering alcoholic. "The running joke was, was he an alcoholic before or after he met Elaine?" Doc said with a laugh.

Josh came up and asked if either of them were interested in dessert. Neither wanted dessert, but they both ordered another drink. When the waiter had left Sarah asked, "What is your doctorate in?" Doc explained that he has an undergraduate in education with a double major in political science, a Master's in Education with a principal's license, a Master's in Advanced Leadership Research, and the Doctorate in Organizational Development and Behavior. Sarah commented that he had a lot of education. "Yes, a lot of formal education, but I'm not sure it rubbed off on me. Like Mark Twain said, I never let my schooling interfere with my education." Sarah said she loved that quote and we often learned more through experience than through formal education.

Doc asked, "What do you like to do for entertainment or in your time away from work?" Sarah replied that she was an avid runner. Loved to read, liked music of nearly all kinds. Doc said, "I used to run a number of years ago. It was a good routine when you travel on the road a lot, as I did for twenty years. Now, I can only really walk at a brisk pace and sometimes that is a problem." Sarah asked, "Why." "A couple of years ago I had a brain tumor removed from a nerve that controls my balance. When they were in there, they discovered the tumor was larger than originally thought and in removing it they scraped facial nerves that have left the left side of my face somewhat paralyzed." Sarah said, "I really didn't notice the paralysis in your face, I was drawn to your incredible blue eyes." "Are you flirting with me Sarah?" Doc said. "Maybe," she said.

Doc looked at his watch and noticed that they had been at Drake's for over three hours and it was approaching nine o'clock. "I hate to bring this evening to an end, but I have an early flight in the morning and I still haven't packed a bag," said Doc. "Oh, I was really having a nice time talking to you," said Sarah. Doc acknowledged he was having a good time too. "Why don't we do this again next weekend?" Doc suggested. Sarah agreed and suggested next Saturday, and they made a date for 5:30 pm again at Drake's. Doc asked, "Can I walk you to your car?" Sarah replied that she lived so close that she had walked to Drake's. "Then can I give you a lift home?" asked Doc. Sarah agreed and they walked to Doc's Range Rover.

"Wow, a Range Rover?" said Sarah. "Yes, I just bought it a couple of days ago and I am loving it," said Doc. Sarah went on to talk about how nice it was and that she drove an older Volvo station wagon. "Well, we don't keep our investments in cars. I had a Volvo wagon a few years ago and that was one of the best cars I had ever owned. Loved the way it handled," Doc said. It was only a few minutes when they reached Sarah's small house in a lovely St. Matthews neighborhood. Doc got out of the car and walked around to Sarah's door and opened it for her and then walked her to her front door. He thanked her again for a lovely time, gave her a peck on the cheek and a friendly hug and said, "I am really looking forward to Saturday." Sarah said, "I am too, and by the way I owe you a dinner. You've already paid for two, so I'll pick up next week's check." Doc replied, "We'll see about that," and gave her another quick peck on the cheek and said, "Good night Sarah." She said, "Good night Henry, and thanks again." Doc got in the Range Rover and began his drive home to Betsy and a walk.

On the drive home, Doc was thinking about Sarah. He thought that he hadn't felt this "light" and good since his first date with Molly. But maybe he was getting ahead of himself; he was an "old man" what would someone Sarah's age sees in him. He would follow Kathleen's advice and let things fall in place naturally. He was remembering when he gave Sarah a pick on the cheek and the wonderful scent of her perfume. It was going to be difficult to keep his mind on business this week that was for sure.

When he got home, he put a leash on Betsy, grabbed his cane and took her on about a one-mile walk. When they returned, he gave Betsy a treat, packed his bag for his trip, and gathered his files and notes for his briefcase and threw his laptop in the briefcase. Even his briefcase looked old. It was an old lawyer's briefcase that he had bought second hand several years ago. It was battered and had seen better days, but he liked the style and besides, a new lawyer's brief could go for $500 to $800. He could reason overpaying for an automobile, but not for a briefcase.

He had two quick calls to make. One to Kathleen to tell her about his dinner and one to Patrick to confirm him watching Betsy. He quickly called Patrick to remind him to be sure to give Betsy her treats after her walks and where the veterinarian's number was in case Betsy got hurt or sick. He called Kathleen and told her what a good time he had and that he was seeing Sarah again next weekend, and that he felt incredibly happy for the first time in a long time. She told him he deserved happiness and to embrace it and again, just let things unfold.

Meanwhile, in St. Matthews, Sarah called Michele to fill her in on her evening with Dr. Morrison. "Michele, he is sixty-four years old, sweet and charming, and with the bluest eyes I think I have ever seen," said Sarah. She went on to say "He told me about his late wife Molly and how he married her within three months. But he did not say how she died. He told me that when he saw me, he thought he had seen a ghost, we looked that much alike." Michele said, "Oh my gosh that's wild Sarah. Are you going to see him again?" Sarah told Michele about the dinner the following Saturday evening and how she was looking forward to it. Michele asked what the man looked like. Sarah described him as six feet one with just a very slight paunch, casually dressed in jeans, a button-down shirt, and a blue blazer. "He also brought me a small bouquet of flowers as a thank you for meeting him," said Sarah with a smile in her voice. "Oh my God, he brought you flowers!" said Michele. Michele asked how she felt about seeing him again. Sarah replied, "I can't wait, he is a very interesting man."

Chapter 46
If I Fell

The Labor Day weekend came around quickly. Henry took Friday off to make it a four-day weekend. On Thursday, Henry was trying to wrap up the week and set plans for travel for the next month with his secretary Betsy. Betsy couldn't help but notice that Henry was looking happier in the last few weeks and knew it had to do with Molly. Betsy asked, "So boss, what do you have planned for the weekend or need I even ask?" Henry motioned her into his office and said, "Shut the door and have a seat." "Oh my, this sounds serious," said Betsy. Betsy was like an older sibling to Henry and could keep a confidence. "I've invited Molly to stay over the weekend with me. I plan to spend an evening at home Friday, a nice dress up dinner hour on Saturday, casual Sunday going to the air show on the lakefront and a casual Monday," Henry informed Betsy.

Henry told Betsy that he made himself vulnerable and laid out all his past history with women and his fear of intimacy in relationships. He also said to Betsy that Molly was committed to going to a therapist with him as she wanted a serious committed relationship with him. "Wow," Betsy exclaimed, "this sounds like things are moving very fast." Doc replied, "I've never been surer of something, I'm in love with her. I even look at the world in a more positive way." Betsy asked, "Have you slept together?"

Henry replied "Yes, but truly only slept." He said to Betsy, "By the way I have a research project for you."

Across town in Oak Park, Molly was on her way home from school and thinking about what to pack for the weekend. Henry said that Saturday night would be an elegant dinner out, so bring something to dress up. When she got home, she decided to go ahead and pack so she would be ready to go when Henry picked her up on Friday afternoon. As for Bear, one of her students, Siobhan, lived in the next building, and she would pay her to come over and look in on the cat. She packed a couple of pairs of jeans, tennis shoes, high heels, necklace, earrings, bracelet, underwear, Henry's shirt she used as pajamas, toiletries, and her "little black dress for Saturday evening, and of course her running clothes. She had no idea where he was taking her Saturday evening, that was a surprise. That night she couldn't sleep she was excited and a little bit nervous about the weekend and whether the relationship would go to the next level of "physical." She thought to herself as she laid there in the dark, am I ready to make love to him? She answered herself, yes, she was ready.

Friday at school dragged dreadfully slow as Molly anticipated the weekend with Henry. She knew she would have a good time with Henry, but she couldn't stop thinking about sleeping with Henry. As she thought about it, she knew she was ready for sex or more appropriately with Henry, making love. Finally, the school day ended, Molly packed up her bag and headed to the car for short drive home. Siobhan was riding home with her today as she would be going to the apartment to learn what she needed to know about taking care of Bear. Siobhan said, "Miss Kniss, where are you going this weekend." "Oh, actually just staying in the city with a friend for the weekend," Molly replied.

Before Henry left the office, he asked Betsy if she would research the best marriage and family therapist in Chicago on Friday. Betsy said she would and have the information on his desk when he came back to work on Monday. Henry planned to start their couple's therapy as soon as they could. On Friday morning, when he had the opportunity to sleep late, he couldn't, he was too excited about the weekend. He got up showered and shaved, then walked down the street to a breakfast diner for eggs and coffee and the morning newspaper. When he returned home, he picked up Robert Caro's recent biography of Lyndon Johnson. Having double majored in political science, he loved biographies of key political figures. He loved biographies in general, as that's how you learned about life, how people became who they became. How events in childhood affected their personalities.

Late in the afternoon, Henry went to the garage and the drive to Oak Park and Molly. He could hardly contain his excitement. Ever since he and Molly began their relationship, he felt as if he had a permanent smile on his face. As he moved through the city streets, he kept telling himself to just let things happen naturally over the weekend. If something physical developed, then it developed, but he would focus on just enjoying being with Molly reveling in her beauty and her personality that drew him to her.

As he drove up to the Oak Park exit, it felt as if the Porsche was just as excited as he was to take the exit, as he flew off the exit and geared down to make the stop. He pulled into the lot and bounded up the steps to her apartment. Molly was already coming out of the door with a young girl as he reached them. The young girl gave him a quizzical look as she knew that Miss Kniss was spending the weekend in town with "a friend." Molly introduced Siobhan to Henry and told him she was looking after Bear for the weekend. Siobhan said, "Hello, nice to meet you, oh so you're the man with the Porsche!" Both Molly and Henry blushed when Siobhan said that. After Siobhan left Molly looked at Henry and said, "Well that will be all over the school before I walk in the door on Tuesday." Henry apologized for his timing, but that he couldn't wait any longer to see her. He pulled her in close and gave her a long kiss, and Molly said, "That's nice and a great way to start the weekend."

They drove into the city and when they got into Henry's flat, no sooner was the door shut, then Molly pulled Henry close and kissed him saying "I really just needed another one. I'm becoming a kissaholic she laughed. "So, what do you have planned this evening?" Molly asked. Henry explained that a walk and dinner on Navy Pier, then a walk along the lakefront and back home. Before we go to sleep tonight, I want to get a bottle of wine and take you up to the top of the building. The view of the city and lakefront from up there is beautiful. We can sit, talk, sip wine, and enjoy the view and the night air.

They found a spot on the Navy Pier, then walked arm in arm along the lakefront. Henry stopped periodically to just hold Molly and give her a tender kiss. After a couple of hours of walking, they made their way back to Henry's building.

It was approaching nine in the evening when they came home. Henry went to the refrigerator and grabbed a bottle of Chardonnay and then two glasses. After a bit of a freshening up, they took the elevator to the roof. They passed the enclosed rooftop swimming pool and walked to the half wall that marked the edge of the building. There were wrought iron patio furniture pieces scattered about. Henry pulled a table and two chairs near the wall. He placed the glasses on the table, stood up and poured the wine into the glasses giving one to Molly. He put his arm around her and made a toast to them, then hugged and kissed Molly. They looked at the view of the lighted buildings, the John Hancock building, south to Meigs Field, Soldier Stadium. The night was warm with a slight breeze and comfortable.

They stayed on the roof for a couple of hours till 11:30, then went downstairs to the flat. They both got ready for bed, Henry in a pair of gym trunks and Molly in Henry's shirt. They got under the sheets, cuddled, kissed, and held each other until they fell asleep.

They awoke on Saturday morning to the aroma of coffee brewing from the automatic coffee machine in the kitchen. Henry got up while Molly was asleep. He went to the kitchen and got a tray, two coffee mugs, and he toasted two English muffins and got out some cream cheese, butter, and jam. When the coffee was done, he took it back to the bedroom, set it on the nightstand, then bent over and kissed Molly good morning. "Ready for breakfast sweetheart?" he said. "Oh, how sweet of you," said Molly.

After breakfast, Henry showered, Molly got into her running short and then sat in the living room for a few minutes. Henry invited Molly to ask her sister to come up for the air show on Sunday. Molly said, "That will be great she'd love it." "Maybe your mother would like to join us too?" asked Henry. Molly suggested he might not be ready for that. "Well, there's no better time than now," he replied. "That would be great, thank you for inviting them both," Molly said excitedly. Molly called them both, and Bridget would pick up their mother and bring her up. Henry said, "I'll arrange for a guest parking pass for the garage and I'll leave it at the Doorman's desk."

Molly went for her run along the lakefront up past the Shedd Aquarium and Soldier Field and back. When she returned, Henry opened the door and gave her a hug and kiss. Molly said, "Eew, I'm all sweaty." Henry replied, "He didn't care." He said, "Get your shower and I'll fix a couple of burgers for lunch, if that's okay? "Fine by me," she replied. A while later she returned and the two had burgers and fries. "I guarantee you that tonight the cuisine will be slightly better than lunch," Henry said with a smile. Molly asked where dinner was that evening, and Henry replied that the whole evening was a surprise from beginning to end.

The afternoon was spent listening to music and talking and finding more out about each other. He told her that he had Betsy researching couple's therapists for him. He asked, "You're still serious about this right?" "Yes, I love you and if this will help us develop in our relationship and resolve your intimacy problem, yes I am totally committed to therapy and to you," Molly replied with deep sincerity. The afternoon passed quickly. Henry said, our evening begins at exactly 7:30. Just let me retrieve a couple things from the master bedroom and I'll get ready in the guest bath.

An hour later, Henry sat in the living room in a dark gray suit, starched white French cuff shirt, and a purple and thin white stripe necktie. Molly emerged in a "little black dress," black high heels, diamond earrings, and a silver necklace. "You look absolutely beautiful my love," said Henry adoringly. "Why thank you, and you look rather handsome yourself," said Molly. Henry said, "I am so happy you wore black because it will go perfectly with these," he said presenting her with a large gift jewelry box. She opened It slowly and found pearl earrings and a pearl necklace. Molly gasped with surprise and excitement and said, "Henry, you shouldn't have. They're beautiful." "Yes, I should, any woman that would agree to go to therapy with me deserves an awful lot more." She came in close to him and gave him a hug and kiss.

Henry looked at his watch and said it's about time we go, we have an eight o'clock reservation at Spiaggia. "Oh, said Molly, I've heard its very nice, and expensive. You are spoiling me Henry."

Chapter 47

Money

Monday morning, Doc got up early, had his coffee, walked, and fed Betsy, and got his briefcase and bag ready to go to the airport. He bent down to give Betsy a pet on the head and said, "Patrick will be here this afternoon, now go lie down." Betsy ambled across the room to her dog bed, picked up a toy in her mouth and laid down for a nap. Doc went down to the first-floor garage and put his bags in the Audi TT.

He drove through the village to the highway and couldn't resist opening up the Audi on the highway. It accelerated quickly and handled like a go-cart. He reached the airport a bit early but that was okay, you never knew how backed up security might be. He checked in, made it through security relatively quickly and proceeded to the gate. American Airlines had just introduced a non-stop flight to and from Louisville to Los Angeles. The flight would leave at 7:30 am and arrive in LA a little after 9 am LA time. The return flight was a red eye that would arrive in Louisville by 6:30 am. He would be returning to Louisville on Thursday morning this week, after a couple of days of meetings with Jamal and with John Donati, a very good friend from his old "online" pre internet days.

The flight was smooth and uneventful, but he wondered if the airline could possibly squeeze one more seat onto the plane. It's getting ridiculous. Jamal was there to meet him at baggage claim. "Welcome my friend, how was your flight?" asked Jamal. Doc responded that the flight was just fine. "How many meetings do we have with potential investors?" asked Doc. "We have one late this morning, two this afternoon, and two in Las Vegas tomorrow afternoon. "We can make that drive early in the morning and be back tomorrow evening," said Jamal. Doc added, "It will be a long day."

Doc's meetings with potential investors went well. Out of the five with whom he met, two had made commitments for nearly $100,000, which would carry the company for three months with extra contractors working to speed product development for Gary. On Wednesday morning, Doc and Jamal had breakfast to wrap up their business before Doc flew home that night. "Jamal, for your help in setting up these meetings, you will get a ten percent finder's fee/commission when the $100,000 hits our bank. I thank you for all of your help," said Doc. "It was my pleasure my friend. It seems we don't get to see each other very much unless we have business to conduct," said Jamal. Doc and Jamal had known each other for twenty-five years when Doc was traveling extensively in the Middle East. They had met at the Beirut Times newspaper in the Los Angeles office. They were both in their early forties then and near the peaks of their careers. Jamal had helped introduce Doc to contacts in the publishing business in Egypt and Kuwait. The two continued their talk to include family updates, planned vacations. Doc and Jamal bid each other farewell with a "man hug."

Doc had lunch scheduled with John Donati. John had been a friend for thirty-five years and now ran a consulting firm that helped startups win their first big clients. Doc had wanted to meet with John to get some advice on the startup. Over a two-hour working lunch, John listened to the fundamentals of the startup as Doc described it to him. John then went into detail describing a list of questions that the startup team needed to ask themselves. He also suggested some questions the team needed to ask Gary about his company and industry to more accurately make their financial projections. It was a productive meeting. John invited Doc to come up to his Vancouver home over the summer and Doc said he would.

After John left the hotel restaurant, Doc went back up to his room, set his phone alarm, and laid down for a long nap before the overnight flight. He slept from about three in the afternoon until six in the evening. He got up, went back down to the restaurant for a light dinner, returned to his room and gathered his bags together. After watching a bit of television, he picked up his bags and went to the lobby for the shuttle to the airport.

The flight left on time, and thirty minutes into the trip Doc fell asleep. It was a pleasant sleep with a dream of Sarah. He liked the young woman and was looking forward to their next dinner. He still could not get over how much Sarah looked like Molly. He must put that fact aside and observe Sarah as her own person.

He landed in Louisville on time and after claiming his bag, headed to the car and then straight to the office to meet with Brandon and Jesse and relay the news of the trip. Doc arrived at the office at about 8:30 and the guys came in about 9:00. He told them that $100,000 should be hitting their account today from two different investors. He turned over the paperwork that secured the funds. The funds gave the team some running room to get the product developed quicker. After talking with the boys for a while, Doc left the office for home.

When Doc came in the door, Betsy was happy to see him and he took her on a long walk and a puppy treat afterwards. Doc spent the afternoon reading and relaxing. He was looking forward to Saturday evening's dinner with Sarah.

Chapter 48

She Said She Said

Sarah's work week was a hectic one. She was still managing the discrimination case on the west coast and communicating daily with those company officials. Things seemed to be settling down and the officials were putting the agreed upon plans in place. It was Friday, and Sarah had made plans to get together with the girls tonight at Drake's and she knew the topic of discussion would be about Dr. Morrison.

She was looking forward to talking to the girls. She had not been dating a lot in the last couple of years and had been focusing on her career. Her career was blossoming at the expense of her personal life. She was torn between her career and her personal life, but she also heard her biological clock ticking. How did all this square with developing a relationship with Doc? Was she interested in this older man that way? Was he interested in her? Life can be so confusing. She thought he was certainly a handsome man, who was thoughtful and intelligent. Sarah was becoming impatient, after only one dinner, about where things could or would go.

At 5:30, Sarah arrived at Drake's and quickly found the table where Jackie, Janet, and Michele were seated. The three women welcomed Sarah with a round of applause which embarrassed her thoroughly. She threw up her arms in mock thanks and very red faced took a seat next to Michele. "Okay, Jackie said, after you get your drink you have to spill the beans on this guy." Sarah replied, "Well there's not a lot to tell yet." "Yet!" said the three women in unison. Janet asked, "You mean you're seeing him again?" Sarah nodded yes.

The waiter came by and took drink orders and left the menus. When drinks arrived, the questioning began. Janet asked, "So what is he like?" Sarah replied that Dr. Morrison or Henry or Doc, was tall, very blue eyes, thoughtful, and intelligent. Michele added "He brought her a bouquet of flowers." "Really," said Jackie. Sarah added that he brought them as a thank you for agreeing to meet with him. Just then Sarah's phone lit up, it was an email from Dr. Morrison. The women all said she had to read it to them. "Okay, okay, I'll read it," said Sarah. Sarah read aloud, "Okay it says; Dear Sarah: I just got back from Los Angeles this morning. Thought about you on the flight home and how much I enjoyed your company last week and am looking forward to seeing you tomorrow evening. Yours, Henry."

Janet said, "He sounds very sweet." Sarah nodded "He is." Janet asked, "What else did you find out about him?" Sarah went on to tell the women that Doc had traveled extensively in Europe, South America, and the Middle East. That he had lived in Dallas, New York, London, and Hong Kong. Sarah added, "He also drives a new Range Rover." Michele said, "Well that indicates a little bit of money." "Or he's in debt up to his eyeballs," added Janet the accountant.

Michele asked, "Did he mention anything about his late wife?" Sarah said, "Only that he thought I was her ghost, that I looked that much like her. I literally took his breath away and that he was immediately flooded with happy memories." Jackie asked, "So what are you going to talk about tomorrow?" Sarah replied, "I hope to find out more about his late wife, how she died, and more about her." Michele added, "Well tomorrow could end up being a real downer of an evening." Sarah added that Doc/Henry was an inquisitive person and a particularly good listener. "He has this ability to make you feel like you are the most important person in the world when you are talking to him. He listens closely and asks questions that demonstrate how close he listens."

Chapter 49

I'll Follow the Sun

H enry and Molly made their way to the elevator. Before leaving the condo, Henry picked up a house phone and asked Lawrence to hail a cab for them. When they walked into the lobby, Henry slipped Lawrence a tip and thanked him then escorted Molly out of the door to the waiting taxi. He told the driver the destination and they settled back in their seats for the ride. Henry looked at Molly and said, "Have I told you today just how beautiful you are?" Molly nodded and said, "I think a couple of times as a matter of fact."

They arrived a few minutes later at the restaurant which was atop a building that overlooked Oak Street and Lake Shore Drive. Music was playing as they walked in, nothing loud but understated soft jazz from a combo. They were shown to a corner table for two. The waiter came for drink orders and Henry ordered his usual Amaretto and Bourbon and Molly ordered a Martini. When the waiter returned, he told them of their specials for the evening. Henry ordered a Caesar salad and a filet mignon, while Molly ordered a small salad and the pasta special.

Over dinner, the two talked about family, and Henry asked Molly, "I can't help asking what your brother might wear to a place like this?" Molly did not take offense, but laughed and said, "You know it is an interesting thought." Henry apologized. He added, "You know, sometime soon you're going to have to go south with me and meet um, gulp, my mother. Then feel free to make comments about the person who is responsible for any and all of my neuroses."

At the end of dinner, the waiter asked if they wanted dessert. They both said no, and Henry asked for the check. Henry looked at Molly and said, "I have dessert at home, and I don't mean that in a dirty way, I bought a cherry cheesecake." They left the restaurant and took the elevator down to Michigan Avenue. They walked along the avenue window shopping here and there and walking off dinner. They passed the John Hancock tower and Henry hailed a cab for the short ride back to his building.

As the taxi pulled up, Lawrence was there to open the door for Molly, while Henry paid the driver and came around from the other side. He thanked Lawrence as he held the door for them both and tipped him. In the elevator, Molly put her arms around Henry and gave him a kiss and thanked him for a wonderful evening. "Well, I'm not sure it's over yet. There is still dessert and maybe coffee if you like?" said Henry. Molly acknowledged that dessert would be good.

Inside his home Henry said, "I have another surprise for you" as he pulled an envelope out of his coat pocket and gave it to Molly. Her name was on the front of the envelope. She opened it to find a credit card looking pass key and a key. She looked quizzically at Henry. He said, "It is a pass key to the garage and a key to my home." Molly said, "Oh my, you are serious, aren't you?" Henry replied that he was that serious and asked her if she was, Molly nodded yes, and they hugged each other. Henry said, "Now for dessert, and it comes in two parts, part one coming up." He went to the kitchen, made coffee, and cut two slices of cherry cheesecake (his favorite) and brought them to the living room.

As they finished dessert Molly asked, "I believe you said that dessert was in two parts, what is part two?" With that, Henry dimmed the lights and went to the stereo and put in a special cassette he made. He motioned Molly over for a dance, out of the stereo came Neil Young's "Harvest Moon." While they danced close, Tim sang to the stereo in Molly's ear.

As the music played, they danced closely and slowly, holding each other tight. After the song ended, Henry leaned in and gave Molly a passionate kiss. Molly started to speak, and Henry put a finger to his lips as the next song began. It was the Beatles song *I Will*. They continued to dance slow and close and again toward the end of the song, he leaned closer and sang in a whisper the last words of the song.

At the end of the song, Henry held Molly and kissed her again. He took her hand, turned off the stereo and led her back to the master bedroom. He looked at her and said, "Are you ready to go further?" Molly nodded yes. Henry lit a candle on each nightstand and pulled down the covers. Molly noticed there were two chocolates on the pillow. She said, "When did you do this?" "While you were in the bathroom just before we left for dinner," Henry replied.

They stood holding each other, and Henry loosened his tie, but Molly finished taking off his tie, removing his cuff links, and untucking his shirt. Henry reached behind Molly and unzipped her dress, which then fell to the floor revealing, for lack of a better phrase, some out of the ordinary lingerie. He said to her, "Either this is your normal underwear, or you were anticipating something?" Molly replied, "Maybe I am a former girl scout and am always prepared," Henry said, "I don't really care which it is, I just like it on you my beautiful girl." With that, Henry kicked off his shoes, removed his socks, and Molly removed the rest down to his boxers.

Henry then picked Molly up and placed her on the bed where he began to caress every part of her lovely body. She reciprocated by drawing him to her and kissing him deeply. She stopped for a moment and said, "You need to know that I am a good Catholic girl, I am not taking birth control." He replied, I am a good Catholic boy and don't own any condoms so." They both said together, "We have to be careful."

Having said that, Henry continued caressing Molly to her distinct delight. They went under the covers and continued kissing and caressing. Henry was gentle and tender as he entered Molly and began making sweet tender love to her. They made love all through the night much to one another's pleasure. In the morning, Henry got up and got coffee and bagels and brought to the bedroom. He got back under the covers and drew Molly near to him kissing the top of her head and her cheek, then her lips. Molly woke up and gave Henry a long kiss. She said, "Good morning, and thanks for dessert." Henry laughed and said, "No, thank you sweetheart, last night was amazing." Henry was in his boxer short and a tee shirt, Molly was in Henry's shirt, her pearl earrings, and necklace from the night before. Henry looked at her and said, "Have I told you today how beautiful you are and how much I love you?" Molly replied, "No, but say it as many times as you like today. By the way, I love you!"

Molly got dressed in her running clothes and prepared to do a long lakefront run once again to well past Soldier field and back. Henry took a shower and started tidying up the condo for the visit of Molly's mom and sister. As she was going out the door she stopped and gave Henry and big hug and kiss, he said, "Do you have your key?" She shook her head no. Henry picked the key up from the counter and put it on a rubberized elastic wrist band Molly would wear while she ran. He hugged and kissed her again and sent her on her way. As she was descending in the elevator, she thought about how happy she was. She felt even lighter as she began, he run down the lakefront.

Chapter 50

I'm Down

Late Saturday afternoon, Henry hopped in the Audi TT, put the top down, and headed to the grocery to pick up a small bouquet of spring flowers for Sarah. After leaving the grocery, he sped the little Audi towards Drake's in St. Matthews and his second dinner with Sarah. He was dressed casually with a white button-down shirt with sleeves rolled up and untucked, a pair of jeans, and his Sperry's, he told Sarah to dress casually in an email he sent last evening.

Sarah was making her finishing touches to her ensemble. She wore a pink polo shirt, jeans, and a pair of Sketcher's as she was instructed to dress casually. To add to the casual look, she put her hair in a ponytail and wore a baseball cap. Today, even though it was "casual," she put on Chanel No 5 perfume. She then began to walk the few blocks to Drake's and her meeting with Henry.

Henry rolled up to the back parking lot of Drake's, put the top up on the Audi, grabbed the flowers and went in. He found Sarah at one of the front tables, which was becoming their spot in the restaurant, and tapped her on the shoulder, then presented her with the bouquet. She said, "More flowers?" He replied, "A pretty lady deserves pretty flowers." She blushed and thanked him for the flowers. The waitress appeared asking for their drink orders, Henry replied, "I believe the young lady will by having a

Pinot Grigio and I will be having Bailey Hayden bourbon and Amaretto, is that right Sarah?" Sarah nodded yes.

Henry asked, "Well, any crises this week?" Sarah replied, "No, just very busy wrapping up things from the event on the west coast." They continued to make small talk, ordered, and ate their dinners. After dinner, they each ordered another drink when Sarah asked, "If I am not being to forward, tell me what happened to your wife." Henry lowered his head for a few seconds, he said, "I was wondering when we would get to that, and I believe I owe it to you to tell you the story. Would you like to go or a ride?" Sarah said sure. Henry said if you don't mind, I am going to take you to my house on the river, it's quiet there and we can sit on the deck, listen to the river, and I'll tell you the story." They exited the restaurant and headed to the Audi, Sarah asked "Where is your Range Rover? He answered, "I drove my treasured little sports car today, my Audi TT. Would you like the top down? "Sarah replied that she would love it. They drove through the city to the downtown bridge and up the river road to Henry's house.

As they pulled into the garage, Henry said this will give you a chance to meet Betsy. They went upstairs and Betsy came to them wagging her tail. "Hello girl, meet Sarah, Sarah meet Betsy." Sarah bent over and petted Betsy. They took Betsy for a quick walk down the road and when they returned, Henry gave Betsy a puppy treats and let her out onto the deck, where she found her dog basket and laid down. Henry asked, "Would you like a drink? I have Chardonnay, but not Pinot Grigio." Sarah said Chardonnay would be fine. Henry poured a glass of Chardonnay and poured his bourbon and amaretto, and they went to a small sofa on the deck where they sat next to each other.

Henry told Sarah how he and Molly had met and the whirlwind romance that had ensued. He knew after the first date that he was going to marry Molly. He had even told his secretary that and asked her to be a witness to the ceremony, even before he asked Molly. They had begun dating in late July and by Thanksgiving they were married. Their marriage lasted from 1990 to 1996 when Molly was killed. In that time, there had been a total of three pregnancies, two were lost to miscarriages in early stages and the third was in the seventh month, a little girl, killed with her mother.

Molly had been a French teacher when they met and remained so until the day she died in Normandy, France. Molly and the Spanish teacher had taken a group of girls from the school on a study trip to Spain, Gibraltar, and France. They were only two days away from coming home when the accident happened. Molly and the group were on a bus headed to Normandy on a narrow French country road, when a motorcycle pulled out in front of the tour bus. The driver over corrected with a quick turn of the wheel causing the bus to flip into a ditch. Molly sustained a severe head injury as well as massive internal injuries. She was trapped between seats with bags and girls on top of her. When she was extricated from the bus and rushed to the hospital, her injuries were too severe, and she did not survive. Sarah reached over and held Henry's hand as he was telling the story.

With a deep sigh Henry said, "At the time of the accident, I was in London setting up my new office. I had been offered a job with Reuters News to cover the Middle East and Latin America in securing publishing rights for English speaking business news journals. Molly and I were going to move there after the baby was born, I would take a short leave and then we would move. I received the call about 10pm that night at my hotel and I believe that I went into a kind of shock. The Spanish teacher had called me, and I could not believe what I was hearing.

Henry went on to say that the next few years were very tough. He threw himself into work to ward off the depression and the occasional foray into hedonism to try to erase the pain of the loss. After three years of traveling the world and living in London, he said, "I sold the condominium in Chicago and I moved back to southern Indiana and followed my first passion of teaching. Got my master's degree in education and my principal's license. Truly, the kids brought me out of the depression." Sarah squeezed Henry's hand and leaned over and gave him a kiss on the cheek.

"Well, it's getting late and I better get you home," said Henry. Sarah replied, "Let's just sit here a little longer and watch the river traffic and listen to the waves." She then leaned her head on Henry's shoulder. After a little while, Henry said, "Can I freshen your drink?" Sarah said, "You just sit here, I'll take care of that and I'll freshen yours." A few minutes later Sarah returned with their drinks, she patted Henry's knee, handed him his drink, and gave him a kiss on his forehead. Sarah said, "You are a dear man, and I am so glad I met you. I cannot imagine what you have gone through." Henry conceded it was a very rough patch and at times he behaved in ways he wished he hadn't.

After sitting in silence for a while, Sarah said, "Can you show me your house?" Henry said, "Sure, follow me." He showed her the kitchen, his office, the master bedroom, guest room, and a loft bedroom. They returned to the deck where Betsy stood waiting for them. They both gave Betsy a pet on the head and she laid down. They both sat on the sofa again and once again Sarah leaned her head on his shoulder. Henry thought to himself "I wonder what type of relationship Sarah wants. I was happy to be a mentor and friend, but she seems a little more affectionate than that." Sarah was thinking to herself too, "He is really a nice man and has been through so much, I just want to take care of HIM."

As it approached midnight, Henry said, "As much I hate to say this, are you ready to go, and believe me I'm not rushing you." Sarah said, "I like this a lot, can we just hang out for another hour? And I'd like it if you put your arm around me?" Henry said, "Yes, I'd like you to stay a while longer. Just sitting here quiet is nice." So, they continued to silently enjoy each other's company. Sarah asked out of nowhere, "What is your favorite memory from teaching school?" Henry replied, "There are so many of them. One girl after she graduated, asked me to walk her down the aisle at her wedding, as her father had died when she was an infant. I was so honored to do it." "That is so sweet," said Sarah. As the hour passed by Sarah looked up at Henry and said, "Do you go to church?" "I do, I go to both St. Michaels and occasionally to the Cathedral of the Assumption in Louisville." Sarah replied, "I go to the Cathedral too. Would you consider going to five o'clock Mass with me tomorrow. "I'd love to. I'll pick you up about twenty till five tomorrow," replied Henry.

They both got up and Sarah gave Henry a gentle hug. She then bent down and gave Betsy a hug too. They walked to the car and Sarah said, "Can I have a go at driving your sports car? I've never driven one before." He gave her the keys and said, "Do you know how to drive a manual transmission?" Henry asked. Sarah said she had learned on a stick. They backed out of the garage and Sarah took off laying rubber in three gears as they drove down the road. She looked at Henry and said, "Sorry about that." A few minutes late, they arrived at Sarah's house and as a gentleman, Henry walked her to the door as Sarah led him there holding the flowers, he had given her. After she unlocked the door, she gave Henry a gentle tight hug and a kiss on the cheek. Henry said, "I look forward to Mass tomorrow." "Me too," said Sarah.

Chapter 51

I'm Happy Just to Dance with You

When Sarah entered her home, she noticed there were several messages and missed calls on her phone, all from "the girls." Well, she would have to call them all tomorrow and give them the run down on tonight. But now it was time to make sure she took time to cuddle Binx a bit and then off to bed.

When she arose the next morning, it was already ten o'clock and the phone was ringing. Sarah answered. It was Michele who immediately said, "Well, what happened, how was it, are you going to see him again?" Sarah said, "Hello Michele, I had a good time. We went to his house and just sat, talked, and had a couple of drinks." Michele practically shrieked when she said, "You went back to his house." Sarah told her that Henry had a lovely house on the river, not big but comfortable with a beautiful deck overlooking the river and they sat on the sofa on the deck and just talked. Sarah said, "I hugged him and kissed him on the cheek a couple of times, and I hugged him and kissed him on the check when he walked me to the door." "Oh," said Sarah, "he has an adorable old Golden Retriever named Betsy." Michele asked Sarah, "What did he say about his late wife?"

Sarah told Michele that it was a sad story, that his late wife Molly was killed in a bus crash in France. That she was a chaperone on a school trip of schoolgirls studying French and Spanish. She was seventh months pregnant, and the baby did not survive. She told Michele how Henry was in London and was not with her when she died. He didn't go into detail, but I felt so sorry for him. He told me when he saw me, he thought he had seen a ghost. I looked that much like her.

After a pause, Michelle said, "How terrible." Their conversation continued and Michele asked Sarah if she was seeing him again. Sarah responded, "We are going to Mass together at the Cathedral this evening." Michelle asked, "Sarah are you in love with this man?" Sarah said, "I don't know, but I am deeply in "like" with him. And I believe I would have to be the one to move things forward as I think he is too gentlemanly and probably thinks he is too old."

Michele asked if Sarah thought he was too old for her. "Michele, I've dated a lot of guys my age, a little older, some a little younger, but I don't think he is too old. But I definitely want to see more of him," said Sarah.

Just then, Sarah was getting another call, from her mother. "Michele, I've got to go. I'm getting another call. It's my mom," Sarah said. She clicked off from Michele and picked up the call from her mom. "Hello, Mom," said Sarah. Her mom called to ask about her evening with Dr. Morrison. Sarah told her mom everything she told Michele, how she was deeply in "like" with Henry and the story of his late wife. Mom advised, "Now Sarah, don't rush into anything, he's old enough to be your dad." Sarah said, "I know, I know, I am not rushing, I just really enjoy his company and the fact that he is older does not make a bit of difference to me." Sarah explained. "And before you ask, I am seeing him again. We are going to Mass together this afternoon." Her Mom said, "Okay, okay, I won't say anything else except just be careful."

Chapter 52
Lovely Sarah

Doc left Sarah's house with a lot of thoughts running through his head. How serious was this young woman? How did he feel? Where did he want the relationship to go? Thinking to himself as he drove through the night air, he went into this out of curiosity with no expectations of anything. Now, things were changing. He genuinely liked the young woman, and it wasn't because she reminded him of Molly, to be sure it was not that. She definitely had her own personality, a take charge type of individual. He liked that. As he drove, he thought "I'm old enough to be her father, does that or should that matter?"

He was settled in his life, and that was the point, he was too settled. The boys in the company had begun to make him feel younger and now Sarah. Doc was a fatalistic person. He believed that things definitely happened for a reason. Whether you believed in God's plan, divine intervention, karma whatever, he believed people were placed in your path for a reason.

On river road, he turned on satellite radio and the U2 song "I Still Haven't Found What I'm Looking For" came on and he thought what timing. It was a song that played to and tapped into he doubts, his faith, and his lifelong restlessness. Maybe this was a time when he needed to not doubt so much, not question or analyze so much but to give it up to faith. Yes, he was fatalistic, but the relationship with this young woman testing that faith and fatalism. He still hadn't found what he was looking for but maybe "it" found him. Happiness had possibly found him.

He finally pulled into the garage. He walked up the steps and there was faithful Betsy waiting for him. He took the elevator down to let Betsy go out one last time for the night. They came back up; Betsy got her puppy treat and Doc went to bed. It would be a fitful night's sleep, as he kept thinking about Sarah and turning the relationship over and over in his mind. He was too old for her, no he wasn't, yes, he was. It just wouldn't stop. Finally, about four in the morning, he drifted off to sleep.

Around nine, Doc arose with Betsy laying on his chin on the edge of the bed. I know girl it's time for walkies. Doc got the leash, took Betsy down in the elevator, and out the door they went. They walked their usual two-mile route through the village, Doc felt that he heard every bird that was singing that morning and almost felt that he didn't really need his cane. When he got back, Betsy got her usual puppy treat and Doc fed her. He picked up his phone off his nightstand and saw that there was a message from 1:45 this morning. He listened to it and it was Sarah telling him what a wonderful time she had that evening and was looking forward to seeing him later today. "For an old man, she sure is making me feel good with the flattery. Why would a beautiful young woman want an old man like him," he said to himself?

He decided to call Kathleen, since he hadn't talked to her in a few days. He told his sister all about the two dates with Sarah and that while flattered, he didn't know why Sarah would be interested in him. Kathleen told him, "Would you just relax and let things happen or unfold as they will? If you quote me on what I'm about to say, I'll choke you. You're a handsome man who doesn't look his age. You're intelligent and have a good sense of humor and most of the time you can laugh at yourself, so lighten up," she said. Kathleen asked Henry about Sarah. He told her that she was the mirror image of Molly. She was funny, self-confident, and assertive and she made him feel happy. Kathleen said, "So be yourself and relax and whatever your age difference, it just doesn't matter if you both know what you're getting into and you're both happy."

Chapter 53
Love Me Do

After about an hour and a half, Molly returned from her run, Henry stopped her and gave her a hug and kiss. Molly said, "Eww, I'm sweaty." "And I don't care," replied Henry. He asked what time her Mom and Bridget were coming over. Molly answered, "About noon." Henry informed her that she had about an hour to get ready. Shortly before noon Molly emerged from the master bedroom and Henry already had a picnic basket ready to take to the air show; he had packed fruit, cheese, crackers, and a selection of sandwiches. Drinks were bottles of water and a few cans of soft drinks.

Just then the house phone rang, it was Lawrence announcing that two guests were on their way up. Molly said, "Well, here comes your ultimate test, you're meeting my Mom." "I think I'll be able to charm her," said Henry. Momentarily there was a knock on the door, Molly answered it and let her Mother and sister inside. Bridgit made her way to Henry and gave him a hug and whispered, "Good luck." Henry made his way over to Molly's Mom and said, "Welcome Mrs. Kniss, I'm Henry and I'm glad you could make it today." She thanked him for the invitation and presented him with an apple pie for dessert. Henry told the group there were two choices for viewing the air show; they could take their things early to the roof and grab a table up there or they could try to find a spot on the lakefront.

The group chose to go to the roof as it provided access to shade, a table and chairs, and access to a restroom. The air show lasted for three hours and when it was over the group came back down to the condo for some coffee and dessert. The whole afternoon Henry sat next to Gladys Kniss and explained the types of planes that were flying overhead, asked her about her job as a school secretary and the school. He paid a lot of interest to her and made her feel special. After dessert, Bridgit and Gladys left after hugs from both Molly and Henry. As Gladys left, she looked at Molly and gave a wink to her, a wink of approval.

Molly and Henry sat together on the sofa and both released a collective sigh of relief. Henry asked, "Well did I pass the test?" "Oh yeah, she totally likes you. You took time with her and focused on her. She liked that a lot," said Molly. "Let's sleep in tomorrow and I'll forfeit my run for the day. Henry agreed with the plan and gave Molly a passionate kiss. "Do you want to stroll along the lakefront later?" Molly asked. Henry said that he would love too.

That weekend cemented the seriousness of their relationship. Over the coming weeks, they began seeing a counselor to help Henry get past his fear of intimacy. The counselor gave them both techniques to help. By the first week of October, Molly and Bear had moved in with Henry and Henry bought another parking space in the garage.

In late September, Henry took Molly to southern Indiana to meet both his mother and his sister Kathleen who were both important influences in his life. Kathleen just adored Molly and they got along famously. Henry's mother on the other hand acted standoffish but maintained politeness. Henry told Molly on the way home not to worry about his mother. She likes to try to exert whatever control she could over his life. When he graduated college, he was close to going in the Navy as an officer. His mother literally fell to her knees crying and begged him not to do it because his father was in the Navy, and she hate his father.

At the end of October was the Chicago Marathon. Bridgit and Molly were both entered, and Henry was going to meet them at various points along the race route and supply them with supplements to help them through the race. At the end, he was there to cheer them on to the finish and then take them back to the condo to rest and recover. Bridgit spent the night rather than drive home as tired as she was. Both twins finished the marathon in under four hours which was impressive. They celebrated over wine and a pasta dinner.

On Halloween, they attended a company Halloween party together, Molly dressed as Napoleon and Henry dressed as Saddam Hussein complete with battle fatigues, red beret, combat boots, fake thick moustache, and skin toner. Molly talked a lot with Henry's secretary Betsy, who came as Betsy Ross, and discovered what a mothering effect she had on Henry. Betsy looked out for him at work and a bit on the personal side as well.

In early November, Henry called Betsy into his office along with Mike Mackowiak his boss and asked them to close the door. I wanted to tell you both something and ask you both something. "Oh my God," said Betsy "You're going to ask Molly to marry you!" "Well thanks for taking the proverbial wind out of my sail Betsy. Yes, I am going to ask her Saturday evening to marry me. I want the two of you to be our witnesses. I plan on the day before Thanksgiving going to city hall and doing a civil ceremony. Are you two available?" They both said they were, so the plan began to take shape. Henry had bought an engagement ring of emeralds with diamonds around them. He didn't believe in getting a traditional diamond, he wanted something special for Molly.

On Saturday evening, November 3, Henry took Molly to Spiaggia where they had their first romantic dinner together. That night he had given Molly the pearl necklace and earrings. Tonight, she asked, "Is there some special occasion tonight?" "No, no, nothing special. I just like to see you looking so glamorous," said Henry. They had a lovely dinner, with that beautiful view of Lake Shore Drive at night. Over dessert of chocolate mousse, Henry reached into his jacket pocket and pulled out a jewelry box, looked at Molly sweetly and said, "I would be honored if you would say yes to marrying me." Molly got tears in her eyes and said, "Yes," as Henry slipped the ring on her finger, she added "I love you so much Henry." With that they were officially engaged. Henry asked what type of wedding she wanted, and Molly replied, "I don't want a big public ceremony. I want something private." "What would you say to getting married at city hall the day before Thanksgiving and we leave for our honeymoon the day after Thanksgiving? "asked Henry. "I can go for that," said Molly, "Where are we going for honeymoon?" "Well, I know you have to teach, and you still have your master's classes to take, so I'll give you a couple of choices; long weekend in New York, Los Angeles, or San Francisco," said Henry. "Are you serious? I'd love to go to San Francisco!" replied Molly. All the way back to the building, Molly leaned in close to Henry in the back of the cab.

Once home, she asked him to keep the lights dim and put those two songs on the stereo that he played the first time they went to Spiaggia. He did and they danced in the dimly lit living room with mainly the lights of the city showing through the big picture window. After they danced to the second song, Molly led Henry by the hand to the bedroom.

Chapter 54
Baby It's You

Late Sunday morning, Henry began thinking about going to Mass that afternoon with Sarah. He loved going to the Cathedral, on Sunday mornings they had a full choir accompanied by an awesome pipe organ. Saturday evenings, it was usually just a piano, the cantor, and the music and the musicianship were just as good, but more intimate. Some masses he had attended at smaller churches used a cheap organ and the music always sounded like a funeral dirge, but not at the Cathedral of the Assumption. The music, in itself, was a spiritual experience.

Henry decided to call Kathleen. He updated her on where things were going. Henry said to Kathleen that Sarah was being very affectionate and caring towards him and asked him to go to Mass this afternoon. Kathleen said, "So she's a good Catholic girl. That's good. If you ask me, she see's something in you, God knows what it is! Just kidding." "Thanks sis, I appreciate the confidence that you boost me with so freely," said Henry. "If I were you, I would let her drive this thing and let it go as far as you feel comfortable, you can slow it down anytime you want. But I know you, you'd be afraid of hurting her by stopping her," said Kathleen.

Henry usually listened to his sister. They had grown closer as they had gotten older and he trusted her. He would let Sarah take charge and anyway, Sarah had that type of personality. He decided to spend the afternoon reading on his deck and just watching the river and the day go by. About 3:30, he shaved and showered, put on a blue and white striped button-down shirt, khaki slacks, and a blue blazer. He decided to drive the Range Rover today and headed off to Sarah's house. He arrived just a bit early at 4:30 and was welcomed into her house with an affectionate hug from Sarah. Sarah introduced Henry to Binx the cat and showed him around the small house. After running to the bathroom, she was ready to go.

On the way to the Cathedral, they both chatted about how much they liked the music at the church. They arrived about five minutes before mass began. Sarah asked if Henry minded if they sit in the back. Henry replied, "You're not going to sneak out after communion, are you?" "No. silly, I like to sit in the back and just take in the whole of the church. The altar, the beautiful stain glass windows, the blue ceiling with the stars. I just enjoy the whole experience," said Sarah.

After Mass, as they were walking to the car Henry asked, "Would you like to get a bite to eat and maybe browse a bookstore?" Sarah replied that she would love that. They drove out to the East End of Louisville to the Paddocks Shopping Center. There were several restaurants and a Barnes and Noble bookstore to browse. He suggested that get a quick bite at Zoë's Kitchen, which featured a fresh Mediterranean style menu. They both ordered the Spinach Feta rollup and a soft drink. After dinner, they wondered over to Barnes and Noble to browse. Henry browsed the new novels with Sarah. She looked over the new Stephen King book, James Patterson's latest, and she got interested in a book called *Where the Crawdads Sing*, which she set aside to purchase. Henry browsed history and biographies. He picked out the new Erik Larson book "*The Splendid and the Vile*," about the leadership of Winston Churchill. They made their purchases and walked to the car.

Sarah asked, "Can we go back to your house and sit on the deck for a while? I really like the peacefulness of listening to the water." Henry replied sure. They drove the few miles from the east end, across the bridge to Henry's home. Once inside, he said, "Sarah, do you want to go with me to walk Betsy?" She replied, "love too." They took Betsy on a short walk, returned home, and gave Betsy her treat. Henry made two drinks and the three of them went out onto the deck.

Henry and Sarah sat on the sofa and Sarah said, "Would you do me a favor and put your arm around me?" Henry immediately did as he requested, and Sarah snuggled her head between his shoulder and chin. There they sat quietly, sipping their drinks for several minutes. Sarah finally broke the silence and said, "How do you feel?" "I feel fine," he replied. Sarah told him "No, about us?" Henry asked her if she thought it was a little too soon to be asking that question and she replied "No, I think after being with me several times you should have some sort of feeling or indication." "Well, I like you very much. You are pretty, you are highly intelligent, driven, and most of all you make me smile. My concern though is our age difference," he replied.

Sarah said, "I knew you would bring up the age thing. I have dated men my age and I find them lacking. You, on the other hand, have so many life experiences good and bad and yet you seem very centered and calm. You have a great sense of humor and you don't take yourself seriously. I love that about you. And you are a handsome man, so don't you dare bring up age again!" "So how do you feel," asked Henry. "I like you an awful lot. I think about you often through the day," Sarah replied. A long silence hung in the air between them until Sarah broke the silence. "Can I ask you another favor?" asked Sarah. Henry replied that she could. Sarah asked, "Would you please kiss me?" "Excuse me," he replied. "Would you please kiss me?" He turned toward her and gave her a tender kiss. She replied, "That wasn't a kiss!" She took his face in her hands, drew him near and gave him a passionate kiss and said, "Okay, now we've gotten that out of the way, so relax and put your arm around me again."

Chapter 55
Can't Buy Me Love

S unday morning and Henry and Molly slept late. It was just three weeks until they would get married. Molly called her sister first and talked to her for well over and hour. Then she called her mother and talked to her for an equal amount of time. Henry had shaved and showered while Molly was on the phone. "Molly," Henry called out "Are you going for your run this morning?" "Yes," she said, "But just a five mile as I need to take it down a couple of notches after the marathon. I should be back in a half hour or so." He asked her if she would like to go to the Bandera Bar and Grill for lunch today. She replied, "Yes."

Molly returned from her run, showered, and changed clothes and the two walked to the Michigan Avenue restaurant. They enjoyed people watching the folks walking along Michigan Avenue. They talked about the honeymoon in San Francisco in just three weeks. Henry, in fact, was going to make the arrangements that afternoon when they returned to the condo. He was going to use some of his frequent flyer miles to upgrade their airline tickets to first class to make the trip a little more special.

Henry made their plans; they would be flying first class from Chicago to San Francisco and staying at the Hyatt Regency Hotel. Molly was in charge of picking out things that she would like to see and visit. They planned to host Thanksgiving for the family and then fly out the day after

Thanksgiving, returning on Monday evening. Molly would have to arrange for a substitute for Monday and Tuesday.

The three weeks passed quickly and at last the wedding day had arrived. Henry and Molly were up at seven. They were going to meet Mike and Betsy at city hall at ten for the ceremony. Molly was wearing a winter white tea length dress. Henry was dressed in a navy-blue suit, white French cuff shirt, cuff links, and a blue and white striped Repp tie. When they arrived at city hall, they were in line with several couples most dressed like they were for a civil ceremony, but there was a young Marine in dress blues and his bride in a full white wedding dress. When it came their turn, a secretary introduced them to the retired Judge, Julia Shaw, who would perform the ceremony. She asked the two if they had their own vows, Henry answered no but he did want to read something before they started. He pulled out of his jacket pocket the lyrics to the Beatles song *I Will*. The judge then performed the ceremony ending with, "You may now kiss your bride." Henry then gave Molly a tender sweet kiss. After the ceremony, Henry treated the four to lunch at the Drake Hotel on Michigan Avenue. They had a lighthearted lunch and Henry and Molly thanked Betsy and Mike for their support. As they were leaving, Henry shook hands with Mike and Betsy gave him a big hug and kiss on the cheek. Henry said, "Thanks Mom." Then Betsy punched him in the arm.

The newly wed Mr. and Mrs. Morrison walked happily down Michigan Avenue and back to THEIR home to prepare for Thanksgiving Dinner. They walked hand in hand in their building and were greeted by Carlton the doorman on duty. Carlton said, "Mr. and Mrs. Morrison, the guys and I got you this for your special day." Carlton handed the two a bouquet of roses and a gift certificate to Marshall Fields' Department store. Henry gave Carlton a man hug and said, "You guys didn't have to do this." "We know, said Carlton, "but we wanted to." In the elevator alone, Henry said, "That was so nice of the guys." Molly suddenly pushed Henry against the wall and started kissing him passionately, then said, "Let's get a start the honeymoon." The two made love all afternoon, Thanksgiving preparations could wait till this evening.

On Thanksgiving Day, they awoke early and began sprucing up the condo, setting the table and putting on the final touches for the day. Molly had prepared the turkey and dressing, Mom and Bridgit were bringing the side dishes and dessert. About eleven, Bridgit and Mom arrived. Bridgit and Gladys gave Henry and Molly hugs and kisses and words of congratulations. Gladys handed the happy couple a card in an envelope. The card was filled with a handwritten happy sentiment and a check for $5000. Henry said, "Oh Gladys, this is too much. You don't have to do this!" Gladys said, "You're saving me money; I would have spent more than this on a wedding ceremony." They all laughed and Molly hugged Gladys and said, "Thanks so much Mom, I love you."

As they started their married life with a family Thanksgiving, they knew that marriage was work and the therapy would continue to help them, especially Henry, along the way. The honeymoon was a joyous trip of fun, exploration, and new experiences for the couple. Their first Christmas together was emotional and moving, as Molly told Henry that she was pregnant. They were both ecstatic, but two weeks later Molly suffered a miscarriage. It was an emotional ride that neither of them planned on. Their counselor told them to support each other and allow each other to grieve the loss.

Their first year not only saw them experience the loss of a pregnancy, but the death of Henry's father. Both events were emotionally crushing for both Henry and Molly. They both grieved the loss of their child. Henry did not necessarily grieve the loss of his father as they weren't that close, but he grieved the loss of time he had. Henry received word that his father had terminal cancer and had weeks to live. His father received the diagnosis in early June and died twelve weeks later. Henry spent the summer working two weeks, then flying to California for a week throughout the summer. By the time his father passed away and Henry flew out to the funeral, he returned and collapsed with exhaustion from emotional stress and just plain exhaustion. He was so frail and weak, that Lawrence the doorman had to help him to his condo, where he collapsed on the sofa. Molly managed to get him to the bed, where he slept in his clothes for sixteen hours. He had lost twenty-five pounds that he could not afford to lose.

Molly was so concerned for her husband's health (physical and mental) that she called Betsy to say that he would be out for the week ill. Betsy knew she had seen her boss deteriorate and lose weight the past few weeks. Molly called both the therapist for an emergency appointment and his doctor at Northwestern University Hospital for an appointment. The therapist told Molly her husband needed a good month of rest as he was very nearly close to a nervous breakdown. Henry's physician Dr. Brenda Kaufmann said that he was severely dehydrated and recommended a couple of days in the hospital for rest and to run various tests.

The twelve weeks of dealing with his father's illness and passing took a toll on Henry mentally and physically. Physically, he had a severe case of mononucleosis and mentally near the breaking point. Molly took a four week leave of absence to take care of Henry. He told her that three days before his father died, his father wanted Henry to tell him he loved him as a father. He told Molly, "I couldn't do it. He hadn't been there. He hadn't earned it." Henry reminded his mother that many times he had gotten he and Kathleen to go see him and he just didn't show up. That he had probably had a fight with Henry's mom. Henry called his dad out and said, "No you don't get to say that. If I had wanted to see my kids bad enough, I would have sucked it up and taken a few minutes of verbal punishment." He said to Molly, "Then three days later he died. I felt guilty for not telling a dying man what he wanted to hear. I told him I loved him as a human being, but he hadn't earned fatherhood. Then I began thinking, would I be a good father?" Molly sat next to him on the sofa and cradled him in her arms as tears began running down his face. She told him "You will be a good father. I could think of no better person to be a dad. As for feeling guilty, don't. You told him the truth as gently as you could, and you made the extreme effort to be there for him." Henry started to cry more, and Molly held him tightly and kissed his forehead. Henry sobbed. He was thinking how thankful he was to have Molly. If it had not been for her, he would have come unglued. He loved her so much.

She told him, "Why don't you take a nap and when you get up, we'll have dinner." She helped him up and walked him to the bedroom, tucked him in and kissed him tenderly on the lips. Within seconds, Henry fell asleep. Molly went to call her mom and talk about taking care of Henry. "Mom it's as if he is a broken man. He came back from that funeral barely able to walk," Molly told her. "Is he any better?" asked Molly's mom. "Well, he still cries, sleeps a lot, but a little less than at first, and he's gained a couple of pounds. I'm going to walk him down to the lakefront after dinner and just sit there for a little while," said Molly.

Just before Molly was to wake Henry up for dinner, there was a knock at the door. It was Carlton (one of the doormen). "Mrs. Morrison, how is Henry?" said Carlton. She told Carlton he was getting stronger and if he could spare a minute, she was just going to get him up. She excused herself and went to the bedroom to wake Henry up. She bent over the bed and kissed him on the forehead, she said, "Time to get up sweetheart, and you have a visitor. Carlton came up to check on you." She helped him up and helped him walk slowly to the living room. Carlton said, "How are you Henry?" Henry replied, I'm fine, come sit with me a few minutes. Carlton handed Henry a box of chocolates from the doormen. "That was so thoughtful of you, please thank the guys for me," said Henry. Carlton told him they were all concerned. Lawrence had told them how bad Henry had looked and that he had been in the hospital. Henry and Carlton talked for about fifteen minutes before Carlton left.

Molly put dinner on the table and tried to get Henry to eat just a bit more than he did the day before. She said, "Do you feel like trying to walk to the lakefront and sit there for a little while?" Henry said, "I'd like that." And so, it went day after day for four weeks. Getting a bit stronger each day and going to counseling once a week for his mental health and always with Molly accompanying him. At the end of four weeks, Henry was well enough to start back to work doing half days. Betsy was a big help to him in getting reorganized and up to speed. After two weeks of working half days, he felt well enough to get back to his regular routine.

Chapter 56
Another Girl

Sitting next to Sarah on the deck felt easy and comfortable. Even after she asserted herself and planted that wet kiss on him. He reflected for a bit, and said, "So I'm guessing this is starting to get serious?" "Yes, I'd say that's fair. I've been thinking that I really don't want to keep dating all these guys my age who are on the career climb. I feel like I am in competition with them but am also to stay in my assigned spot as a woman, do you understand that?" she said. He understood all too well. He was not a threat to her. "By dating me, you get a boyfriend, although I'm too old to be a boy, and a mentor of sorts," Henry said. Sarah replied, "You make me sound sort of mercenary and calculating." "No, I didn't mean it that way. I just mean it makes perfect sense. But what about a family? That is the ultimate dilSarah for women, career versus family?" he added.

They sat in silence for a long while just listening to each other's breath. Sarah finally broke the silence and said, "Do you want a child." "I've always wanted a child. I've lost three, and I think about my little girl every day. I'd like to think I'd have another chance, but it looks like time is passing me by," said Henry. Sarah said, "Here's me taking charge. What if we became a couple, would you want to have a child with me? It got quiet for a couple of minutes. "Are you proposing?" Henry asked. He added "We have been out together three or four times, is that enough to know? Sarah said,

"I know that I am falling in love with you and I know some will accuse me of wanting to marry my father but that's not it. I want someone stable." "I may be stable, but I have not fully retired. I'm working with two young men in a startup company and I don't really plan to fully retire, but I do make my own hours and often work from home. "I know you are still active, and I love that about you, that you are engaged and want to be."

"Okay, I'll paint a picture and you tell me how it fits for you. We date, get more serious, and get married. We have a baby, since I work out of the house a lot, I'm able to help quite a bit. Then we decide, oh, this is one sharp cookie, she needs to be running her own crisis consulting firm, or, PR, or whatever, but you're smart. So, we rent you an office downtown on this side of the river, hire a secretary and we both split our out of home time. How's that sound?" suggested Henry. "That sounds perfect! I love the way you think, and I, well, just love YOU!" Sarah exclaimed loudly. "What just happened?" said Henry. "What just happened is that we have made a plan?" Sarah replied. "We made a plan? I thought I painted a hypothetical picture," said Henry. "Yes, but it was such a good blueprint it just has to happen. Would you mentor me? asked Sarah. "Of course, I would," Henry answered. "Do you think you could marry me?" Sarah asked. "Yes, I could, but why don't we have at least two or three more dates first. I got it, let me meet your friends you were with that night. I'm sure they'll talk some sense into you and wave you off this older man," said Henry. Sarah thumped Henry in the forehead and said, "I told you to stop mentioning the age thing, I don't want to hear it!"

They again went silent for a few minutes. Out of nowhere Sarah leaned up and gave Henry a long, soft, tender kiss and wrapped her arms around him. "What was that for?" Henry asked. "It was for, just being you?" Sarah replied. "Do you want another drink?" asked Sarah.

"I think I better have another drink," replied Henry. A few moments later, Sarah returned with their drinks and snuggled into Henry. "Let me ask you a question, do I need to do any real thinking in this relationship, or can I just sit back and relax and let you plan everything?" asked Henry.

"I wouldn't say everything. I'll let you choose where you want to go for our honeymoon, since you're paying for it," said Sarah. "You know what we could do. We could take the next ten days off. Go get the license tomorrow and get married by a justice of the peace and take our honeymoon. Notify everyone from our honeymoon destination and just blow their minds, wouldn't that be wild?" said Henry. Sarah said, "Don't tempt me because I would do it!" "In all seriousness, you're not really thinking you want to get that serious to marry me, are you?" asked Henry. Sarah thumped in the head again and said, "Snap out of it, haven't you been listening to me old man." Henry thumped Sarah in the head for mentioning the age thing.

"I knew that first night we met that I wanted to get serious with you. I kind of felt a longing to take care of you," said Sarah. "Take care of me? I'm not an invalid," replied Henry. "No, goofy, you've been dealing with a lot of hurt and you've been alone a long time. I wanted to be with you. You're in my thoughts daily," said Sarah. "Well, I have to say you've been in mine a lot too," added Henry. "Is that the truth, you mean it?" asked Sarah. Yes, of course. You're lovely, bright and sexy, I mean what's not to love," asked Henry. "I have it," added Henry, "Let's go away somewhere next weekend, a four-day weekend and see how we get along, separate rooms, how about it?" asked Henry. "No way separate rooms, if this is some sort of test, every-thing gets tested. I'm sleeping with you in whatever sense you take that. This is the twenty first century man!" exclaimed Sarah. He thumped her in the head again, and she thumped him in the head right back. "I said man, not old man," said Sarah. He immediately pulled her close and gave her a tender kiss as an apology.

"Okay, how about next weekend we take a trip to Los Angeles. We can have a meal with my good friend Jamal and do Hollywood touristy stuff. I mean real corny stuff," said Henry. Sarah said, "That will be great, but I think I'll take Tuesday off too, as we will probably be coming back on the red eye." Henry said he would make the arrangements and they would leave on Friday morning. Henry looked at Sarah and said, "Can you do me a favor?" And right away Sarah kissed him. "Wow and you're psychic too, you read my mind," said Henry.

The work week went quickly for Sarah as she was still helping the California company through their problem. She started thinking that Henry was right, she is sharp enough to be doing her own thing and she is networked in with a lot of companies. Maybe the first three or four months would be slow, but she felt confident she could build a business. After work on Thursday, she had dinner at Drake's with Michele. "You said you wanted to marry him!" said Michele when Sarah had told her about the conversation. "And you're doing what?" Michele continued when Sarah told her about the long weekend trip to Los Angeles. "Henry said he would get two rooms, but I told him no one room would be fine that I could sleep with him," Sarah said. Michele replied, "Are you crazy? Did you have too much to drink?" "No, and no, I did not have too much to drink."

By the time Thursday came around, Henry was anxious and excited about the trip. This young woman was certainly assertive, and he was certainly flattered by her words and actions and honestly a little frightened. He had never been with a woman that assertive and sure of herself. He decided to call Kathleen; he hadn't talked to her all week and boy she would get a kick out this. Kathleen was stunned after Henry told her about last Sunday. Kathleen said, "She said and did all of that? Really, and after going to Mass. Well, I guess it's a new week and you can always confess the following weekend. So, you are sharing a bed with her?" "Kind of looks that way sis," Henry replied.

The Friday flight was an early one leaving at 7:30 am, but it was non-stop and would get in at 9:30 am Los Angeles time. He picked Sarah up at 5:30 am, kissed her hello and loaded her bag into the Range Rover. They made it to the airport in just a few minutes, he dropped Sarah and their bags at departing flights and then went to park the car. They checked in and made it through security smoothly and proceeded to the gate. When they began calling for boarding, she was surprised to learn that Henry had procured first class tickets.

The flight was a smooth one and they landed in Los Angeles on time. Henry said, "Let's get the rental car and get checked in at the hotel and freshen up, we have lunch with Jamal in West Hollywood." They got the car and drove to their hotel, the famous Beverly Hills Hotel. They checked in and found it had one king bed as requested by Sarah. She immediately ran and laid on it. Henry immediately unpacked and began putting his clothes in drawers, Sarah on the other hand just opened her bag and left things in, fishing around for her toiletries. They relaxed and talked for a while. Just before noon, they got in the car and headed to Hedley's restaurant in West Hollywood to meet Jamal.

They parked the car and as they entered the restaurant, they saw Jamal waiting for them at the entrance. Jamal had a red rose for Sarah. As Henry introduced the two, Jamal presented Sarah with the rose and gave her a kiss on the cheek. The three got a table and began to chat. Jamal said, "My friend here told me he was bringing a beautiful woman with him, I didn't know you were this beautiful." "You better be careful Sarah; Jamal will try to charm you away from me and you may find yourself missing your flight home," said Henry.

On Friday afternoon, they drove to see the famous Hollywood sign and then the Griffith Observatory, and Griffith Park and The Greek Theater. Their afternoon complete, they drove back to the hotel. They showered and dressed for dinner in the hotel. After dinner, they had a couple of drinks before heading back up to their room. Once inside the room, Sarah took Henry by the hand and led him to the bed. Sarah looked at Henry and in a husky voice said loudly, "Take me to bed Henry or lose me forever!" "You do know that was a Meg Ryan line from Top Gun, don't you?" said Henry. "I'm going to say it once more, take me to bed Henry or lose me forever!" Sarah repeated. Henry moved closer to Sarah, she grabbed him by the shirt and pulled him down on the bed and got on top of him. She began kissing him and unbuttoning his shirt and undressing him. He reciprocated undressing Sarah. When it came to sex, Sarah pushed Henry down and made love to him. They made love a couple more times before morning.

They got up early on Saturday and drove to Anaheim to go to Disneyland for an exciting day of theme park rides. They returned late in the evening having gotten a day of sun and tired from walking around the park and waiting in line. They both showered and again Sarah took the lead on making love to Henry. Afterwards, Henry got a strange look on his face of excruciating pain. "Sarah, Henry said, call an ambulance and then help me get dressed. I'm having a heart attack." Sarah said excitedly, "Are you serious Henry?" "Deadly," he replied, "in agony."

Within a few minutes, the ambulance crew arrived, and Sarah let them in. Sarah answered all questions for the crew except for medical history. She did tell them "He has had three previous heart attacks." The crew inserted an IV, EKG lines, and blood pressure cuff and then loaded Henry onto the gurney. Henry looked up at Sarah and said, "I'm sorry about the trip honey." Sarah said with a tear in her eye "I'm coming with you; I'll be with you. Henry tell them to let me be with you." He did.

Chapter 57

All You Need
Is Love

November 1991 marked their first anniversary and Henry took Molly to lunch at the Drake hotel where they had lunch right after they were married last November. It had been a rough year for them both. Henry looked at Molly and said "I love you so much. You went through such pain and trauma and later in the year you supported me through going to California to see my Dad and nursed me back to health. You're an amazing woman Molly and I'm lucky to be married to you." "No, I'm just as lucky. You're a sweet and dear man who does the right thing no matter what it does to you," said Molly.

Henry told Molly that he had a combination anniversary and Christmas present for her, a present that they both needed after such a year. He handed her an envelope. She opened it to see an itinerary for a trip to Hawaii. They would leave on December 26, the day after Christmas and spend eight days in Maui and two days on Oahu. "I'm glad you're my husband. You treat me like a queen," said Molly.

This year their Thanksgiving would be spent at Bridgit's house. They left the condo at about 10:30 for the drive to Park Forest and Bridgit's house. They got in the Porsche and Molly drove. Henry still hasn't been driving much as was still recovering. On the drive, they talked about their trip to Hawaii, clothes they would have to buy and maybe a couple or few pounds to be lost after Thanksgiving.

Thanksgiving was a joyous affair. Bridgit and Gladys were happy to see Henry feeling a bit better, as they had been worried about him. Both women gave him a hug and a kiss and hugs for Molly too. The turkey was good, as were all the side dishes and dessert. Christmas this year would be celebrated at Henry and Molly's. Christmas came quickly and the family gathered at Henry and Molly's. Gifts were exchanged, and a wonderful meal was shared. Everyone was excited about the Hawaii trip.

In the morning, Henry and Molly grabbed their bags and went to the lobby to meet James from the car service, who loaded their bags in the trunk and off they went to the airport. When they got to check in, Henry checked to see if he could upgrade their coach seats to first class. There were seats available for upgrade, so they got first class for the nine-and-a-half-hour flight. Both were grateful for the upgrade on a long flight. The opportunity to get and move around without crawling over people or people crawling over them was a blessing to say the least.

The two days they spent on Oahu, they drove around the island, and they climbed to the top of Diamond Head. Maui was a place to lay by the pool, go to the beach and simply relax. On Maui, they rode bicycles down the steep mountain road from Haleakala, they enjoyed a catamaran cruise and snorkeling. They made love with their hotel balcony door open and ocean breezes blowing across them. They talked a lot about their first year of marriage, the loss of the baby, and Henry's near nervous breakdown. They went through a lot through that first year and came out emotionally healthy. They were looking forward to the new year and facing whatever came their way, much stronger than they were at the beginning of the year.

In February, Molly discovered she was pregnant again. When she told Henry, they both had tears in their eyes but decided to tell no one until Molly was close to three months along in the pregnancy. One evening in early April, they were sitting on the sofa together when Molly said, oh no, I need to get to the bathroom, Henry helped her. When they got there, they discovered that Molly was bleeding badly. Henry grabbed the house phone and called Lawrence and the door stand and told him to hail a cab to go to Northwestern University Hospital, it was an emergency. Henry picked up Molly in his arms and carried her to the elevator and down to the front door and the waiting cab. Lawrence said, "I already paid and tipped him to get you to Northwestern Hospital ER." Henry thanked Lawrence and off they sped to the hospital. When they arrived, Henry carried Molly in while yelling for help. A nurse and an orderly brought a gurney and they took Molly to an examining room with Henry close behind.

The doctor came in to examine Molly, who told him what happened. The doctor did an exam while Henry waited in the hall a nervous wreck. After a seemingly long time, the nurse invited Henry back into the exam room. The doctor looked at Henry, who was ashen faced, and asked the nurse to get him some juice, as he looked ready to pass out. The doctor suggested that Henry sit down. Henry moved a chair near to Molly and held her hand. The doctor told them that they had lost the baby, a girl, and Molly was otherwise physically fine after the D and C.

Henry stood up and then bent over the bed and hugged Molly tightly as they both began to cry. The doctor said: I'll give you two a few minutes alone, but I would like to admit Molly for a couple of days just for observation and to be safe. Henry said, "Thanks, Doctor." Henry turned to Molly and said, "Are you alright sweetheart?" Molly shook her head no, "Just stay with me for a while okay?" she said. Henry told her he wasn't going anywhere. He said when they get her settled in a room, he would ask for a cot so he could sleep there tonight. He said, "I will run home for a few minutes to get some toiletries and a change of clothes and anything you might need."

Once Molly was settled in her room, Henry went home to pick up a few things for each of them. First, he had to clean the bathroom of the blood and tissue. It was a gruesome job that caused tears to stream down his face. He had to clean the hardwood floor down the hallway where blood had dripped. On his way back to the hospital, Henry stopped by the doorman stand and repaid Lawrence for the cab and tip. He told Lawrence they had lost the baby and Lawrence hugged him. He told Lawrence he would be staying at the hospital for a couple of days with Molly. Lawrence said, "Tell her me and the guys asked about her." "I sure will Lawrence," said Henry.

Henry called both of their employers and explained what had happened. He called family members and told them what happened, and that Molly was okay physically. Gladys, Bridgit, and Kathleen all cried over the phone. Kathleen offered to come to Chicago for a few days to help out, but Henry told her they would be okay. For two days, Henry stayed with Molly in the hospital and tried to comfort her. He suggested that when she felt like it, they need to talk with their counselor about grieving this loss.

Molly and Henry attended their regular therapy session, but for the most part now they were discussing how to grieve the loss of a child, a daughter. Henry suggested a getaway for a few days when Molly felt up to it. They settled on ten days in June, as Molly would be out of school and Henry would take some accrued vacation time. They chose to go to London and tour the city, spend time in the parks people watching and not adhere to any kind of a tourist schedule.

Their time in London was spent at the John Howard Hotel on Queensgate near Hyde Park. They took the Tube (London subway) to see Buckingham Palace and the changing of the guard, then to Westminster, and the Houses of Parliament, where they watched a session of the House of Commons and saw Prime Minister John Major. They took a daytrip to Canterbury Cathedral, Leeds, and Dover on the English Channel. They walked in Green Park, Regents Park, and Hyde Park. Henry rowed Molly in a boat on the Serpentine in Hyde Park. They shopped at Selfridge's and Harrod's. While rowing on the Serpentine, Molly asked Henry if he thought she would have been a good mother. "Of course, you would have been, and you will be a good mother."

One night they took the "Jack the Ripper" tour which started at a pub at ten p.m. It was a walking tour through Whitechapel, the areas of the Ripper murders. Whitechapel had pubs and still the occasional street prostitute like it did in the days of the Ripper murders. The guide pointed out where the murders occurred, and where the police were. The tour ended at midnight at a pub. Over Lager, the history professor that led the tour discussed the theories of who "Jack the Ripper" really was.

The trip was just what both of them needed. They landed back in Chicago on the Friday of the Fourth of July weekend. They had three days to rest and relax before Henry had to go back to work. Molly would begin her running on Tuesday and gradually build up her distances, but not run a marathon this year.

Chapter 58

Doctor Robert

On the way to the hospital, Henry handed Sarah his mobile phone and gave her his password to unlock it. He asked the paramedic for a pen and piece of paper for Sarah. He gave Sarah the list of people to call. First his sister Kathleen, his brother Patrick, his business partners, Jesse and Brandon. When they arrived in the ER, he informed the doctor that Sarah would be with him as he had no family nearby and she was going to be his family.

The medical team rushed Henry into the Cath lab to see what was going on with his heart. It was determined that he was in the middle of a massive heart attack. His heart stopped beating in the Cath lab and a code was called. The doctors revived Henry and decided to add two more stents to the existing two already in his heart. Within four hours of being brought into the ER, he had been placed in intensive care. Sarah came to see him at about the same time one of the doctors stepped in. The doctor said she had to leave, and Henry said if she leaves, I'll pull out all these wires and tubes and walk out of here as best as I can.

The doctor told Henry to settle down that Sarah could stay in the room. The doctor told the two that Henry had a massive heart attack, that they put two more stents in his heart. That his heart had stopped while in the Cath lab and they had revived him. The doctor said that he would be in the hospital about four or five days and be in cardiac rehab for six weeks. He was to stay off work for six weeks, do some walks and get some rest. Now, instead of going home Monday night, they would be leaving on Thursday or Friday night. Sarah looked at Henry and said, "I will take care of you Henry, I promise."

Sarah called Henry's friend Jamal who came to visit Henry. Sarah extended their stay at the hotel and changed their flights to Friday night. She called her boss and explained what happened and that she wouldn't be in until the next week. She stayed with Henry every day and kept him company. She listened attentively to the doctors when they came to talk to Henry. On Tuesday morning, he was transferred to a monitored unit outside of the ICU. Thursday evening, Henry was released from the hospital and Sarah drove them back to the hotel in the rental car. Once back at the hotel, they went to the restaurant for a bite to eat. Sarah ordered healthy things off the menu for him. There was a one-mile walking trail outside of the hotel and Sarah encouraged Henry to walk the trail. They walked together slowly. Henry had his cane and Sarah took him by his left arm. By the time they were finished, Henry was weak and very tired.

They went back to their hotel room and laid down together on the bed propped up on a couple of pillows. Henry put his arm around Sarah, and she nestled her head between his shoulder and chin. He kissed the top of her head and ran his hand up and down her arm. He said to her "Are you sure you want to be with me?" She replied, "Yes, more than ever. When I saw you being wheeled into the ambulance, I realized just how much I was in love with you and wanted you to myself. I thought I was going to lose you!" "I love you Sarah, and if you help me, I'll get stronger and get back to where I was." She told him she would do everything she could to help him.

They stayed at the hotel until Friday evening when they had to go to the airport. They went a bit earlier as Henry was walking slowly on his cane and was still weak. When they checked in, he asked if there were any upgrades available in first and told the agent what had happened and would appreciate an upgrade if possible. He upgraded with his mileage.

He refused the electric car to the gate and insisted on walking to it even though it took him a bit longer than usual.

The flight back to Louisville was a smooth one. Sarah leaned her head on Henry's shoulder and slept most of the flight. When they arrived, Henry insisted on walking to the parking garage, even though Sarah offered to go get the car and bring it around to arriving flights to pick up Henry. He did allow her to drive back to the house. They took the elevator from the garage to the living floor. Sarah took Henry to the sofa and made him comfortable. Patrick had already been at the house and walked Betsy as he had left a note. The moment Sarah got Henry settled on the sofa, he was fast asleep. Sarah took his bag and sorted dirty clothes from clean clothes. She took the clean clothes to the bedroom and put things away. She took her dirty clothes from her bag and did a couple loads of laundry while Henry was sleeping. She grabbed a book from her bag and took a seat at the end of the couch near Henry's feet and read while he slept, occasionally taking time to rub his feet. As she read, Betsy lumbered over and put her head on Sarah's knees. Sarah petted Betsy.

Thoughts were running through Sarah's head. She thought that she could get used to this life. She also thought she almost killed Henry. She admired this man for things he had accomplished and how mellow he was as a person. He cared about Sarah's dreams and aspirations. She admired that even though he had been weakened by the heart attack, he did not hesitate to walk rather than ride a cart like an invalid. Sure, it was somewhat stubborn, but she admired his steadfastness to not giving into weakness. Now he was out cold from doing all that walking. She made up her mind then and there.

She wrote him a note that she had gone to the store for a few minutes and would be back. She took the keys to the Range Rover and drove to a Walgreen's they had passed on the way home. She browsed the card section looking for just the right card to fill out and give to Henry when he awoke. She bought a card of encouragement and when she got to the car, she took a pen out of her purse and wrote a note inside of it. Then she drove back to Henry's house. When she got upstairs, Henry was still fast asleep. She sealed the envelope and wrote his name on the front. She then returned to her book. After a total of three hours asleep, Henry woke up to see Sarah dozing at the end of the sofa. She was sleeping light and heard Henry moving around and sitting up. She said, "Well good morning sleepy head. How are you feeling?" "Weak," he answered. "Here, this is for you," as she handed him the card. He read the Hallmark words, but it was what Sarah had written that caught his breath.

Do you know what my problem is? I'll tell you what my problem is, I love you. I love your smile. I love your gorgeous blue eyes. I love your name. I love the way you look at me. I love your walk. I love the sound of your laugh. I love the sound of your voice. I love how when you touch me, I get weak. That's what my problem is. I want you to marry me old man!
All my love,
Sarah

He leaned toward her and gave her a hug and a kiss, then a thump on the head for the old man comment. "Yes, I deserved that thump," said Sarah. She added "But you didn't answer the question, will you marry me?" "I have a bad habit that I learned from my mother and it has rubbed off on me. What will people think of a sixty-four-year-old man marrying a thirty-five-year-old young beautiful woman? Nevertheless, I will marry you and the hell with what people think? I love you, it's clear you love me by the way you looked after me in Los Angeles." Henry replied. "I love you with all my heart and soul," he added. Sarah hugged and kissed Henry and said, "I love you so much Henry Morrison." Henry asked Sarah what the next step in the courtship would be and Sarah replied, "To plan the wedding of course and to choose a date. You get to work on the honeymoon plans!" Sarah said joyfully. "Is this going to be a church wedding, small or large, justice of the peace, preacher, Catholic Church?" asked Henry. Sarah replied, "I have never been married before, so I want a church wedding with a couple hundred guests and a nice reception." "Fine by me, I will have to pick out some groomsmen, and a best man, and get to work on the honeymoon plans." Sarah told him that first thing first, they had to get his cardiac rehab started and get him stronger. "How about a Christmas wedding? You're the best gift I can think of receiving," said Sarah. "What a very sweet thing to say, I think you're a pretty nice gift too," added Henry.

Okay, why don't we go set on the deck for a little while and then I fix something for dinner. They went to the sofa on the deck and sat and cuddled and watched the river, the boats, and the barges go by. They listened to the sounds of the birds, watched the hummingbirds come to the feeder and looked at the trees reflected in the water from the other side of the river. They talked about what they saw in the clouds, a game Henry hadn't played since he was a child. Life was beginning to take on new meaning for both of them. Everything seemed to stimulate the senses.

Chapter 59

Get Back

They had been married less than two years and had suffered so much. They still loved and supported each other; it was the only way they could have gotten through it all. By August, Molly was back into her running routine and feeling somewhat back to normal. Henry was back on the road with work and feeling much better. They were getting back into a normal routine of taking long walks on the lakefront, walking to restaurants for dinners.

School was starting again for Molly, which meant a new group of freshman girls for her introductory French course. This year she and the Spanish teacher were planning a tour of Spain and France with their junior and senior students for the spring semester. She was looking forward to that trip and Henry encouraged her to go. He said, "I really think that those girls will love the trip and the cultural experience." Molly said, "Would you chaperone the trip with us?" "Seriously, you'd like me to go with you?" said Henry. "I'd love you to go with us," Molly replied. She added, we're planning on making this an annual trip with possible school credit for making the trip and completing assignments before, during, and after the trip. "That's a great idea, those kids are going to love it!" said Henry.

The fall semester proceeded normally for Molly; she had a full schedule of classes as well as some private tutoring after school. Her running was getting back into form and she was still running longer runs with Bridgit on the weekend. She was also coaching the cross-country team which gave her great satisfaction. Henry said to Molly, "Maybe we should take your mom to Hawaii this year as a Christmas present. Flying every week as I do, my mileage keeps building up and I think I have enough built that I could spare three coach tickets to Hawaii. Would she like that?" "Oh my God, Mom would be over the moon if you did that for her Henry!" said Molly. "My quarterly bonuses have been really good the last year and we haven't touched that money. Why don't you, Bridgit, and I take a long weekend trip? I know how you miss doing things with her, so maybe a long weekend to D.C?" said Henry. She told Henry he was being awfully generous, and he replied, "I love your family!"

Labor Day weekend was coming up in a couple of weeks and Henry had Molly call Bridgit about flying to Washington D.C. for Friday, Saturday, Sunday, and returning on Monday. Bridgit was thrilled to be asked and to go. Henry booked the flight with his mileage and found a deal on a hotel suite where they could all stay in the same place, with two bedrooms on a concierge floor with free breakfast in the morning and snacks throughout the day.

The Friday before Labor Day arrived, Bridgit stayed Thursday night in Henry and Molly's guest room, so they would all be able to catch the 6:30 a.m. flight to DC and arrive about 9:30 a.m. D.C. time. On the way out, Henry gave the extra key to the apartment to Lawrence who was going to go up daily and sit and play and feed Bear while they were gone, for which Henry gave Lawrence a generous amount for the favor. James from the car service picked them all up at 5 a.m. and made the quick trip to the airport. James asked, "So where are the three of you going to this weekend?" Henry answered that they were headed to D.C. and James said, "I love that city, all the history, and the museums."

The flight leaving Chicago was a bit choppy until they got closer to the D.C. area. On final approach, they circled over the Washington monument and landed at Reagan National Airport. They claimed their bags and proceeded to the Metro subway for the ride to Union Station. They were staying at the Hyatt Capitol Hill, which was just within walking distance of Union Station. Their plan for today was to see the Capitol building, the National Botanical Gardens and work their way down the Mall to the Washington Monument. By the end of the day, they had reached the National Air and Space Museum. The three got into a flight simulator that would literally do barrel rolls and all kind of machinations a real plane would do. They screamed as Henry did all kinds of maneuvers, taking off straight up, barrel rolls, etc. It was only a five-minute ride, but Henry terrorized the twins on that short ride.

At the end of the Mall, they reached the Washington Monument. There was a long line to go up in the monument, so that would be their first task in the morning. They decided to get on one of the trolleys that drove around the city pointing out historic places. They got off the trolley at Union Station and walked back to the hotel. They got to their suite and decided to freshen up and find a place for dinner. They decided to take the Metro to the Adams-Morgan district where there were a variety of restaurants with different ethnic foods. After dinner, they walked around the Adams-Morgan district then took the Metro back to the hotel. They sat around the suite just talking about the day and planning the next day. They would start with the Washington Memorial, then walk along the reflecting pool to the Lincoln Memorial, the Korean War Memorial, and the Vietnam Memorial.

On Sunday, they took the Metro the National Cathedral for church services. Following church, it was to lunch and then for a walk through the National Gallery. Shopping made up the late afternoon and then back to the hotel for a swim in the pool and then a late dinner. Each morning of the trip, the twins went for runs in the early morning hours. On Monday, they arranged for a late checkout time of three which gave them time in the morning to see a couple more things. They took a tour of Ford's Theatre and took the Metro to the White House, where they saw President Clinton land on the south lawn in Marine Helicopter One.

They arrived back in Chicago about seven in the evening after a nice long weekend. James was waiting to load their bags and drive them to Henry and Molly's. Bridgit hugged them both goodbye and thanked them, then went to the guest parking area and headed home to Park Forest. Henry grabbed their bags and the two of them got in the elevator. "That was thoughtful of you to invite Bridgit and thoughtful of you to try and include Bridgit and mom in things as often as you do," said Molly. "They're my family too," answered Henry.

Through the summer and fall, Henry and Molly took long walks on the lakefront, went out to dinner once per week and took the occasional getaway weekend drive. They drove to southern Indiana to visit Henry's Mom and Stepdad a couple of times. This year they flew to the Louisville Airport for Christmas Eve with Henry's folks, sister, and brother and his two nieces. On Christmas Day, they flew back to Chicago early in the morning and gathered their gifts to drive to Gladys' apartment for Christmas. Henry got to meet the girls' brother. "He seems awfully normal; I wouldn't think he was a cross dresser," said Henry. "You don't know what kind of underwear he's wearing, do you?" said Molly. Henry said, "Now that is a thought that's going to fester for a while."

After Christmas, Henry, Molly, and Gladys caught a flight non-stop from Chicago to Honolulu. Henry had booked two rooms next to each other at the Outrigger Hotel, two blocks off the beach. They toured during the mornings and afternoons were spent on the beach. They took Gladys to historic places, the north shore, and walked and shopped along the shops and designer stores in Waikiki. The week passed quickly as it tends to do in a place like paradise.

The beginning of their third year of marriage looked like a better year already. The past two years, Molly had been pregnant, and miscarriages were the result. Henry had dealt with his father's death the first year which was rough, but so far this year everything was going along smoothly. In April, Henry and Molly, along with the Spanish teacher at Molly's school, chaperoned a group of junior and senior girls to Spain and France in the first of what Molly hoped to be an annual trip. In Spain, they landed in Madrid. They visited Gibraltar, Madrid, Barcelona (which was Molly's favorite place), then to Granada and the Alhambra. After six days in Spain, they caught a flight to Paris' Charles de Gaulle International Airport. Their tour guide met them at baggage claim for the trip to the hotel. In their time in Paris, the group saw the Louvre, the Cathedral of Notre Dame, the Palace of Versailles, among other sites. They ventured by their tour bus to Normandy and the site of the World War II D-Day landings. They visited American Cemetery at Normandy, taking the St. Lo road to get there.

The group returned to Chicago with a lot of memories and for the students a lot of work to do regarding their trip. For nearly all of them, this was their first trip out of the country. Molly had lived in Paris for a semester to enhance her study of the French language. The girls would never forget this trip. It was the first time Henry had been to Spain and France. His travels had taken him frequently to London and Frankfort.

Nineteen ninety-three so far had been a good year. Henry and Molly were continuing their counseling, they were still very much in love. Nineteen ninety-three ended up being an exceptionally good year for the couple and apparently, they got better with the rhythm method as she did not get pregnant that year. Their sex life was active, and their timing was a lot better.

Chapter 60
Fixing a Hole

S arah decided that she would stay with Henry for a while to take care of him, make sure he ate healthy, went to cardiac rehab, and exercised by walking every day beyond the work he did in rehab. She also went to the first visit with his cardiologist to hear his condition. The cardiologist told them that Henry's heart was strong, he did exceedingly well on the stress test. There was damage to the heart muscle, but if he exercised and ate healthy that would go a long way to getting healthy. The doctor said delicately, no sex for about a month and limited him to one cigar per week and two bourbons. The doctor asked if Henry could work from home as much as he could and keep it to twenty hours per week, Henry said he could. Sarah looked at Henry, as if she meant to be the enforcer.

On the drive home, Henry looked at Sarah and said, "Hey, do you want to have your friends over for a cookout on the deck?" Sarah said, "Do you feel up to it?" Henry answered, "Yes, in a couple of weeks I think would be fine. Maybe a Sunday afternoon if that works for you." Sarah said that would be great that she wanted her friends to meet Henry. Sarah asked, "Are you okay with me staying with you, I just kind of barged in really." While Sarah was driving, he leaned over and kissed her cheek and patted her thigh, he said, "Of course I am, I love having you with me."

It was nearly lunch time when they pulled into the garage. Sarah said, "I'm going to drop you off here and I have to run to the grocery for a couple of things and I'll fix lunch when I get back okay?" Henry agreed and took the elevator up instead of climbing the steep set of stairs to the living area. While Sarah was at the grocery, he picked up the leadership book he had been reading and continued with the book. Within the hour, Sarah returned from the grocery with several bags of items. She said, I bought healthy things for you and the two of us are going to turn into quasi vegetarians. For lunch she said, "We are having a salad, a bacon lettuce and tomato sandwich with soy bacon and a cup of low sodium tomato soup." "Boy, you really mean to take care of me, don't you?" said Henry. "I want you around for a long time. I love you if you haven't figured that out yet!" Henry asked what she was going to do about work. Sarah replied, "I've been giving serious thought to that since your heart attack and since the advice and encouragement you gave me before your heart attack, and I think I am going to go out on my own and start my own firm with your help. Would you help me?" asked Sarah. "Of course, I will. We'll work on the business plan together," said Henry.

Sarah told Henry she still had ten weeks of vacation stored up, she would give her notice this week and work until July 1. That would give her until mid-September to get things rolling and generate income. "How do you feel about me moving in with you?" Sarah asked. Henry replied, "Well, between spending several nights together and you being with me in the hospital and the last week here at home, I kind of like the idea. I'd love it if you would move in, I haven't been this happy in a long time Sarah." Henry went on to say that he had concerns about the age difference and there were things to be considered. The age difference could create problems. The appearance for one thing that Henry is chasing a younger woman, a stereotype of older single men. The perception that a younger woman only wants and older man for his money. Importantly to consider, at sixty-four, Sarah may only have twenty years with Henry before he passed away. Additionally, if they had a child together, the child would lose their father possibly before he or she were in college. Also, he told her, they were a couple of generations apart in their outlooks on life and their life experiences, they might not fit in with each other's friends. "Are you saying you don't want to be with me?" asked Sarah. "That's not what I'm saying at all, I'm just telling you the realities, especially that I will die long before you and our child will be young when I die. I do love you I am just laying out realities that you have to consider," Henry replied. Sarah said, "I will be devoted to you, I don't want your money, I want you and before you say it, I am not looking for a father figure. I find you incredibly attractive and I don't think about the age." Henry said, "Okay, then give me a kiss." Sarah kissed Henry sweetly and she moved in close to him, gave him a hug and laid her head on his chest, then she looked up to receive a warm, passionate kiss from Henry. He asked, "Do you need a business partner?" "You mean it! "Sarah exclaimed. "Yes, I do. I have my own work to do with my partners, but I'm here with you and will put some money in, give you advice and possible some sales leads through the network of people I know," said Henry.

Sarah got lunch ready and set on the table. She said, "By the way you have some company coming in about an hour." "Who would that be?" asked Henry. Sarah told him that his partners had called her to ask if Henry was up for a visit. He hadn't seen the guys in a couple of weeks and was anxious to catch up on business. Sarah said that they had some good news to share with him. As they ate lunch, they talked about how to start her company and how to fund the venture. Since they were officially living together, Henry suggested Sarah could sell her house to partially fund an office and an assistant for a few months. Sarah was open to selling the house but wondered about an office yet. Henry told her that he would be happy to put in some cash to help the company get started. He was willing to commit $50,000 to the venture. That would help towards a logo design, an assistant, and small office space in the city of Jeffersonville, just next to Henry's village and across the Ohio River from metropolitan Louisville.

The two decided to sell Sarah's house and put half the proceeds into an investment account and the other half as an investment in her company.

She started making a list of potential clients, a list of people she could network, and Henry's list of people to network. Just then the doorbell rang, Sarah went downstairs to answer, and it was Jesse and Brandon. Sarah had never met the two men, but only spoken to Jesse on the phone. The three introduced themselves and made their way upstairs. Henry was out on the deck waiting for them.

They man hugged each other, sat down around the coffee table, and enjoyed the breeze coming across the deck. "Can I offer you coffee, soft drink, water, watermelon Red Bull?" asked Henry. Both guys answered, "Red Bull." Henry got up to get the drinks, but Sarah stopped him and said, "I'll get them." Henry said, "Sit and talk with us when you come back." The boys told Henry that a sale that he had been working on since December had come through and would mean a first payment in about a month of $300,000. The contract was logistics work for a sub-Saharan African government. It would mean a trip to Los Angles in two weeks and in eight weeks a trip to the African country. Henry said he would check with his cardiologist the next day about the LA trip and the African trip. He really wanted to go as it was his client.

Sarah returned with the Red Bulls for the boys and lemonade for Henry. Sarah sat down next to Henry. He asked the boys how the work with Gary was coming along and Brandon answered, "We are ahead of schedule and with the money coming in from the African project, we can hire another programmer to speed the product to market." Henry said, "That's great!" Jesse thanked Henry for the hard work on the African project, which would lead to a couple of other contracts. Henry said, "Sarah, why don't you tell the guys what you are planning?" Sarah sketched out what her company would be doing and when she would be starting. Jesse suggested that Sarah go to some networking events with Jesse and Henry and that would get her name out there. Sarah said, "I need to get my office established, and my logo and website established. I could be up and running in a month." "I have an idea for an office in downtown Jeffersonville. A friend of mine owns the building and I think he has a space available," added Henry. Henry said to the guys, I'm going in as a silent partner with Sarah, but don't worry I still have my mind focused on our company." Jesse volunteered, if you'd like me to look at your financial projections, I'd be happy to do so." Brandon said he knew a good guy to do the website and could get a good deal for her. Sarah was overwhelmed with the help and support she was getting from Henry and the guys and was visibly moved. "Thank you so much," said Sarah.

After Jesse and Brandon left, Sarah hugged Henry and said, "Your partners are really nice guys and I appreciate all three of you, but you most of all my darling man" and then kissed him. "Do you want to take Betsy for a walk?" asked Sarah. "I think that's a great idea, I could use the exercise," said Henry. They put the leash on Betsy, then took the elevator downstairs and went out to the street. Sarah took Henry by the arm to steady him for a short walk while Henry held the leash. They walked to the center of the village and back, about two miles. When they came home, Sarah suggested that Henry take a short nap, which he did.

While Henry was asleep, Sarah called her mother for a talk. Sarah told her all about the trip, the heart attack and how she had taken time off to help Henry. Her mother was cautious in her tone and asked Sarah if she knew what she was doing by moving in and selling her house. Sarah replied, "I'll tell you the same thing I told Henry. I'm not looking for a father figure, I don't want his money, I'm not a gold-digger, and yes, I know I will probably only have twenty years or so with him. She told her mother about the new business of going out on her own and how Henry and his partners were helping her. Her mother replied, "Well I always thought that your company undervalued you and overworked you, so I'm behind you starting your own firm." Sarah replied that she was really excited about doing her own thing and she would work half the time from an office Henry found for her and half the time out of Henry's home office. "I really love him Mom. He is sweet, thoughtful, smart with a lot of business experience around the world and he knows some of the most interesting people," Sarah told her mother. Sarah added, "The sad thing is I will only have twenty years with him."

Chapter 61

Baby's in Black

Nineteen ninety-four began as a good year. Henry's first quarter bonus for the region's performance was gratifying to say the least. Molly was preparing for another spring trip to Spain and France with another group of junior and senior girls. Molly enjoyed these trips as she got to see the expressions on the faces of the girls as they traveled internationally for the first time and to see the sites they were experiencing. Henry donated some of his bonus to a fund for worthy students who could not afford to make the trip.

Henry took Molly to the airport to meet up with the girls and the other chaperones on the trip. Henry was not going this year and Molly was in charge of the whole trip from coordinating with the tour operators, working with the tour guides in each country and enforcing curfew on the girls in the hotels. They started their days with six a.m. wakeup calls for a full day of touring. The girls were excited during the whole trip. After ten days, they left from Charles de Gaulle airport for Chicago O'Hare. Henry waited at the International Arrivals terminal watching for Molly and her group to exit. He spotted her and called out her name, she gave him a big hug and kiss and said she had to stay with the girls until each one had been collected by their parents.

At last, the last student had left, and Molly made her way back to Henry. They hugged, kissed again, and walked to the parking lot. Henry loaded Molly's bag in the trunk, and they headed back downtown to the building. On the way he asked Molly how tired she was. "I'm actually okay, I slept nearly the entire flight, why?" Molly said. "I thought we could order pizza, or get Chinese takeout, cuddle up on the couch and you can tell me all about the trip," suggested Henry. Molly liked the idea of staying in and cuddling, which she was hoping would lead to other things, as she really missed touching his body.

They arrived at the building at about five o'clock. They decided on pizza and Henry called in the order for delivery. The pizza arrived about a quarter to six, Henry tipped the delivery guy and went to the kitchen for plates and drinks. Both Molly and Henry had a beer with the pizza as Molly began to tell Henry about the trip. They lost one girl for about an hour somewhere in a museum in Spain. Some guys in Paris were hitting on a couple of the girls and Molly put a stop to that. She went on to talk about all the sites they visited, her two most favorite were always the Alhambra in Spain and the Louvre in France.

Toward the end of Molly's stories, and after the pizza and beer were finished, they began kissing and fondling on the couch. They began undressing each other and made their way back to the bedroom. The lovemaking was fast and furious and extremely passionate. Molly had only been gone about two weeks, but the lovemaking was as if they had been apart for a year. They made love a couple more times throughout the evening throwing their usual caution to the wind.

Molly became pregnant for the third time. They told absolutely no one about it. They were terrified daily that they would lose this baby too. At eleven weeks, Molly saw the obstetrician who assured her that everything was fine so far and to come back in three weeks. Henry was relieved that everything was progressing normally. The following week, Molly began bleeding and Henry rushed her again to Northwestern University Hospital where she was told she had miscarried again. The miscarriage sent Molly into a terrible depression. For the first two weeks after the loss, she cried easily and would often wake up in the night crying. She took a week off work as did Henry. They continued to go to therapy but now focusing on managing the depression. It wasn't long before the depression turned to anger. Molly was angry with God and felt that she was being punished for something. She was the most devout Catholic Henry knew, but this deeply religious woman was questioning God and venting anger at the Creator.

Molly stopped going to Mass for months. She called into work sick three or four days per month. She even stopped running for a while and became a fast-food junkie and gained weight. She was trying to comfort herself and Henry was totally useless about knowing what to do for her. Henry would hold her tight and try to comfort her as best he could, many times he cried with her. All he could do was be there for her.

Finally, after several months, as if a switch had been flipped, Molly began to return to her old self. She was still angry with God but returned to attending Mass every week. Counseling helped Molly as she talked through her anger with their therapist. The second half of 1994, Molly and Henry considered adopting a daughter from China. Molly wanted to be a mother but was rationalizing that for whatever reason her body couldn't carry a baby to full term. Her doctor, however, said that there physically was not a reason why she couldn't carry a baby to term.

They began the adoption process by choosing an agency, setting up appointments with social workers, doing police and FBI background checks. They went to the FBI office and were fingerprinted. The social worker would do a series of interviews with them as a couple and individually. The social worker would also interview friends and relatives to determine their suitability as parents.

By the time they had their background checks completed it was the end of the year. The social worker visits would begin in January of 1995. The social worker's visits would take place monthly for six months. After the reports by the social worker, they would either be approved or rejected as adoptive parents. Just as they were approved and were awaiting the call to go to China, the Chinese government placed a temporary hold on foreign adoptions. They would not restart the adoptions for six months. Again, Molly and Henry could do nothing but cry, this time out of frustration. They went to bed each night holding each other as if the world were coming apart, which for them, it was coming apart.

The Labor Day weekend was spent on a weekend trip to San Antonio. They stayed in a hotel along the River Walk, walking along the river holding hands and holding each other. They made love and they talked, and they made love again. They were both very near a breaking point. When they returned to work on Tuesday, Henry received a call from a competing company wanting to talk to him about an opportunity. He took Wednesday off for a half day interview and lunch with the hiring Vice President Sean Fansler.

Fansler said that Henry had been recommended for this job by both clients, colleagues, and past managers. He was known in the industry for his detail to service and completing projects ahead of schedule and under budget. The job he was being offered would be split between Chicago and London. The salary was one and a half times his current salary, plus the job offered generous bonus and vacation schedule. Henry told Fansler that he wanted to talk the position over with Molly and would call him back within forty-eight hours.

When Molly got home for work, he told her about the job and where they would be living. The assignment sounded exciting and since the money was good, their mortgage was small, and Molly could tutor in London she encouraged Henry to take the job. Henry immediately called Sean and accepted the job if he would add other ten percent to the base salary. Fansler matched Henry's request and asked if they could meet over lunch the next day and Henry agreed.

Over lunch, Sean explained the project in more detail which was essentially licensing publications for a world business news database. Most of the time would be spent in London managing a staff of five licensing agents that would literally cover five continents. The agents were all women located in different places around the world. He would particularly be of help to the two women working in predominantly male cultures, Latin America, and the Middle East. The women were capable, but the culture demanded a male influence. He and Molly would be flown to London to search out a place to live. Fansler asked how soon he would be available, and Henry answered two weeks, but since he was going to work for a competitor he would probably be released immediately.

On Wednesday, Henry went into the office as usual. He asked Betsy if Mike was going to be in today and she said yes. Betsy could tell that something was amiss in the way Henry carried himself and he acted edgy or nervous. Betsy asked Henry if he was okay and Henry responded, "Yes, I'm fine." Thirty minutes later, Mike arrived at the office and Henry asked if he could talk to Mike and Betsy in Mike's office. When all three were in the office, Henry shut the door and said that he had something serious to tell them. They looked at him wondering what the news was going to be. "Mike, Betsy, I am resigning my position and taking a position with Reuters News. The job will be split between here and London, but mostly in London," said Henry. Mike replied, "I really hate to see you leave but I understand that you need to move up and we can't hold you back. If you are totally sure this is what you want, then I'll accept your resignation. Is there anything we can do to keep you?" "No, this job has a VP title and room to move up and I think after everything Molly and I have been through, it will be an adventure and a nice change," said Henry. Mike said then since you are going to work for a competitor, I have to ask you to clear things out today and leave the job ASAP. Betsy will help you sort your things." They stood, shook hands, and gave each other a man hug. Betsy stood and hugged Henry and cried. Henry said, "Look I will keep in touch with you guys, I promise."

Betsy went to Henry's office with him, collected hi ID card, pass key, and desk key while Mike requested to the IT department that Henry's email password be taken down that afternoon. Betsy said, "Check your email and grab anything you think you'll need and between you and me, print out your contact list so you have it. I'd do that first actually. Betsy and Henry worked for two hours clearing out his office and putting his belongings and personal files into two bankers' boxes. By 11:00 a.m., Henry and Betsy had packed up his things and he was ready to get a cab back to his building. He said goodbye to Mike, and Betsy rode the elevator down to the street with him. She gave Henry a big hug and kiss on the cheek before he got into the cab. She said, "You'd better stay in touch!" "I will," promised Henry.

Henry got his boxes home just in time to turn around and go back out to meet Sean Fansler at Catch 35 for lunch. He freshened up just a bit before Lawrence hailed another cab for him to the restaurant. Henry arrived a bit early and waited in the lobby for Sean to arrive. Ten minutes late, Sean arrived, and they were seated. Over lunch, Sean asked if Henry and Molly could fly to London in the next week. They would be flown business class and Henry would be briefed on his new job and he and Molly would meet with an estate agent to find a flat to live. Henry said they could fly on Monday. Sean told Henry that they would have a week to ten days to find a residence and the company would pay their first three month's rent on the flat, which Henry believed to be more than fair. The two parted after ninety minutes with flights scheduled and hotel for Henry and Molly booked.

When Molly got home from school, Henry told her they would be flying to London on Monday and returning ten days later. He gave her all the details that Sean had told him, and Molly was excited and ready to go. She called her boss and arranged her time off and began organizing lesson plans for her substitute. Molly told Henry she would resign near the end of the year, but still wanted to chaperone the spring trip to Spain and France.

The two were excited about this new chapter in their life. They called their respective families, and all were happy for them. After dinner, Henry and Molly began to talk about their relationship and marriage and the things that had happened over the last four years. Molly had finally accepted that God wasn't punishing her with miscarriages or changing Chinese policy. Moving to London would be like a restart from all the bad things.

And Your Bird Can Sing

On Friday, Henry had arranged for his realtor friend, John Baker, to show he and Sarah an office space downtown. Henry and Sarah hopped into the Audi TT with Sarah at the wheel for the short trip downtown. They met John at ten in the morning to view the office space. John led the two to a second-floor office suite. The suite had a two private office, one slightly larger than the other, and a reception area. Henry watched and listened to Sarah negotiate the lease agreement with John.

Sarah negotiated a fair rate for the office, and she would take possession of the space at the first of the month in two weeks. Next, they needed to see a lawyer to set up her company, which Henry suggested a Limited Liability Corporation (LLC), which at this stage would work best for Sarah. They found a lawyer who did the paperwork for her. After the papers were filed, she could then establish a bank account in her company name. The last thing to do was to procure office furniture and office decorations. Henry knew of a wholesale office supply warehouse where they could shop. They spent three hours shopping, picking out two desks for the offices and another for the reception area. They also picked out chairs for the reception area and offices. Sarah would shop around various shops for the artwork to hang, but that would be for another day. She was excited about the office and her new business.

It was late afternoon and they drove home. Henry suggested after a long day, they should go out to dinner. She said, "Are you feeling up to it, it's been a tiring day." Henry said to her, "I want to celebrate your first day as an entrepreneur." Henry called a nice Italian restaurant called Vincenzo's for a reservation. It was three in the afternoon and Henry laid down for a short nap while Sarah set about laying plans for her new firm. First, she would submit her resignation on Monday morning. Next week, get a logo designed, a bank account established and initial business cards, so she could begin networking. She was feeling excited about doing her own thing and either seeing it succeed or fail based on her initiative and decisions. She was also excited about working with Henry. True, he was going to be a one third silent partner, but he had a vast knowledge base, knew a lot of people and his partners were willing to help as much as they could.

Henry woke up from his nap about 4:30 and walked to the living room to find Sarah. Sarah was in his office working at her laptop. She didn't hear him come in the room, he bent over the chair and kissed her on top of her head and said, "Hello Madam President." Sarah replied, "Hello man who has my heart." He told her, "We have a 7 p.m. reservation at Vincenzo's for dinner. Do you need to run to your house for anything to wear?" Sarah told her she did need to get a dress, shoes, and some jewelry for the evening. Henry told her to take either car, so she took the Range Rover.

Sarah was back within the hour ready to shower and change into her evening wear for their celebratory night out. She was concerned that Henry would tire out, after all, this was only the first week after his heart attack. She showered, dried her hair, applied her makeup, and slipped into a traditional "little black dress" for the evening. She put in diamond earrings, a diamond necklace and bracelet. Henry was putting on a dark blue pinstripe suit and a blue and white striped repp tie. It was 6:30 and about time to leave for dinner. Henry said to Sarah, "You look absolutely stunning." Sarah replied, "And you are a very handsome man." "I think I'll drive the Audi; the valet car park guys love it," said Henry.

They arrived at Vincenzo's and were shown to their table. The waiter asked if the two were celebrating any occasion this evening and Henry said yes, we have a new CEO in our midst. Henry ordered a Pinot Grigio for Sarah and a Whiskey Sour for himself as they browsed the menu. Henry said to Sarah, "I am proud of you for what you are doing. Most people won't take the initiative to go off on their own, but you are and that's only one of the things that I love about you." "Well, I couldn't do it without your encouragement to believe in myself. Now I feel confident and know that I can do this," said Sarah.

For dinner, Henry had a salad, grilled salmon (heart healthy) and sides of green vegetables. Sarah was giving looks at him if he strayed from healthy choices. She had a salad, and Rainbow Trout with vegetables. They did not order dessert, but Henry ordered two glasses a champagne. Henry held his glass and toasted Sarah, "To my rising star and the woman who holds the key to my heart." Sarah added, "To you, who I love deeply." They clinked their glasses and sipped their champagne. They continued talking and finishing their drinks. Henry asked for the bill. He left cash with enough to cover a generous tip. They walked to the valet stand and Henry presented the ticket. Moments later the car arrived, he tipped the valet, and motioned for Sarah to drive.

They put the top down and drove along the river on the warm summer night. Sarah, probably because she was driving a sports car, drove just a little faster on the two-lane road. She liked the feel of fresh air on her face and wind in her hair. A few minutes later, she pulled the car into the garage. When they got upstairs, she suggested a glass of wine on the deck. They sat on the sofa on the deck, Sarah kicked off her shoes, tucked her feet under her and leaned her head on Henry's chest. Sarah said, "I'm lucky to have you and I don't care what people think about our ages. I love you for who you are, for you." They cuddled and sipped their wine for about an hour. Sarah turned assertive and began kissing Henry. Sarah asked, "Do you want to dance? I have a playlist on my phone." Henry said, "I'd love to dance." "You wouldn't know it by looking at me, but I love older music. Stuff recorded actually before I was born," said Sarah. She told him that she would listen to music with her mom and dad, the stuff they liked and "I guess it rubbed off on me," she told him. She started the music on her phone and as they started to dance, Henry recognized the music. It was Neil Young's *Harvest Moon*. As he held Sarah in his arms, dancing with her, his mind was transported back many years to when he played that same song and danced with Molly.

Sarah had just a handful of slow dance music on her playlist, as the last song ended, she looked up at Henry and kissed him sweetly on the lips. They sat down and Sarah went back to the kitchen to freshen their wine glasses. When she returned, she sat closely and laid her head on Henry's chest. He said to her, "You're not going to believe this, but I played that same song, *Harvest Moon* and danced to it with Molly. I love the song, but it was an eerie feeling when it was the first song on your playlist." Sarah apologized for playing the song. Henry replied, "Don't apologize. It brought back nice old memories and it just made beautiful new memories. I love it that it's on your playlist."

Chapter 63

Here, There and Everywhere

The estate agent showed Henry and Molly several flats, but they settled on a small two bedroom flat in Marylebone on Wyndham Street. The flat was a short walk from Baker Street and Regent's Park. It was also near several Tube stations and bus lines near King's Cross and St. Pancreas. The rent on the flat was 1000 pounds per month. They would be able to afford it as Henry had a small mortgage on the condo in Chicago. The flat was unfurnished, so it would mean that they would have to do some shopping. Molly would make this place her own. She felt excited to be living in a new city and a fresh start after all the setbacks she and Henry had experienced.

They would stay in their hotel for another few days. Henry had meetings to attend and his staff to meet along with his assistant Fiona. Fiona was a young university graduate from Newmarket, a city an hour north of London that is famous for horse racing worldwide. Fiona was helping Henry get set up with phone service at home and a mobile phone to be used in the United Kingdom. She volunteered to help Molly out in navigating the Tube and the bus system and the city. Henry invited Fiona to have dinner with he and Molly the next evening.

The new job would see Henry traveling two weeks out of the month, so it was important that Molly get comfortable with getting around and managing on her own. To help out, she had talked with Bridgit about coming over for two weeks to stay when Henry went on his first trip. When Henry arrived back to the hotel after work each day, he and Molly would spend time walking around the city, and now that they knew where they were going to live, they spent time walking around their new neighborhood.

The next evening, they met Fiona at the Baker Street Tube station near King's Cross. They had dinner at a pizza place along Edgeware Road. Fiona warned them both that the first thing they had to constantly remind themselves is to LOOK RIGHT when crossing streets, as the cars are coming from a different direction than in the United States. Americans were hit by cars every year because they looked the wrong way before crossing a street.

Fiona was a great help; British Telecom would be coming the next day to put the phone in and the gas and electric were already engaged. Fiona told Molly, "Here is my mobile phone number and you can feel free to call me if you need help or just would like to talk." Fiona added, "We need to get you set up with a mobile phone. I can help you do that after dinner if you like," Molly said, "That would be great, thank you I'd like to get that accomplished. One more thing ticked off the list."

After dinner, Henry and Molly took one of London's Black Cabs back to the hotel. Their hotel was a quaint building called the John Howard Hotel, just two blocks from Hyde Park on Queen's Gate. Once they got back to their room, they freshened up and decided to go for a walk. They walked up Queen's Gate to the entrance to Hyde Park. They walked along a wide pathway, Henry with his arm around Molly. Once inside the park, they could barely hear the noise from the street. "How do you think you'll like living here honey?" Henry asked. "I think I'll like it once I get used to the Tube and the surroundings of our neighborhood." Henry told her they would try to walk around as much as they could the next few days to get the hang of things. He told her that the company would ship over whatever they thought they would need, but the flat was so small they would only ship clothing and a few knick knacks. The rest they would buy locally. They turned back around and walked back to the A315 and Queen's Gate, where they turned left and walked along the Edge of Hyde Park to the Royal Albert Hall, where they crossed the street to Exhibition Road and walked past the Imperial College Business School and the Royal School of Music. They then decided to head back to the hotel and call it a day. They made love that night and afterwards Henry just held Molly in his arms. He was happy to be married to her and excited about starting this new chapter in their life.

Toward the end of their visit Henry would have three free days to explore with Molly before they would have to pack up and leave. They would get two weeks back in Chicago before they had to be back in London. They would have to arrange shipments, storage of the Porsche, the sale of Molly's Festiva and storage of all the other things they weren't going to ship to London. In the last three days they had in London, they went to Westminster Abbey, St. Paul's Cathedral, and The Tower of London. They also took a train from King's Cross and went to visit Windsor Castle.

Finally, it was time to pack and go home? Well, what had been there home for the past four years. Henry was quite sure that his residency in London would be for a few years before any kind of a promotion that would put him back in North America. On the flight back to Chicago, he discussed with Molly the prospect of putting the condo up for sale. He did not want to sublet the condo and be an absent landlord. They agreed to hire a realtor when they returned and put the condo up for sale.

Touching down in Chicago, both Henry and Molly felt bittersweet as they realized they would be leaving the city for a few years. Waiting for them at baggage claim was James ready to take them home. "Well James, this will be one of the last times we ride together," said Henry. Henry told James that he and the Mrs. were moving to London for a few years. "I'll be sad to see you go Mr. Morrison, you're one of my favorite customers," said James. Henry told James that he had always enjoyed his rides to and from the airport. James picked up both of their bags and escorted them to the car and loaded the bags. Henry and Molly settled in the back and Henry held Molly's hand as they made their way downtown. Before they left London, they had picked out living room and bedroom furniture for their flat and arranged delivery for the afternoon that they returned to London in two weeks' time.

Once they were back in their home, Henry poured both of them a glass of wine and they sat down on the couch together. Henry pulled Molly to him, hugged her, and gave her a kiss on the top of the head. He got up to get a pad of paper and pen. They listed all the things that they needed to get done. Henry looked for storage facilities for his Porsche and storage facilities for their belongings. He began to make phone calls and arrangement for storage. He also called and made an appointment with a realtor to sell the condo. He also called a moving company to come pack up their things and take to storage and pack up some things to be shipped to London. The realtor would visit with them the next day, as would the moving and storage company. Now they just needed to put the car up for sale. Molly would put a posting up at school where she had to give her notice as well.

The next day, Molly drove her Festiva to work so that if anyone were interested in buying it, they could take a look at it. She walked into the principal's office before school started. She said to Mrs. Schultz that she needed a few minutes of her time and Mrs. Schultz invited her into her office. Molly told her that Henry took a new job and for the next few years they would be living in London. She added that they had to be back in London in two and a half weeks and that she was officially giving her notice. Molly said, "I will write lesson plans that will get through the next six weeks and I would like to come back in the spring to help chaperone one more trip to Spain and France. Mrs. Shultz said she was sad to see Molly leave and yes, she could come back and chaperone the trip in the spring. They would keep in touch via email.

Chapter 64
Every Little Thing

S aturday morning Sarah was up early making oatmeal for breakfast. A few minutes later, Henry got up shaved, showered, and dressed and made his way to the kitchen and gave Sarah a hug and a kiss on the cheek. He said, "Do you want to go on a walk with Betsy and me after breakfast?" "I'd love to honey, I already let Betsy out for a few minutes," said Sarah. They ate together on the deck and discussed Sarah's new business, and Henry's upcoming trips. Henry had made a follow up appointment the coming week with both his primary care physician, Dr. Tailor, and his cardiologist, Dr. El Refai, to get the clearance to travel. Each day Sarah seemed to get more excited about being in business for herself. She called a realtor to arrange the first of the week an assessment of her house, what price to ask and to take photos. Monday they would go together to buy computers and finish picking our furniture and paintings to decorate the office.

Sarah got Betsy and put her on a leash and she and Henry went out the door to walk through the village. It was a quiet morning and as they walked Sarah said, "I've been thinking about the wedding. I don't really want something big. Why don't you and I get a couple of witnesses and get someone to officiate for us. Let's put whatever money we would put towards a wedding and put it towards an awesome honeymoon." Henry asked her if she were sure she wanted to give up a ceremony and she said she was. "We can have a celebration reception when we come back from the honeymoon," added Sarah. "When do you want to get married then?" asked Henry. "Why don't we get the office set up, business cards made, an assistant interviewed, and a job offer made, then we could get married and take off for two weeks and start the new firm when we get back?" 'Sounds good to me," said Henry.

On Monday, Sarah put her house up for sale and she and Henry bought three MacBooks for the office. They got phone lines put in, then ordered business cards online. They picked out and scheduled delivery of the office furniture and decorations. Tuesday morning, they went to a local bank and set up an account for the company. Henry moved the $50,000 into the account from his and Sarah would add her ten week's pay to the account. Tuesday afternoon, Sarah went with Henry to see both of his physicians. He got clearance to make the Los Angeles trip and of course the honeymoon, but neither wanted him to make the South Africa trip in five weeks. But, if he were going to go, he needed to make sure to get all his vaccinations and his primary care physician would arrange for them.

When they returned home, Henry was very tired and worn out from the day of appointments. Sarah was driving the Range Rover and she looked over to see that Henry was dozing off to sleep. When she pulled into the garage, she gently woke him up and he was shortly wide awake. Sarah asked Henry, "Do you want Chinese takeout tonight?" He said, "That sounds good, I'll call in an order and go get it." Sarah told him to call in the order and she would pick up the order and told him to "Chillax."

When Sarah returned with their dinner, they talked about a honeymoon location as they ate. They wanted to go somewhere that neither of them had visited. They finally decided on Aruba for two weeks. They would book a private ocean villa just off the beach. Sarah said, "There is so much for me to get excited about. I can't wait to marry you. I am excited about the honeymoon, and I am anxious and excited to start my new company. I am so in love with you Henry." "And I am in love with you, now let's get this honeymoon confirmed. Then we'll make a list of people to invite to a wedding celebration/reception and get invitations sent well before we leave," said Henry.

On Wednesday, they met with a small company to build a website, just basic to start with, so they could have up in a week. Sarah had officially resigned her job early Monday morning as she and Henry started their busy week. When she told her boss that she was starting her own firm, she was told she needed to leave the building with her things within an hour. She was leaving a firm where she had spent the last fifteen years climbing up the corporate ladder and now, she was on her own. It was a shock to her system, humbling, and really a bit humiliating. Her colleagues watched her leave with a box full of her belongings and a few other things that Henry helped her carry out. He had asked if she was okay, she had a tear in her eye as people watched her leave the building not knowing the circumstances for her leaving. She would have to call a few colleagues this week to let them know what was happening.

On Thursday, she and Henry worked on two job descriptions for an associate for Sarah to mentor and a personal assistant to manage the office. Once written and edited, they posted the position on a couple of career networking sites. Henry suggested that Sarah talk to the career offices of the University of Louisville and the regional campus of Indiana University for likely seniors that would fit or recent graduates, in addition to the networking sites. Hopefully, within a week or so they would have some candidates to interview. Sarah immediately got on the phone to the universities and asked if they could help set up interviews for her. She would email job descriptions later in the day. She asked Henry if he would be willing to sit in on interviews with her and develop some interview questions.

Henry told Sarah he needed to get some work done today and do a conference call with the guys. His doctors had told him to take it easy, so he was only working a couple of hours per day, but he had been spending a lot of time and energy helping Sarah, not that he minded. He would book time for a long walk and a nap this afternoon. Sarah left Henry to work in his office while she sat on the couch to work. She created a list of contacts to make and search online for networking activities in the next couple of weeks, so she could get started getting her name out there.

Henry worked until noon and he and Sarah went to lunch at a local deli. When they got back, they got Betsy and put her in the Range Rover and drove to a state park with hiking trails to give Betsy a good long walk through the woods. They walked a two-mile trail that was not too strenuous. The trail meandered up and down some small hills and a couple of bridges across a small stream. The shade of the trees and the breeze made for a nice walk. After about an hour and a half, they headed back home, and Henry laid down on the sofa for a nap. He told Sarah to not let him sleep more than ninety minutes.

It was seemed like a remarkably short time Henry felt something on his lips. When he awoke, he realized it was Sarah kissing him awake. She said, "Time to get up sleeping beauty. Have I told you today just how much I love you?" He replied, "I don't think so." Sarah told him that she loved him more than she could ever describe and if he weren't under doctor's orders, she would jump his bones right now." Henry replied, "Well here's the thing, in my weakened condition I wouldn't be able to fight you off." Sarah started kissing Henry and licking his neck. She said, "You taste salty, I think we need to get you a shower." Sarah led Henry by the hand to the master bedroom and to the shower. They undressed each other and started the water.

Chapter 65

She's Leaving Home

Before Molly left London, she had looked for all-girls' schools in central London, hoping she might be able to find a job as a teacher, supply teacher (substitute) or a tutor when she returned. She applied at several. When she returned, she would make follow up calls to those schools to check her status and their needs. At the moment, she and Henry were frantically taking care of things to prepare for the move. Henry found a car storage company and arranged for the Porsche to be picked up the following week. The two of them separated those things that would be shipped to London and those that would stay in storage here in Chicago.

The condo was officially up for sale and they had two prospects that were interested in looking at it the agent told them. Henry called Mike Mackowiak to ask if he would act as a power of attorney if the condo sold while they were in London. Mike would not have to negotiate, that would be done, he would just have to sign papers for Henry, Mike agreed. All the formalities of the move had been taken care of and now all that was left was to spend the remaining time with their families before leaving. They drove from Chicago to Madison, Indiana to stay with his sister Kathleen and visit his mother, stepfather, and brother Patrick.

Henry's mom was critical and just couldn't see why anyone would want to move halfway around the world for a job. She was always critical of Henry and just about anything he did. He would share successes with her, but his whole life he never received praise or encouragement from her. Molly always saw this on their visits and as sweet as she was, she built up a resentment towards Henry's mom. Henry's mom had always sensed that resentment and consequently she and Molly did not get along. Molly was protective of her husband and felt for him. It was sad, he was like a child seeking approval he would never get. Molly and Kathleen got along famously and loved spending time together. Henry's stepfather and brother loved Molly; it was just Mom that was the problem. Yet, Henry would defend her saying that's just how she is, don't let it bother you.

Everyone in Henry's family were happy for the opportunity he had in London and to further his career. The family went to dinner together and Henry and Molly spent time at his parent's house, but also a lot of time with his sister and her husband and Henry's nieces Susan and Sarah. On Monday, Henry and Molly left Kathleen's house at 10:00 a.m. for the five-hour drive back home to Chicago. Molly slept almost the whole drive until they got to the Chicago Skyway as they came into Jackson Park and then Lakeshore Drive.

All their remaining furniture would be picked up on Thursday by the moving and storage company. Thursday evening, they would fly British Airways to London checking two large bags each of clothing. Tuesday and Wednesday, Bridgit and Gladys would visit with them while on Wednesday the packers would be there from the moving and storage company. The car storage company would be there to collect the Porsche. Wednesday evening, Molly and her sister and mother started to get teary eyed as the time for Molly to leave for London got closer and closer. She reminded them that they would be home for Christmas.

Friday morning came quickly. The two were tired mentally and physically from the week's activities. The company had paid for Business Class seats for the flight over and that made for a measure of comfort. No sooner had the plane left the runway than Molly fell asleep and slept half of the six-hour flight. When they landed, it was 6:30 a.m. London time. By the time they cleared customs, retrieved their bags, and got a cab it was 8:00 a.m. They were taken to their new address on Wyndham Street. When they walked into the flat, it was of course completely empty except for the stove and refrigerator. The furniture they had selected would be delivered that afternoon by the department store. First, they needed to get some basic supplies. They walked down York Street to the Tesco's on Baker Street to get a few food items, toilet paper, paper towels, etc. to hold them over until they could get to a larger grocery store on Saturday.

By Friday evening, all the furniture had arrived and was set up in the flat. They did have to go to a department store and by drapes to cover the windows. By the time they turned in for the night, they were both exhausted. Exhausted from the overnight flight and getting the flat set up. There were still a few things that were being shipped, but for the most part they were good to go as far as the flat was concerned. The weekend was spent shopping for groceries and other things for the flat. They opened their overflowing mailbox, most of the mail was advertisements, but there was a letter from St. Paul's Girls' School. Molly opened the letter and read that they requested that she call them to make an appointment to come talk about a position. Molly was excited and grabbed her mobile phone to make the call to the Headmistress of the school, Mrs. Palmer.

Molly spoke with Mrs. Palmer for about fifteen minutes and scheduled a time to meet the following Tuesday. She was excited and walked over to Henry, hugged him tight, and told him she had an interview. She could hardly contain her excitement. It was a nice day and Henry suggested a picnic in Regent's Park. They walked down York Street to Baker Street and to the mini-Tesco to grab a couple of premade sandwiches, drinks, and little cakes for dessert. Three doors down from Tesco was a small general type store where they were able to buy a cheap blanket they could spread on the ground for their picnic. They walked back down Baker Street to the Regent's Park entrance. Once they were inside the park, they noticed that lots of other people had the same idea. They spread their blanket out and had their lunch. After they were finished, Henry laid his head on Molly's lap as she sat, and people watched. Within minutes, Henry had fallen asleep. Molly watched him sleep and thinking how happy she was. The two had weathered some storms and tragedy in their marriage but were doing okay. As she sat there, she thought she felt different. Not just happy, but joyful and light. It was a good feeling she thought. She looked down at Henry and stroked his cheek with her hand thinking how much she loved this kind man. She decided that tonight she would do something out of the ordinary for her, she would take charge and make love to him. She would take the lead.

After about thirty minutes, Henry woke up and they decided to gather up their things and take a walk through the gardens of the park. They held hands and walked at a leisurely place. They talked of making a visit to the park a weekend event in the warm months when they could. After walking through the park, they stopped at a bookstore in King's Cross Station as they made their way back to the flat. Henry picked a copy of Richard Preston's book *The Hot Zone*, while Molly grabbed a copy of *The Alienist*. They spent the rest of the afternoon relaxing and reading on the sofa.

That evening, after dinner, as they were watching TV, Molly began some heavy petting with Henry. She kissed him on the mouth, the neck, then began unbuttoning his shirt, then began unfastening his pants when she began feeling strange. She thought the feeling would pass so she returned to her task, but there it was again, a feeling of nausea. Then it hit, she hurriedly went to the bathroom and vomited. After a few minutes, she returned to the sofa and sat next to Henry who said, "Hope you're okay. Most women don't have that kind of vile reaction to me. Are you okay?" Molly replied, "I'm so sorry honey, I don't feel so good and it just came on all of a sudden." "It's okay, I hope you're not coming down with something. Can I do anything for you sweetheart?" asked Henry. Molly thought to herself he might have already done it, as she began calculating the times they made love. Maybe that weekend a few weeks ago in San Antonio. Oh my gosh, I may be pregnant. As she thought that, there was at once of feeling of joy and elation mixed with fear based on her last three pregnancies.

She went to bed early still feeling sick and vomiting. On Sunday, she felt better, and she told Henry she may be pregnant and could he go to the chemist to get one of the early pregnancy tests. Henry immediately walked to Baker Street and found a chemist and bought one of the tests. He returned within the hour. Molly used the test and a little while later they discovered she was pregnant. They were happy to be pregnant but given their history, they were also scared. They only really knew a couple of people in London and that was Henry's boss Sean and his assistant Fiona. Molly decided to call Fiona for a recommendation for an OB-GYN. Molly would ask several other questions first about places to shop for certain things, who might know a doctor for Henry and an OB-GYN for her.

Molly dialed Fiona's mobile number and Fiona gave her the name of a good OB-GYN named Dr. Book and gave her the number.

After talking to Fiona for thirty minutes she hung up the phone. Monday she would call Dr. Book and Tuesday she would meet with Mrs. Palmer at the school. Both Henry and Molly were a bit worried about the pregnancy. Molly had not yet been able to carry a baby to term. She would express her concerns to the doctor and try to make appointments for more frequent checkups.

As the week began Molly made the appointment for later in the week with Dr. Book and on Tuesday was told that there was a part time French teaching position open at the girls' high school. She interviewed for an hour or more and was offered the job. Molly thought it was offered quickly because the school term had begun, and they were desperate to fill the position quickly. She was upfront about the fact that she may be pregnant and about having time in March to chaperone a trip with her former school during the U.S. spring break.

Chapter 66
The Ballad of Henry and Sarah

L ying in bed after their shower, Henry said, "Sarah, you're a temptress and you're going to cause another heart attack, but I'd have to say it would be worth it." "You're too cute old man," replied Sarah. Henry gave her a light thump in the head for using the taboo "old." "Oops, I'm sorry I used that word, it just sort of slipped out," replied Sarah. The two cuddled and talked about their wedding. Henry told her that he found a wedding planner in Aruba that would arrange everything for a wedding on the beach in Aruba and arrange witnesses as well. Sarah liked the idea of the wedding and honeymoon all being arranged.

As Sarah and Henry made their wedding and honeymoon plans, the following week there were candidates to interview for her assistant position and for the receptionist position as well. Sarah called each candidate to schedule a time and the candidates sent their resumes to her via email. The interviews for the assistant position (the person that Sarah would mentor) were scheduled for a week from Monday and the interviews for the receptionist position were scheduled for a week from Tuesday. Sarah received a call from the realtor to set up visits for four viewings of her house in St. Matthews. Sarah's mother called to negotiate keeping her cat Binx permanently. Sarah was reluctant to let Binx go, but with the new business she was going to be busy and mom needed company, so she agreed.

The week for the interviews arrived, so Henry and Sarah went to the new offices to do now a total of five interviews for the assistant position. There were two young men and three young women applying for the job. Three of the five interviewed well, one of the young men acted as if he didn't want to be there or care about the position either way, he just went through the motions. The last candidate, a young woman named Cheryl seemed the best suited for the position. She was a graduate of the University of Louisville with a degree in political science and a minor in communications. She said she had planned to start an MBA in the next couple of years to help further her career. Cheryl had excellent references from work experience and professors in the portfolio she provided. When the interview was finished, Sarah asked if Cheryl would wait a few minutes in the reception area. Sarah closed her office door and she and Henry discussed the candidates, but Henry pointed towards the reception area and said, "There's your assistant right outside the door." Sarah replied excitedly, "I know, she is perfect." The two needed to know if Cheryl had any other interviews or offers in the works. "Let's start her at $36,000 per year rate for the first ninety days and see how she works out. If she is doing well at that point, bump her to $41,500, which would be par for the industry and be eligible for another raise at her one-year anniversary," suggested Henry. Sarah agreed and called Cheryl back into the office. Sarah asked Cheryl if she had any other interviews or offers at the moment. Cheryl told them she had one offer she had to respond to soon and an interview the next afternoon. Sarah told her the offer that she was making and the group insurance that she was offering as part of a small business network. Cheryl told them the other offer was for more, but she felt working with Sarah in a new company was worth the risk with doing more hands-on work. Cheryl accepted their offer. Sarah exchanged mobile phone numbers with Cheryl and told her that the job would officially start in a month and that she would be calling off and on in the meantime to bring her up to speed with developments.

With that, Cheryl Sanders became the first employee of the firm as Public Relations Coordinator. The next day, Sarah hired Isabel Perez to be the firm's receptionist/secretary.

By the end of the week, the staff was hired, the office was ready to go except for a copy machine, coffee maker, some white boards, and a few other odds and ends, but that could wait. In four weeks, the firm would officially be open for business, in two weeks she and Henry would be flying to Aruba to get married and enjoy a two-week honeymoon, and next week Sarah would tie up the odds and ends and finish making a few networking calls. She told Henry, "You know on second thought, let's have Cheryl start next week working part-time. While we are in Aruba, I'll forward my calls to her phone or the office phone and she can set up meetings for me for when I return." Henry told her that was a good idea. Sarah made the call to Cheryl and the two would start meeting half days in the office the following week.

The next week flew by with Sarah making calls, returning calls, setting up meetings on a shared Google Calendar with Cheryl and eventually Isabel. Cheryl was a joy to work with, she was efficient, anticipated things, and helped Sarah with planning things for their first quarter in business. On Friday, Sarah asked Cheryl to call Isabel a couple of days before her start date to make sure she would be there on day one. Previously in the week, Sarah had introduced the two on a Zoom call. Sarah told Cheryl she would be holding down the fort until she returned in two weeks and then she left the office.

Sarah drove the Audi TT with the top down on the fifteen-minute drive along the river road to home. As she drove, she was feeling on top of the world. She had a new business, an office, a staff, and soon a wonderful husband whom she loved and adored, but also was a tremendous help to her. When she got home, Henry met her at the top of the stairs, he said, "Welcome home boss." Sarah dropped her briefcase and purse on the floor as Henry wrapped his arms around her, lifted her off the floor, gave her a warm hug and kiss, and told her how much he loved her. Sunday morning, they would be flying to Aruba via Atlanta. They went ahead and packed their bags including a suit for Henry and a nice dress that Sarah had picked out for the wedding. Saturday morning the realtor called Sarah to tell her that there was an offer on her house. There had been two buyers bidding and finally there was an offer over what she listed the house and she accepted. The realtor was coming by straight away to have Sarah sign papers. She had made a $80,000 profit; that along with the $50,000 Henry put in would give her a twenty-week runway to get business generated.

Sunday morning came quickly and the two left for the airport in the Range Rover. They boarded their flight, changed planes in Atlanta and by three p.m., they were in Aruba.

Chapter 67
Honey Pie

By November, Molly was three months into her part-time teaching job. She loved teaching in England as she found the students to be much more respectful that in the states. She was also three months into her pregnancy, and everything was normal. Henry had already made a couple of trips to the Middle East, South America, Western Europe, and to Asia. Over twelve weeks at his new job, he had been gone five weeks. He felt guilty about leaving Molly alone while he traveled, especially while she was pregnant.

While Henry was gone, Molly made arrangements to meet up with Fiona and a couple of her friends. Molly and Fiona were becoming fast friends and Molly came to rely upon Fiona for tips on where to go for various things she needed and the best bus routes and Tube routes to get around the city. In the nearly three months they had lived in London, Molly was getting used to the transportation, the stores, and was becoming known in the neighborhood. She and Henry were feeling more confident about the pregnancy and were making plans to decorate the second bedroom as the baby's room. They began talking about the prospects of being parents and the responsibilities. They were even talking with Molly's mom about spending a couple of months in England to help Molly with the baby when it arrived.

They were planning on going home to the states just before Christmas to visit family and Molly was looking forward to seeing Bear. Because of England's rules on bringing animals into the country, Bear would have had to spent six weeks isolated at a government facility to make sure no diseases were brought in, so Bridgit took Bear into her home. Two weeks before returning to the states, Henry and Molly went to Harrod's to shop for gifts from England to take home to the family. They also wanted to get a gift for Fiona and small gifts for Henry's team around the world who would be in town for a meeting right before the two left for the states.

Things were going well for Henry and Molly. Both loved living in London and were adjusting nicely. Both loved their jobs; Henry found his challenging and financially rewarding and Molly loved teaching the teen aged girls. Molly was thriving at the school and the girls liked having an American teaching them. The last day of the school term, Molly's students showered her with all kinds of gifts at a Christmas party the last day of class.

Four days before Christmas, Henry and Molly boarded a British Airways flight for Chicago and Christmas with the family. Before leaving, Henry had called James in Chicago to arrange a ride to Bridgit's house where they would be staying while in Chicago. They would be home for one week before heading back to London. The two of them were excited about coming home and neither slept on the flight. Molly was now four months pregnant and grateful everything was still going well. Hopefully at this time next year, they would have a child celebrating its very first Christmas. She wouldn't allow herself to have many of those thoughts as she was still somewhat afraid that something might happen.

Henry and Molly were a happy couple. They were expecting a baby, Henry's career was doing well, Molly was happy with her teaching job and both were happy living in London. It was a joyful time at home with the family. Everything was set up for an exceptionally good 1995. The family was supportive of the couple and Molly's health and pregnancy were good. For two days of their ten days home, Henry and Molly drove to Southern Indiana to spend some time with his family. Kathleen as usual was upbeat and supportive of her brother and Molly and extremely happy for them. They had driven down one evening and stayed at the Seelbach Hotel in Louisville, as his parents did not have enough room and it probably wouldn't have been a good situation between Molly and Henry's mom anyway. The next day, they drove to Madison, Indiana and spent the day with Kathleen and her husband George. They had a wonderful time having dinner with George and Kathleen and preparing and exchanging gifts. Henry and Kathleen always ribbed each other with stories from when they were growing up, which Molly thoroughly enjoyed.

They left Kathleen and George's house and headed back to Louisville and another evening in the Seelbach. Kathleen hugged Molly goodbye and told her how much she loved having her in the family and "Don't let mom get under your skin," she said. Then she hugged her brother and kissed him on the cheek and told him how happy she was for him and how much she loved Molly. That night in their hotel room, Henry and Molly recounted to each other how lucky they were. The move to London had been good for both of them.

As they were lying in bed, Henry rubbed his hand across Molly's growing belly with affection. He was and had been deeply in love with Molly since they first dated. Everything for them had moved quickly. Dating, living together, marriage, pregnancy, miscarriages, and all the other trials and tribulations of marriage. One of those tribulations would crop up again tomorrow with his mother. No one he ever brought home seemed to be good enough for her. Henry thought that since her first marriage to his dad was disastrous and her marriage to his stepfather wasn't happy, she didn't believe anyone should be married.

The next day. Henry and Molly drove to visit with his mother, stepfather, and younger brother Patrick. The visit was cordial with his mother. Henry's stepfather loved Molly and always warmed up to her and made her feel special as did his brother Patrick. Gifts were exchanged and a fine meal was eaten. Throughout the entire day, Henry's mom had only been cordial toward Molly. As if someone were threatening her with punishment if she did not smile and say something nice occasionally to Molly. This was hard for Molly to accept. She hadn't done anything to upset his mom, but she sure could not get any warmth or a small bit of affection from her. Now she was a little warmer when talking about the baby, but not by much.

The day after Christmas, the two packed up their bags and gifts and drove the four and a half hours back to Chicago to spend a few more days with Bridgit. Henry and Molly would also go into Henry's old office to have lunch with Betsy. Betsy was happy to see both Henry and Molly, but she had been close to Henry. She congratulated them both and over lunch, Betsy quizzed them both about living in London, how Molly was feeling, how she liked her job and many other questions. Henry told Betsy that he had an assistant named Fiona who was fairly good, but not nearly as good as Betsy. They all had a good laugh over that. Betsy told Henry she missed having him around the office as it wasn't nearly as humorous. Mike was funny but Henry could imitate people so well. Betsy added that they both looked incredibly happy and Molly looked wonderful and she was saying prayers for them both.

After a long lunch, Henry and Molly drove back to Bridgit's house and then had Bridgit follow them to return the rental car. Afterwards, they all returned to Bridgit's house for dinner and some board games with their mother. The four of them had fun playing the games, laughing, and talking. Towards the end of the evening, tears started to appear as everyone knew there was a flight leaving for London in the morning and two of them would be on it. Mrs. Kniss started to cry first, followed by Bridgit, and then Molly. "Ma, I'll see you in March before I chaperone the girl's trip, and then you'll see me for a couple of months in May when you come over to help me with the baby. Bridgit, I'll see you in March too," said Molly. The night ended early as Henry and Molly had a morning flight to Heathrow. As usual, Henry had booked James to pick them up at Bridgit's for the ride to the airport.

The morning came quickly, and James was ringing the doorbell. Henry brought the bags to the door and James placed them in the trunk of the car. After tears and goodbyes with Bridgit, Henry and Molly got in the back of the car and James drove them to the airport. It was a sad ride for Molly as she was close to her mother and sister. She loved the life she had with Henry and the life she had in London, but she did miss her twin terribly. The twin connection was extraordinarily strong.

Their flight was on time and they landed at ten in the evening in London. They hailed a Black Cab after clearing customs and headed to their small flat. Even though they missed people back home, it felt good to be back in their home. They had two major events to prepare for in the spring, Molly's trip with the French class from the school back home, and the delivery of the baby in May. Henry would be traveling back and forth to the Middle East and South America a few times, but as the due date got closer, he would schedule himself to stay close to home to be with Molly.

Chapter 68

Blue Jay Way

The ocean breeze from the Caribbean was refreshing as Henry and Sarah stepped into their rented bungalow at the Aruban Resort. The breeze and the splashing of the waves was relaxing and intoxicating. As they unpacked, there was still time for a swim in the ocean before dinner. They quickly found their swimsuits and went for dip. They walked into the surf hand in hand feeling the sand between their toes and the warm water splashing on them. Henry put his arms around Sarah and told her he was the luckiest man in the world to have a woman as young, vivacious, bright, and beautiful as Sarah interested in him. Sarah said, "No, I'm the lucky one, I am so in love with you and to know you love me and care for me is bliss." "Well, tomorrow by this time, we will be married, and you will be stuck with me forever," said Henry. For that "stuck" comment, Sarah thumped Henry in the forehead.

After their swim, they changed clothes (a sundress for Sarah and shorts and an open collar shirt for Henry) and went to the restaurant in the resort for dinner. Tomorrow morning, they would meet the wedding coordinator who would brief them on the day. The coordinator had arranged the preacher, music, and the beach site for the sunset wedding. After dinner, Henry and Sarah strolled hand in hand along the beach back to their bungalow. Henry ordered a bottle of white wine from room service and within thirty minutes the wine was delivered. Henry poured them each a glass as they sat on the lanai overlooking the ocean. Sarah leaned in and gave Henry a passionate deep kiss and said, "I love you Henry." Henry began to say, "I love you," when a pained look came across his face and he grabbed his chest.

Sarah said, "Honey are you okay?" He said, "I'll know in a few minutes. Can you go to the bathroom and in my shaving kit is a tiny bottle of Nitroglycerine tablets, can you bring them to me? Sarah returned with the bottle and Henry took two tablets out and slipped them under his tongue to relieve the pain from angina. Sarah said, "What's wrong?" Henry replied, "I think it is only angina. Probably from swimming this afternoon. If the pain goes away with the Nitro, that's what it is. If it doesn't go away in thirty minutes, I probably need to go to the ER." Henry told Sarah not to worry that his cardiologist told him that angina was fairly common after heart attacks. Sarah looked worried and Henry tried to put her at ease by cracking a couple of jokes, but Sarah wasn't laughing. Henry said, "Look, if it would make you feel any better, call a cab and I'll go to the ER. Would that make you feel better sweetheart?" Sarah said, "Yes, I would feel better if someone checked you out."

Sarah called a cab, and they went to the nearest hospital which was the Dr. Horatio Oduber Hospital. When they arrived, Sarah told the nurse that Henry was having chest pains and he was quickly moved to an exam room. The doctor ordered an EKG to be run and IV nitroglycerin. A few minutes later, the doctor was back in the room. He told Henry and Sarah that the EKG was fine and that likely the extreme angina was from exercise exertion which was common. He could keep Henry overnight for observation if they like or he could simply go back to the hotel and rest and call if he had more chest pain. Henry opted to go back to the bungalow.

By the time Henry and Sarah got back to the bungalow from the ER, it was eleven p.m. They both showered and got ready for bed. They left the door to the lanai opened so they could hear the waves and feel the cool evening breeze. Sarah leaned over and gave Henry a kiss and said, "You really scared me tonight. I don't know what I'd do if I lost you." "Let's hope you don't have to find out," Henry replied. Sitting up in bed, Henry held Sarah in his arms and gently stroked her cheek. They talked about the big day tomorrow and there future together. Sarah was shaking a bit after the trip to the ER. "I'm okay and I'll be okay," Henry reassured Sarah. Let's just keep thinking about tomorrow and all the many tomorrows we're going to have together. We love each other, we support each other, and we have a great future together.

The morning came quickly, but they were already awake when they heard the knock at the door. "Who could that be" asked Sarah. "Before we went for a swim, I arranged for breakfast room service. I also added to the coffee and juice, Mimosas to start the day. "You think of everything don't you? "said Sarah. Henry told her he tries to think of everything but doesn't often succeed. He reminded her to dress casually as they had a meeting at ten with the wedding planner. They would eat lunch at a beach side eatery and then come back to the bungalow to relax before the wedding ceremony at seven on the beach.

The wedding planner coordinated flowers for the wedding. A flowered archway on the beach. A wedding photographer, an extra witness, preacher, and music performed by a soloist and a guitar accompaniment. Everything was arranged and ready to go. Henry and Sarah spent the afternoon sitting together on the Lanai catching the breezes. Henry fell asleep and Sarah sat next to him gently stroking his face watching him sleep. She woke him up at five thirty so they both could start getting ready. He was wearing a dark suit with white shirt and subtle blue paisley necktie. Sarah was wearing a shoulder less tea length white dress.

The wedding planner arrived at the bungalow at 6:45 p.m. for the short drive to the beach wedding site. They walked to the site and the flowered archway. An Episcopal pastor was standing slightly behind the archway and Henry and Sarah moved just beneath it. The soloist and musician were in place as was the other witness. The pastor conducted a brief traditional wedding ceremony. In the exchange of rings, Sarah had not had time to get a wedding band for Henry, so Henry gave her a cigar band to use. Henry presented a Sapphire engagement ring with diamonds and a matching wedding band. Henry happily kissed the bride. If it weren't the best kiss he'd ever been given, it was damn close. The soloist and guitarist played two songs to which Henry and Sarah danced. The two songs were *Harvest Moon* by Neil Young and *I Will* by the Beatles. As they danced, Sarah had tears in her eyes as they shuffled on the hard sand of the wedding site.

Chapter 69

Blackbird

Soon after the first of the new year, Henry and Molly settled back into their routines. Molly saw her OB-GYN regularly and the pregnancy was progressing normally. In his travels to the Middle East, he met Jamal who would come to be of great help to him over the years and become an incredibly good friend as well. Life in London was good, expensive, but good. They both liked the pace of a big city and the life of a big city. Places in walking distance to dine and shop were appealing to the both of them.

The weekends found the couple shopping for "baby things"; they bought a pram and baby furniture for the second bedroom. They began to buy clothing that was not gender specific and they began to stock up on diapers. Soon March came around and Molly was nearly seven months pregnant, the longest she had ever carried a baby, and everything was normal. In two weeks, she would be flying back to Chicago to meet up with the French and Spanish classes at the school to prepare for their ten-day trip to Spain and France. She was excited about the trip and ready to go. She was a little concerned about the trip as now she was starting to tire more easily, but she couldn't wait to be with the students again.

Finally, the time came for her to fly to Chicago. It would be nearly three weeks before she returned to London. Henry and Molly took a black cab to Heathrow airport. Henry escorted Molly through security to the gate where they nervously held hands until the last possible minute. They kissed and embraced a long time before Molly was called to board. Henry said, "Keep yourself safe and come back to me, I love you." Molly stepped back for one more kiss and told Henry how much she loved him and what a great dad he was going to be, then turned and boarded the plane. It would be the last time he saw her alive.

Henry took the tube back to the city and to work at his office. He would be leaving in two days for a week in the Middle East to include Cairo, Doha, and Kuwait City. He and the representative in the Middle East were close to closing a deal with the major publication in Cairo, which would be a coup for the company, so he was looking forward to the trip. He could not take his mind of Molly and her safety on her travels. Henry was a worrier.

On the flight to Chicago, Molly teared up as she took her seat. While she was excited about seeing the students and the trip, she was emotional about being away from Henry this long. They really had not been separated for more than a week even with all his traveling. He had promised to try and call every day and he had her itinerary for the trip so he could reach her at hotels. She couldn't wait to be home with Henry and await the arrival of their daughter. They had just recently decided to learn the sex of the child. They had settled on the name Olivia for her. Olivia Claire Morrison. She looked down at her expanding belly and patted it. "Olivia, I can't wait for you to meet your daddy. You will definitely be a daddy's girl," she said to herself and the unborn Olivia.

When Molly landed in Chicago, Bridgit was there to pick her up. She would stay with Bridgit for a couple of days before the trip as well as visit with her mother. It was Thursday afternoon and Molly would be meeting the group at the airport on Monday for the flight to Barcelona. Molly's family were getting together on Saturday to visit with her, including her brother and a couple of cousins.

Her family all marveled at how beautiful she was pregnant and how she glowed with a sense of happiness and contentment. She told them she was feeling fine but tires very easily. She told them all about life in London, how she loved her job and her students. They went to Mass every week at St. Mary's, which was a two block walk away and how they enjoyed taking weekly picnics in Regent's Park. It was a nice gathering and a chance to catch up with everyone. Her mother would be coming over in mid-May to stay for a couple of months to help with Olivia.

On Monday, Bridgit took Molly to O'Hare Airport for her flight to Barcelona. Bridgit got Molly's rolling suitcase out of the trunk for her and set it on the curb. They hugged each other tightly and Molly said, "Bridgit, you have to come see us in London, I miss you." Bridgit said she missed her sister too and promised to come over. She told her sister to be careful and take care of herself and enjoy the trip. She said, "Give my love to Henry when you get home." Molly promised that she would and then she disappeared into the terminal to meet her group.

Once inside the terminal, Molly immediately saw a group of high school girls gathered around a short dark woman, Mrs. Garcia, the Spanish teacher. The girls saw Molly and started yelling, "Mrs. Morrison, Mrs. Morrison, we're glad to see you." Many asked about the baby and living in London. Molly hugged Mrs. Garcia, and they both began to organize the girls for check in at the ticket counter.

After checking in and getting their seat assignments, the group moved through security and to the gate. Many of the girls had not flown before and they were flying on a large Boeing 777, which was exciting for them. The flight was called not long after everyone made it to the gate, and everyone strapped in for the flight. A few hours later, they landed in Barcelona. The tour guide and bus met the group at arriving flights. The girls would spend nearly a week traveling to sites in Barcelona, Granada, Seville, and Madrid, then fly to Paris. The pace was somewhat grueling as the tour coach would leave by eight in the morning and return to the hotel at six or seven in the evening. Lots of sight-seeing and some free time each day for shopping. One of the sights that Molly enjoyed most were the cathedrals and also the Alhambra, the Moorish Palace near Granada.

The ten-day tour left Spain on the evening of the fifth day and the group flew to Paris for five days in France. The seventh day, the tour coach was taking the group to Normandy and the site of the D-Day Invasion. Their bus was traveling through a misting rain from St. Lo to Normandy when the accident occurred. The bus was traveling at approximately 50 miles per hour when a motorcycle pulled in front of it from a side road. The driver slammed on the brakes and over corrected in turning the bus to avoid hitting the motorcycle. In doing so, the bus slid and then turned over on the driver's side. There was loud shrieking and screaming by all the girls as they were being thrown about on the bus. Molly was thrown across the bus violently and landed on the window on the driver's side as two girls landed hard on top of her. After a very few seconds, the bus slid to a stop on its side and there was about five seconds of deadly silence. Then there was the sound of moaning in pain and weeping throughout the bus. The girls tried to climb off each other, but it was hard to navigate as the windows were now the floor and the floor was a wall. The driver was unconscious with blood coming out his mouth and ears. The two students who had slammed on top of Molly were trying to get up and they noticed that Molly was unconscious as well, blood streaming from her mouth, nose, and ears. She did not seem to be breathing either.

In a couple of minutes, the sounds of emergency sirens in the distance were heard. French police and ambulance crews were on the scene within ten minutes of the accident. The driver and Molly were the first two victims to be removed from the bus and rushed to hospital nearby. Both were pronounced dead on arrival and neither regained consciousness. Within minutes more victims began arriving at the hospital for treatment. About half of the girls received serious injuries, two critical, and the remainder had minor injuries, some broken bones, concussions, scrapes, cuts, and bruises. A hotel was found near hospital for those girls that were treated and released. Mrs. Garcia received minor injuries and spent her time organizing girls in the hotel and tending to the girls in the hospital. She made phone calls home to each parent.

A police office searched through Molly's belongings to find emergency contact information. She found Henry's mobile number and address in London. Officer Leclerc had the most difficult task of contacting Molly Morrison's husband to break the news of her death to him. It was seven thirty in the evening in London when Henry's phone rang. He looked at the phone and did not recognize the number. He hesitated for a moment, considering not answering the call, but finally he did. He answered, "Hello, Henry Morrison." The voice on the other end of the line, a female with a heavy French accent said, "Is zis Mr. Henry Morrison?" Henry replied, "Yes, it is, who is calling please?" "Zis is Officer Leclerc of the Normandy Police, I'm afraid I am ze bearer of zum very bad news sir," said Leclerc. Henry thought to himself, it's Molly, something had happened to Molly. Suddenly, he felt very nauseous and lightheaded. Leclerc on the other end said, "Are you still zer sir?" "Yes, I am," replied Henry. Le Clerc went on and said, "Zair has been a terrible motor coach accident near Normandy." Le Clerc described the incident in detail and finally delivered the blow, "Your wife, Molly was injured very severely. I regret to inform you that her injuries were zo severe that she died from them." Henry sat down and began to sob into the phone. Le Clerc patiently stayed on the line until Henry gathered himself, and asked, "What about our baby?" Le Clerc added, "I am zo very sorry, but ze baby could not be saved."

After a few minutes, Henry got instructions, address, and phone number of the hospital. He would leave immediately for Paris, then find a flight to the Caen airport and then drive to hospital. He rushed to Heathrow and got a late flight to Paris. When he arrived at De Gaulle airport, he discovered he would have to take an early flight in the morning to the Caen airport. He would stay the night at a hotel on the De Gaulle airport property.

Chapter 70

Girl

After the wedding ceremony, Henry offered to buy dinner for all who participated. The wedding planner, two musicians, and the witness were agreeable, but the minister had a prior engagement. They went to a fancy restaurant not far from the beach that the wedding planner recommended. Over dinner there was stimulating conversation and interesting background stories. The wedding planner moved to Aruba after being dumped by her businessman husband and the musicians were a married couple that played all kinds of venues in the country. They couldn't think of better jobs or a better place to work. The witness was actually a boyfriend of the wedding planner, who was also a manager at one of the resorts.

After a two-hour dinner and cocktails, the party went their separate ways. Henry and Sarah went back to their bungalow. They sat together on the lanai listening to the ocean waves and began softly kissing. Sarah said, "You do know that we have a bit of a dilSarah, don't you?" She added, "On the honeymoon evening you're supposed to make love to me, but technically your doctor hasn't cleared you for it." Henry replied, "And I don't see either of my doctors around, do you? Now I may get angina, but it's not going to stop me from performing my husbandly duties!"

The two kissed and petted heavier and more passionately and moved into the bedroom, where they began to slowly unclothe each other, kissing and licking each other as they did so. Henry turned off the lights and lit candles. They dove for the bed and flew under the covers and for the next two hours slowly pleasured each other. Afterwards, Henry looked at Sarah and said, "No heart attack, and no angina. Want to go again? Sarah shook her head yes. Neither of them got much sleep that night, but they didn't really care much either.

In the morning, Henry and Sarah took a sunrise walk, hand in hand, along the beach. It somehow felt different now that they were married. "I bet you I'll be the envy of every other old man we see on the beach today," said Henry. Sarah looked up and gave him a thump on the head for the old man comment. Sarah said, "Have I told you today just how much I love you?" "No, you've just hit me," replied Henry. "I do love you with all my heart and soul Henry," Sarah said. "And I love you madly Sarah," Henry replied.

Sarah and Henry spent the remainder of their time in Aruba, swimming, soaking up the sun, and just relaxing. They talked a lot about Sarah's new business and Henry's upcoming trips to Los Angeles and Southern Africa. Henry was feeling better after his earlier angina attack. He still wasn't fully recovered from the heart attack, and really wasn't adhering to physician's warning about sexual activity and his heart. It all went back to his sense of fatalism and survival, and of course Sarah was a temptress.

After ten days, they flew home and arrived in the house at ten in the evening. They both had a sense of keeping things tidy and getting things accomplished, so the first thing they did was unpack and put their suitcases away. Sarah was anxious to call Cheryl and find out if there were any calls or appointments set up for the next couple of weeks. That would have to wait until Saturday morning. For now, Sarah poured a glass of wine for herself and a bourbon and amaretto for Henry and suggested they sit on the deck for a little while before turning in for the night. They sat quietly on the deck sofa in each other's arms sipping their drinks and basking in their happiness. Their married life and living together had been easy and happy so far and things were looking good for the couple.

Saturday morning, Sarah called Cheryl and was pleased to learn that the first week of official operation, Sarah had three appointments and the second week there were four appointments. Sarah was happy to get off to such a good start. She was so anxious to get to work that she could hardly contain herself. Henry had to chuckle at her enthusiasm and found her enthusiasm contagious.

They just relaxed over the weekend, went to Mass at the Cathedral, and for old times' sake went to dinner Sunday evening at Drakes. At Drakes, they ran into Sarah's friends who joined them at a large table for dinner. The girls made small talk with Henry and joked whether Sarah proposed or if Henry did. They asked about the honeymoon trip, which they did not know was in Aruba. After they were told how beautiful Aruba was, ooooohs and ahhhhhhhs from the group followed and then they chuckled about the trip to the emergency room. Henry got to casually know Sarah's friends so now he could place faces with names.

Monday morning came around slowly as if to torment Sarah's patience about getting to start work. Sarah took the Range Rover for the drive to the office. When she arrived, both Isabel and Cheryl were already there at their desks. As she walked in, Sarah invited them both into her office. Out of a bag she presented them both with a couple of gifts she purchased for them from Aruba. She gave them both crafts made from ceramics and each a box of gourmet chocolates. They soon got down to business and reviewed the appointments that Cheryl had set up for her. She delegated some work on mailings that she wanted to go out to Isabel. She would take Cheryl on several appointments with her as she wanted to mentor and include Cheryl in as many things as she could. Her philosophy would be that if she were gone, the office would be in good hands and could run itself. She wanted to train Cheryl to be able to take on projects and responsibility.

Chapter 71
Cry Baby Cry

H enry drove straight from the airport to the hospital near Normandy. Before leaving the airport, he called officer Le Clerc to tell her he was on the way and would be at the hospital in approximately forty minutes. The drive seemed to pass quickly, and he didn't realize how he had managed to find a place he had never visited before. His mind was not on driving, but on Molly. How could she be gone, and the baby too? This seemed like a dream, he felt as if he were in a terminal fog.

When he arrived at the hospital, he saw a female police officer standing at the entrance, he assumed this was officer Le Clerc. As he walked towards the entrance, Officer Le Clerc spotted him and moved towards him. Henry stuck out his hand to shake an introduce himself. He said, "I'm Henry Morrison, you must be Officer Le Clerc. Thank you for your help." Officer Le Clerc said, "Monsieur Morrison, I am so sorry for your loss. Would you like a cup of coffee before we get started this morning?" The two went to the hospital café for coffee. Over coffee, Officer Le Clerc told Henry the details of the accident and Molly's death. She also explained the process of shipping Molly's body to the United States. Henry needed a funeral director in France and one in the United States to coordinate and make sure he follows procedure; he should contact the U.S. Embassy for assistance. Officer Le Clerc offered to help him with the details.

After forty-five minutes of talking, Officer Le Clerc said, "It is time for you to identify your wife Monsieur Morrison. I'll escort you to the morgue to meet the pathologist there. They moved down a couple of hallways to an elevator and then to the basement and the morgue. Officer Le Clerc introduced Henry to the pathologist and told him she would wait for him at the door. She would call the U.S. Embassy for him and a local funeral director to come meet with him. The pathologist walked Henry into the morgue and to a wall of small, refrigerated compartments. They walked across the room and the pathologist opened one of the small doors and pulled on the end of a tray to reveal a body covered by a sheet. The pathologist asked if Henry was ready and he nodded his head. The pathologist pulled back to reveal Molly's body. Aside from a couple of bruises on her face, Molly just looked as if she were sleeping. Henry felt as if his knees were about to buckle. He reached his hand up and stroked the side of her face, just like he used to do when she was alive. "When she was alive," he said softly to himself, not believing that Molly and baby Olivia were dead. Tears started to form in Henry's eyes, and he broke down sobbing. He stood over Molly for a few more minutes, then kissed her on the forehead and then the lips. He then touched her hand and rubbed his hand on her wedding rings, patted, and kissed her belly.

Henry stood up, nodded to the pathologist who then slowly slid the drawer back into the opened door. He turned and walked to the door, went through it, and met Officer Le Clerc. She put her arm around his arm and walked him to a chair. "Can I get you anything Monsieur Morrison," asked Le Clerc. "No, nothing thanks," answered Henry. A man in a dark suit was approaching the two of them, it was the local funeral director that Officer Le Clerc had called. Henry stood up and extended his hand. He, the funeral director, and Le Clerc moved to the café and to a small table. The funeral director had papers for Henry to complete with copies to go to the embassy. Later in the day, he would call Bridgit, and then Molly's mom to break the news to them and find a local funeral director there.

With the immediate concerns dealt with, Officer Le Clerc excused herself, leaving Henry with her card if he needed anything. Henry was just numb and still in a state of shock. He would need to stay nearby for a couple of days to finalize the transport of Molly's body. He settled into a small local hotel and called Bridgit. Bridgit was heartbroken, she sensed that something was wrong, it was that twin connection. She could not stop crying on the phone. She wanted to break the news to their mother herself. Henry said okay and he would call Gladys later in the day. He also called the office and spoke with his assistant Fiona. Fiona was relieved to hear from Henry as people in the office wondered why he wasn't at work. Fiona was heartbroken as she and Molly had become close friends in the months that she had known her. She asked Henry if he would mind if she flew to Chicago for the funeral. He said, that would be nice, and Molly would have appreciated it. He asked Fiona to inform Sean and that he would call him later in the day. Fiona was crying when they hung up.

Two days later, with all the plans arranged for the body transfer, Henry booked himself on the same flight that Molly's body was on. He booked himself a business class ticket. The flight would be leaving the next day for Chicago. On that morning, he boarded the flight and looked out his window to see the coffin being loaded underneath the plane. Molly and Olivia would be buried in St. Michael the Archangel Cemetery in Hammond, Indiana where Molly grew up and her family members were buried.

After two days of viewing at the funeral home with many students, friends, and family offering condolences, Henry and the family were very moved by the huge outpouring at the funeral home. Henry had looked absolutely lost without Molly. He moved slowly, spoke softly. His assistant, Fiona, stood with him and the family and was helping them all with anything they needed. After the funeral, family and friends came to Bridgit's house. Fiona had spoken to Bridgit quite a bit commenting how identical she was to her sister and spoke of the friendship she and Molly had enjoyed. Fiona said that she would be happy to stay a few days and help Henry sort through details he had to deal with. Henry had told Bridgit and

Gladys that they could have everything in storage except for his photos of him and Molly. They could put things up for sale, donate items to charity, and keep what they liked. He was going to have his Porsche shipped to London as he would be living there for a few years.

The following years saw Henry go through a lot of changes and moods especially in the first two years after Molly's death.

Chapter 72

Glad All Over

After two months in business, Sarah was feeling confident. She had four clients that were on a two thousand dollar per month retainer for public relations work and crisis management work. Those four retainers covered her monthly operating expenses, which meant she hadn't had to tap very much of her reserves. She and Henry had been married a little over two months and they were happy. Henry had been to Los Angeles on a couple of trips and had spent a week in South Africa setting up a project and managing the relationship.

But something was wrong, and that's why she was seeing her doctor this afternoon. She hadn't told Henry, but she had missed two periods, but she didn't have any nausea or morning sickness, just felt a bit off. If she were pregnant, it wasn't the best of timing with the business just starting, but she would be happy, they would find a way to manage everything. Sarah was happy with her employees and Cheryl was learning quickly and taking initiative on projects. Isabel seemed to be able to anticipate the needs of both Sarah and Cheryl almost as if she could read their minds.

At one p.m., Sarah left the office for her appointment with her doctor. Cheryl would run the show while she was out. After spending fifteen minutes in the waiting room, Sarah was called back to see Dr. Melissa Roberts. Dr. Roberts asked how things were going with the new business and the new husband. Sarah said she couldn't be happier. Dr. Roberts said, "Well you do seem to have a glow about you today, so what brings you in?" "That glow might be what has me here, I think I may be pregnant," said Sarah. Dr. Roberts, after conducting a physical exam, told Sarah her hunch may be right, but to be sure they would draw blood and run tests to determine for sure. Dr. Roberts also suggested that Sarah pick up an early pregnancy test on her way home. Sarah left the office and stopped at a Walgreen's Drug Store on her way home. She was anxious to find out. Sarah went straight home to do the test. Henry was working at the office this afternoon and would not be home for a couple of hours. As she came in the door, Betsy came up to her for a pet. Sarah took Betsy outside for a few minutes then came back upstairs. She went to the bathroom and did the early pregnancy test. After a few minutes, she determined that yes, she was pregnant. By the timing, and this would be a funny story, she got pregnant the night Henry had his heart attack.

When Henry came home, he gave Sarah a simple bouquet, as he did once a week since they had been living together. Once a week, he would stop by the local Kroger Grocery to the floral section and pick out a bouquet for her. It was just one of the things that Sarah loved about him. They weren't flashy or expensive flowers from a florist, but every week he thought about her in that way. When he gave them to her this day Sarah said, "Thank you baby, how thoughtful." He asked, "How was your day honey?" Sarah replied, "Oh, lots of developments, things are growing. We are still in our infancy, but I know we'll see lots of growth soon and not without a bump in the path."

"You have such a lovely smile on your face today. That smile is an absolute treasure Sarah, you, you, glow," said Henry. "I have something to tell you and I hope it makes you happy. I think I'm pregnant. I went to the doctor today who did a blood test and I'll know for sure in a few days, but I took an early pregnancy test, and it shows I'm pregnant," said Sarah. Henry was speechless for a few moments, then a smile and a chuckle came to his face and said, "I'm ecstatic!" She threw her arms around him and kissed and hugged him tightly. "I'm so glad you're happy Henry," she said. She noticed while he was smiling there were tears in his eyes, she asked, "Why are you crying?" He said, "Well, I will probably see our child graduate college, but I doubt that my lifespan will go much past that, and that makes me sad." Sarah leaned into Henry and hugged him tight and held him for the longest time, as she began to cry with him.

Henry said, "Let's go out to eat to celebrate." Sarah nodded yes as she was still crying. She disappeared to the master bedroom to freshen up. While Sarah was in the bedroom, Henry had to pinch himself that after all these years, he was going to be a father. He knew not to get too excited too soon from his past experiences with Molly, but he couldn't help but get just a little excited all the same. When Sarah returned, he took her in his arms and gave her another soft, sweet kiss.

They drove to Louisville to a place on the river where there was music and outside seating overlooking the river. As a matter of fact, from the restaurant, they could look across the river and see their home. They celebrated with non-alcoholic beverages, a nice dinner and dancing to the music on the great lawn of the restaurant. It was a wonderful evening and they both were in bliss.

Chapter 73

Bad Boy

I t had been three years since Molly's death. Henry was a changed man during those years. He suffered dark depression, isolated himself from his family and had thrown himself headlong into his work. His sense of humor only rarely surfaced. His performance at work was stellar and he was doing extremely well financially. Emotionally, he was a wreck. After Molly's death, Henry maintained his friendship with Fiona. They went to dinners two to three times a week and after about eighteen months the relationship went deeper. Fiona had moved in with Henry a year ago and they had been living together since.

Their relationship started with friendship and evolved into an intense sexual relationship. After a year of living together, it was all about the sex. It was definitely a hedonistic existence. They were two needy people that eased their pain through physical intimacy. All Henry had by this point was intense work and intense sex. Their sexual exploits involved various role plays, sometimes they were strangers meeting in a bar and would flirt back and forth with each other. It was a lifestyle that Henry would never imagine for himself at any time in his life. He and Molly had gone through therapy to ensure a positive and healthy relationship and theirs had been a beautiful one.

While some would feel a life with an overabundance of sex would be pleasurable, especially men, it was physically and emotionally draining. They both kept trying to "top" the previous sexual experience. In the fourth year after Molly's death, Henry began to finally realize that he needed help. Although to some degree he loved Fiona, it was an unhealthy relationship for two of them. They went to therapy together and worked through separating and living on their own. It was a difficult transition with bouts of anger and tears on both sides, but they successfully separated while remaining friends. By the end of the relationship, Henry had lost a lot of weight and was suffering from migraine headaches. Professionally, Henry was still on a fast track to promotions, but he was mentally and physically spent, he was drained. He decided to make plans to resign his job in a few months and move back to the states and pursue a teaching career. He started putting back money to finance his move and put back enough money to live on until he secured a teaching position and pursued a master's degree in education.

He would leave London in the spring of 1999 for Louisville. He managed to leave the company on good terms. He shipped his possessions and his Porsche to a storage facility in Louisville. In May of 1999, he parted ways with the company. He and Fiona reunited for a weekend getaway before he left. It was bittersweet but they both were emotionally getting to better places in their lives. They would keep in contact for a couple of years and then would fade totally apart.

After graduating from college all those years ago, for some reason he couldn't really explain, he had kept renewing his teaching license. When he returned home, he contacted friends of his in various local school districts. He finally took a middle school social studies position and began working on his master's and getting a principal's license. After a year of teaching and obtaining his principal's license, a friend asked him to consider taking over a "mission" Catholic K-8 school in a financially challenged neighborhood in the west end of Louisville.

He interviewed with the board of the school after touring the building. There were broken windows, the interior was dirty despite a full-time custodian. The halls and classrooms had not been painted in years. Enrollment was decreasing, most student's families could not afford the tuition, the faculty was about ready to leave; it was a school that was dying. Whoever took the position would be charged with turning the school around. After a two-hour meeting with board members, Henry was told to wait in the hallway for a few minutes. After twenty minutes, he was called back into the meeting and was offered the job. His salary would be approximately one fourth of his last year's corporate compensation. The money wasn't a problem, Henry had invested well, made money from the sale of his home in Chicago, he was more interested in the challenge of turning the school around.

His first task was to meet with the faculty before they finished the school year and listen to them about their concerns. He scheduled a meeting with them after school one day and listened to the group's concerns. He came back the next day and met with them individually during their planning periods. He organized all their concerns into three categories; first the things he could definitely get accomplished, the second category those things that he could possibly get done, and the third category of things that would be near impossible at least in the short term. He only lost one faculty person, while the rest agreed to return for the next school year.

After speaking with the faculty individually and collectively he met with the group a second time to review their concerns and tell them what he could do immediately and what might take a while. The main thing the meeting accomplished was to demonstrate that everyone had been heard and a plan would be put in action. The faculty had three concerns; first was the custodian who did not do much work and they thought was a pervert, second the appearance of the building, and third the need for a counselor for the students.

Henry worked hard and diligently over the summer to get the school ready and to try and increase enrollment. He met with the custodian and the two agreed on a certain number of tasks to be accomplished in thirty days. When at the end of that period the tasks were not accomplished,

Henry fired the custodian with three week's severance and unused vacation pay allocated. He also found a benefactor to help fund the salary of a recent PhD child/school counselor for the school. Immediately upon hiring the counselor they set about calling in current students for testing to establish baseline IQ scores as no records of testing could be found in the school.

Having hired the counselor, fired the custodian, and hired two new custodians, he needed to improve the look of the school. The school had been a thriving institution in the 1950s and 1960s, but as the neighborhood changed, the school had lost its luster and enrollment had dropped. Very few in the neighborhood could afford the tuition. He set about uncovering prominent individuals in the community who had once attended the school. He met with a group of them at the University of Louisville club to pitch a tuition fund for students. Many were lawyers, businesspeople, and doctors who still had fond memories of the school and wanted to help. They raised commitments of $150,000 and put an application process in place.

Next Henry tackled the look of the school. He asked himself, why would you send your kid to a school that looked like it was falling apart? He found benefactors to supply windows, flowers, and shrubbery, and to supply paint to paint the halls, classrooms, and the exterior concrete foundation. He contacted a community service group with General Electric in town and they supplied 75 people for the day to do the painting, planting, and landscaping.

In the meantime, Henry was talking to media about the revitalization and attending any community fairs and gatherings so he could to promote the school. In the three months of the summer break, the school had been thoroughly cleaned and painted and all broken windows replaced. With the help of the counselor, each current student had taken the WISC (Weschler Intelligence Scale for Children). By the start of the school year enrollment had climbed from 125 the previous year to 160 for the coming school year.

Henry had one faculty position to fill for a sixth-grade teacher. A young girl, a recent college graduate. The poor girl was so afraid of the neighborhood, she came to the interview with her mother. Henry took the young lady to the newly renovated library for the interview. As they were talking, Henry saw a brick flying through the air coming through a newly replaced window. He excused himself from the interview, dashed out of the building and chased the kid down the street tackling him a block away. He called the police who took a report and took the kid home.

Henry returned to the library and the interview. He had torn his suit pants in the flying tackle. The interviewee's mother looked at Henry as he limped past her with torn pants and walked into the library. He finished interviewing the young girl and asked if she would like to see the classroom. He took her up to the second floor and opened the door for her. She looked around for a moment and said, "Mr. Morrison, may I ask a question?" Henry said sure. The girl asked, "Does the pigeon come with the room?" Evidently the hooligan had broken out an upstairs classroom window and a pigeon was sitting on the PA box. Consequently, the girl did not take the job.

Chapter 74
Dig It

Six months into her business venture, Sarah was enjoying success. She now had several clients on retainer, and she was mentoring Cheryl to handle some of the smaller clients on her own. Sarah, Isabel, and Cheryl were now functioning like a well-oiled machine. They were learning each other's preferences and idiosyncrasies and could very nearly anticipate each other's reactions and thoughts. Cheryl was attending more and more networking events at Sarah's suggestions and was learning how to develop business. She even had developed a couple of clients of her own.

As a partner in the business, Henry would usually drift in on Friday afternoons to catch up with the latest developments and offer advice in situations if he could. He was also a good source of contacts for the women to reach out to for future business. Henry was happy that the business was going well for Sarah. They were in good financial shape with most of the investment money still in reserve and untapped. Sarah was cautious with expenditures, nothing extravagant, just really what was needed. As she was now six months into her pregnancy, she had to start planning for leave time and how to transition the workload to Cheryl.

In the evenings, after work, Henry and Sarah still walked Betsy and talked about how life was going to change for them. After his business landed the deal in Africa, he would be spending one week per month on the continent for at least eighteen months to get things up and running and oversee the relationship. But when home, he said he would devote half of his day to childcare and possibly Sarah could work from home half a day or they could move to a larger home and hire a live in au pair. There were a lot of things to consider in the next couple of months. An au pair would cost approximately $20,000 per year but would allow for an immense amount of flexibility for the two of them.

At home one evening, they continued talking about an au pair. The more they talked about it the more it made sense. Together they decided to move to a larger home to allow for an au pair to have a side of the house with some privacy. They would contact an agency the next day and begin the process. It would be the best of both worlds. Sarah would have the flexibility to build her business and raise their child.

Chapter 75

For You Blue

A fter a year and a half at the Catholic school, Henry was called by the
Archdiocese to a meeting at the downtown office. When he arrived,
he met principals from five other "mission" schools from poor neighbor-
hoods. All the schools, including his, were dependent upon the Archdiocese
for financial support. Even though the enrollment at the school had gone
up, they were still operating in the red as were the other five schools.

The Superintendent of the Schools for the archdiocese invited the six
principals into his office. He looked somber as he sat down at his conference
table and invited the principals to please be seated. He started off by telling
them, "As you may be aware, there are multiple lawsuits against the archdiocese charging sexual molestation by former priests. The archdiocese must
reach settlements with the individuals. We therefore must find a way to cut
our expenses to meet these obligations." The superintendent went on to say
that the six schools that the principals represented would be closed and
their buildings sold to help reduce expenses. The principals would be out of
jobs if there were no other openings. Their teachers would be offered posi-
tions at other schools in the archdiocese. The principals would be offered a
six-week severance at the end of their contracts on June 30th.

The archdiocese would be saving close to six million dollars per
year, plus the proceeds from the sale of the buildings and property. The

principals were given a statement to read to their faculties and staff the next day and the news would become public in three days. Henry felt dejected for his team and his students. So much had been accomplished in a short period of time. The next day he called a faculty meeting after school and informed his faculty and staff of the decision. There were tears and questions but in the end nothing would change. He told the faculty of the process for contacting the principals at the remaining schools. The schools each had to make room for at least two extra teachers to accommodate the soon to be furloughed faculties.

Henry had an idea to work as a principal overseas and discovered a series of teacher fairs throughout the United States. He went to one in Houston, Texas and another in Carmel, California. He was offered a high school principal position in Hong Kong at an international school there. By the end of the school year all his faculty had been placed and he was going for a visit at the school in Hong Kong. Henry was now committed to education as a career for the next few years.

He would spend two years in Hong Kong, before the outbreak of the Severe Acute Respiratory Syndrome (SARS) virus broke out. The school was closed for the last three months of Henry's two-year contract. He moved back stateside and became a high school social studies teacher in a rural high school for the next seventeen years. He developed good relationships with many students who stayed in touch with him after they graduated and became lifelong friends. He officiated three weddings of former students, delivered two eulogies for former students, and walked one young woman down the aisle at her wedding over the seventeen years that he taught.

It was more than teaching to Henry; it was mentoring young people that he loved so much about the work. He taught his subjects; economics, world history, U.S. History, Political Science to be sure, but more importantly, he taught his kids life lessons and he always had an active listening ear.

Chapter 76

A Day in The Life 2

Near the end of May, Sarah gave birth to a beautiful baby girl. They named the child Emily Kathleen. Henry had never been happier. He had a wonderful and beautiful wife, a darling baby daughter, and a comfortable living all for which he was grateful. Henry and Sarah had sold the river house and moved into a larger home shortly before Emily was born.

Sarah took eight weeks off from work as Cheryl and Isabel held down the office. Henry's company was doing well, and he was spending one week a month in Africa, except for the two months that Sarah had taken off work. Seemingly, nothing could change this happy life.

It was Sunday evening and Henry had fallen asleep in his chair with Betsy at his feet. The phone was ringing and ringing and finally Henry awoke and answered it. It was his partner Jesse. "Hello?" Henry said. "Did I wake you, old man?" said Jesse. Henry told him, "As a matter of fact you did, what's up?" Jesse reminded him of their meeting and conference call in his car earlier that evening with their lawyer. Jesse asked a couple of questions and then hung up.

Henry was in somewhat of a fog. He looked around; he did not see Sarah. He was still in his river house. There was no big new house. He looked at the clock and noticed he had been asleep for three hours. He got up and walked around the house. He was alone. Everything had been a wonderful dream, now was the said awakening. Betsy looked up at him and wagged her tail. He said, "Alright girl, let's go for a walk." As he walked Betsy, he remembered parts of the dream were reliving past events, but everything involving Sarah had been fantasy, a wonderful and hopeful dream.

He walked Betsy through the village and returned about thirty minutes later. He gave Betsy her puppy treat and returned to his chair and his book. It was about 11 p.m. so he got a cup of coffee and returned to his book. He was reading Erik Larsson's new biography of Winston Churchill. After about forty minutes of reading, he dozed off again and returned to dreams of Sarah.

He was jolted awake by the sound of a female voice calling his name. He stood up and realized he was in what appeared to be his study, but this was not the river house. He looked around and what trying to figure out if this was another dream or not. He exited the study and followed the voice to a bedroom. He also heard a baby crying in the bedroom. When he entered the room, he found Sarah and a child in a crib near the bed.

It was Sarah, she said "Henry, can you take care of Emily? I have a meeting first thing in the morning." Henry replied, "Sure sweetheart, I'll take care of her." He bent down and gave Sarah a warm hug and a tender kiss and then went for the crying Emily.

Henry bent over the crib and picked up Emily. Eww! She needed changing. He took Emily to her room down the hall and quickly changed her diaper. He then took her to his study where he had a rocking chair.

He sat down in the rocker with Emily and he immediately began to sing to her. Henry only knew a couple of children's songs from his own childhood and often he would simply read to Emily whatever book he was reading himself. He began singing a song that his grandfather used to sing to him when he was a small boy.

Mother, mother give me 50 cents
To watch the elephant jump the fence
He jumped so high, he touched the sky

He didn't get back till the fourth of July
Mother, mother give me 50 more
To watch the elephant jump the door
He jumped so low he stubbed his toe
And that was the end of the elephant show

Henry was not particularly a good singer, he could carry a tune, but he had a baritone voice that seemed to soothe Emily. He though as Emily laid her head on his chest, it was the deep vibration of his voice and chest that soothed her, much like driving a child around in a car. After about fifteen minutes, Emily was fast asleep in Henry's arms. He quietly carried Emily back to her crib and gently laid her down. He stood there for a few minutes just enjoying watching this little miracle sleep and imagining all the things to look forward to in her life.

Henry slowly undressed and crawled in bed next to Sarah and cuddled her. Morning came way too soon. He heard Sarah getting a shower and he got out of bed and quietly went to the kitchen to get breakfast for her. Luckily, Emily was sleeping very soundly. As was their routine, Sarah worked from 7:30 a.m. and came home at noon, when Henry would go into the office and work until 5 pm. This routine would change slightly when they found a qualified Au Pair.

Chapter 77
I Am the Walrus

Sarah loved being married to Henry. He was her mentor, he was thoughtful and loving, and he was great with Emily always doting on her and ready to do whatever she needed doing. But she sensed that underneath all of this, Henry had a sadness and a loneliness that no one could reach. It wasn't anything that he said or didn't say, but it was often an expression or a look in his eyes.

The other evening, after Emily was down, they watched the Fred Rogers film that starred Tom Hanks *"A Beautiful Day in the Neighborhood."* He cried from almost the beginning and will not talk about it. She had seen that look even when he appears to be happy and in a crowd of people. Sarah wished deeply to help Henry. One day she was in his office looking for something and there on the desk was a note pad. While Henry was okay with technology, he very often wrote things out longhand first. On the pad was drawn a table with four playlists for his iPad. His musical choices somewhat revealed to her what he was thinking about himself.

He listed two versions of playlists for his own funeral, a playlist of his favorites, and lastly a short playlist labeled Henry's soul. The note pad looked like this.

Funeral Version 1	Funeral Version 2	Henry's Soul	Favorites
Eternal Father Strong to Save	*Nimrod (From the Enigma Variations, Elgar)*	*I Go to Extremes Billy Joel*	*Ironic Alanis Morrissette*
Abide with Me	*Eternal Father Strong to Save*	*Time Stand Still Rush*	*In God's Country U2*
Morning Has Broken Cat Stevens	*Abide with Me*	*Hand in my Pocket Alanis Morrissette*	*Zombie The Cranberries*
Far Away Places Johnny Cash	*How Can I Keep from Singing*	*All Things Must Pass George Harrison*	*Hand in my Pocket Alanis Morrissette*
Amazing Grace	*Dvorak Symphony No.9 II "Largo"*	*I Still Haven't Found What I'm Looking For? U2*	*I Still Haven't Found What I'm Looking For? U2*
How Can I Keep from Singing	*All Things Must Pass George Harrison*		*Message in a Bottle The Police*
Bridge Over Troubled Water			*Linger The Cranberries*
Here Comes the Sun			*Bitter Sweet Symphony The Verve*
			Every Breath You Take The Police
			Saturday Night's Alright for Fighting Elton John
			Sympathy for the Devil The Rolling Stones
			Synchronicity II The Police
			Here Comes the Sun The Beatles
			Nowhere Man The Beatles
			Eleanor Rigby The Beatles

Sarah thought to herself, there is even a sadness in his music play-lists. Loneliness and angst and fatalism. She began to feel a deep ache for her husband, and she wished there were a way that she could help him. Why all this sadness and loneliness? She remembered the scenes from the movie that seemed to move him the most, it had to deal with one of the main character's mother and father. Somewhere inside, he was hurting.

If she wanted to apply amateur psychoanalysis she thought of the lyric of the songs. The Police *Message in a Bottle* ends with *"sending out an SOS,"* repeated over and over several times. Then there was U2's song *"I Still Haven't Found What I'm Looking For"*. And George Harrison's *"All Things Must Pass"*, the acceptance of death as a season of life. What was it that drove Henry to make these choices? Did they need marriage counsel-ing? Sarah didn't think so. Maybe she would try to get Henry to talk about his playlist selections. She believed Henry needed to talk to somebody, because this loneliness and sadness had to be eating him alive.

Before she left Henry's office to go back to Emily, she began to cry over her husband's sadness and loneliness. She went to Emily's room, picked her up and held her in her arms, sat down in the rocker and rocked her dear daughter and cried.

Chapter 78

Martha My Dear

Henry awoke the next morning to a quiet house. Emily was still sleeping, and Sarah would be getting up in a few minutes. It was 6:00 a.m. He started the coffee and went to get Betsy for a morning walk. He noticed this morning that Betsy was slow to awake when he came near and had a bit of a hard time getting up. He put the leash on her collar and the two went out the front door. Since they were in the new house, their walk routine was a bit different. There was a wooded trail nearby that gave them about a two-and-a-half-mile round trip.

Henry also noticed that Betsy wasn't moving as quickly as she normally does. He hoped there was nothing wrong with her. He made a mental note to keep an eye on her the next few days and let Sarah know to do the same. They walked the trail in much slower time than normal, and Henry realized he was going to have to make an appointment with the vet for old Betsy.

When Henry and Betsy returned from their walk and after Betsy had been given her treat, Henry joined Sarah and Emily for breakfast. Emily was happily being fed by mom. After Emily was fed, Sarah put her down for a few minutes. When she returned, she said to Henry, "Are you dying?" Henry responded with surprise, "Sarah, what did you just say?" Sarah responded tersely, "You heard what I said, are you dying?" Henry answered, "No and why would you ask that?" Sarah explained that she had been in his office and noticed the playlist that he had written and two were for his funeral.

Henry answered that he did not want to leave things to Sarah to take care of and "He was not a spring chicken." He told her except for his heart disease and blood pressure, which was controlled, he was fine. She asked about the other playlists like Henry's soul. He told her that was part of an exercise that he used in graduate management classes. He explained to her that you basically identified your life by five songs, five books, and five movies. He thought his five songs said a lot about what he thought about life. He believed his first song selection, Billy Joel's *"I Go to Extremes"* as he tended to either go full force after something or at a very slow pace and nothing in between. The others: George Harrison's *"All Things Must Pass"* which he attributed to a fatalistic view of life and its seasons, Rush's song *"Time Stand Still"* about growing older in a sense. It was his last selection that Sarah questioned, it was *"I Still Haven't Found What I'm Looking For"* by U2. As for the last song, Henry explained that with his career and life, he always felt that he could do better or achieve more and that left him with a feeling of sadness and not being a success.

"Sarah, I'm not dying, and I am happy with you and Emily. I couldn't ask for anything better," said Henry. Sarah came closer and held Henry tightly in her arms and kissed him on the cheek. "Me either," she said. Sarah added, "By the way the agency I have been working with have identified a potential au pair for us. They are sending the information about her and then if we like, they can arrange a Zoom meeting." Henry was enthused about getting an au pair, as that would allow Sarah to be at work more and allow Henry to be of more help to the guys with the startup.

Henry called the Vet to make an appointment for Betsy. Luckily, they had a cancellation this afternoon just after Sarah would be coming home, so she could take care of Emily while he took Betsy to the Vet. When Sarah came home from work at 12:30, Henry put the leash on Betsy and took her to the Land Rover and drove the short distance to the Vet's office. The

Vet examined Betsy, took X-Rays, and found a mass around her heart. The Vet told Henry she wanted him to take Betsy to a Vet Cardiologist and had arranged for Betsy to be seen immediately. The cardiologist's office was in Louisville about thirty minutes away. Henry led Betsy out of the Vet's office, placed her on the back seat of the Land Rover and they drove to the specialist's office where they were immediately seen. Dr. Jackson, the Vet Cardiologist, performed tests beyond x-rays, using equipment that is used to scan the hearts of human beings.

Dr. Jackson reviewed the results with and interpreted them for Henry. Tragically, Betsy had a tumor that had wrapped around her heart. The humane thing to do would be to put Betsy to sleep. Henry was heartbroken and began to sob. Dr. Jackson apologized and handed Henry a tissue. She told Henry that before long, Betsy would develop severe problems breathing, and simply would not have the energy to carry on and would die. It would be rough on Betsy. He told Dr. Jackson that he did not want to put Betsy to sleep in a clinical office, but at home where she belonged and felt comfortable around people who loved her.

Henry reached down and hugged his sweet companion and kissed the top of her head. He put her leash on and led her slowly out of the exam room and to the Land Rover. He lifted her gently into the back seat and they started for home. Tears flowed down Henry's cheeks for the entire twenty-minute drive home. They pulled into the garage and Henry lifted her from the car and gently placed her on the ground and they walked into the kitchen from the garage to be met by Sarah.

As they came in the kitchen Sarah was there. She could see immediately from the look on Henry's face and the tracks of his tears that something was seriously wrong. "What's wrong sweetie?" said Sarah. Henry replied. "It's not good, we're going to have to put Betsy down soon. There is a tumor wrapped around her heart." Sarah said, "I'm so sorry honey." She gave him a big hug and held him for a while as he wept. She then bent down, and hugged Betsy and Sarah began to cry. Henry told Sarah about the Vet that the cardiologist told her about, who will come to the house to put Betsy down. The question was how long will they wait to put her down.

Chapter 79

I'll Cry Instead

L ate in the evening, Henry received a call from his former Honk Kong
student Rajiv in Los Angeles. Rajiv had finally gotten around to review-
ing the proposal that Jesse and Henry had made a couple of months previously and was now ready to negotiate and sign a contract. He needed Jesse
and Henry to come to Los Angeles the next week for talks. Henry said he
would call Jesse and arrange a day the following week and schedule the
flights. Rajiv said he should plan on spending two days in Los Angeles.

Henry said to Sarah, "Can your mother watch Emily for a couple of
days next week? Jesse and I need to meet Rajiv for a couple of days in LA."
Sarah replied that she was sure her mother would love the time with Emily.
"Great!" said Henry. "I'll call Jesse and get it scheduled." After talking with
Jesse, they decided they would leave on Wednesday the following week and
return on the red eye flight the following Friday evening.

"You know this means we are going to have to put Betsy down
before I go?" said Henry. Sarah acknowledged Henry. The next morning,
Wednesday, Henry called the Vet who euthanized animals in their home
environments and arranged the euthanasia of Betsy for Saturday afternoon.

On Saturday afternoon, Dr. Brown arrived. She was a lovely woman;
very tall, about 40 years old, and very dear and compassionate in her manner. Henry led Dr. Brown into his office where Betsy was lying almost

listless in her dog bed near Henry's chair, where she nearly always was when Henry was home. Dr. Brown carefully explained the procedure to both Sarah and Henry. Betsy would first be given a sedative to let her sleep peacefully. When Sarah and Henry were ready, pentobarbital would be given through an IV to stop her heart. Betsy would not suffer any pain. Henry and Sarah said they understood, and Henry went into a discussion with tears running down his cheek of why Betsy had to be put to sleep and why he felt it was important to do it at home. It was as if he was trying to justify it to himself. Sarah watched her husband as he did this feeling sorry for himself thing and that he had to go through all of this with his dear sweet dog, his friend of nearly fourteen years. Dr. Brown asked if Betsy had a favorite toy or blanket. Henry said she had both and went to get them. When he returned, he had a red and blue plaid blanket, and a piece of something furry and purple. He told Dr. Brown that the blanket often lined Betsy's dog bed in the winter and the piece of purple was what was left of her favorite toy for many years her "purple monkey." Basically, it was the trunk of the monkey and its tail.

Dr. Brown explained that they would lift Betsy up and place the blanket under her and afterward she would wrap Betsy in the blanket. Henry placed the purple monkey near Betsy, and she took it in her mouth. With all the preliminaries explained, Dr. Brown asked if they wanted Betsy to be cremated, which they did. Dr. Brown asked if they were ready to begin.

Henry sat on the floor and placed Betsy's head in his lap. Sarah sat on the floor next to Henry, placed her arm around him and petted Betsy. Dr. Brown explained that she was inserting the IV which would give Betsy a bit of a sting. With the IV inserted, she explained that the sedative was now going through the IV to allow Betsy to gently go into a deep sleep. She would be able to feel the pets and hear their voices. When Henry and Sarah were ready, she would administer the pentobarbital to stop Betsy's heart. Afterward, she would leave the room and give Henry and Sarah as much time as they needed with Betsy. When they were ready, she would wrap

Betsy in the blanket, with her toy and remove her to her car. Her ashes would be ready in about a week.

Betsy was sleeping now. Henry just looked at her, bent his head down and said, "Goodbye old and best friend. I love you Betsy." Henry was sobbing and Sarah was crying when Henry looked at Dr. Brown and said, I'm ready. With that, Dr. Brown administered the pentobarbital. A few minutes later, it appeared that Betsy had stopped breathing. Dr. Brown put on her stethoscope and listened for a heartbeat, there was none. She looked at Henry and Sarah and said, "I'll go into the next room until you are ready."

Henry hugged his faithful companion and friend and cried some more. Sarah just hugged them both. After about fifteen minutes, he called the doctor back into the room. Dr. Brown carefully wrapped Betsy in her favorite blanket and her purple monkey and carried her to the car. Henry walked her out to the car, still crying.

Chapter 80

Flying to LA

The following Wednesday, still grieving over his beloved dog Betsy, Henry boarded the flight to LA with Jesse. The two were flying to meet Rajiv and another member of the board of his company about doing location tracking in Africa. They knew they're technology capabilities, but they were interested to know the details of the project that Rajiv and his partners had in mind.

When they arrived in LA at about 11:00 a.m. they went straight to their hotel (the Westin near the airport) to check in and get lunch. They had a 2:00 pm appointment with Rajiv and the President of his company, Jeff Mueller, to hear the details of the Africa project. They would be meeting at Rajiv's home in Hollywood Hills. After lunch at a restaurant on Sunset Boulevard, they placed Rajiv's address in the car's GPS and proceeded to Rajiv's home. They pulled into the driveway next to a Maserati and a BMW. Their eyebrows raised over the Maserati and they walked to the front of the house and rang the doorbell.

Rajiv answered the door and welcomed them both into his house. He took them on a tour. The home was one story visible from the road with an expansive sub level (not quite what you would call a basement) that opened to a beautiful swimming pool. In a den on the sub level, Rajiv introduced Jesse and Henry to the President of the company, Jeff Mueller. Jeff was a commercial developer by trade and a multi-millionaire by income. Jeff was affable, enthusiastic, and gracious as he wanted to fix lunch for the two visitors.

After thirty minutes of chit chat and Rajiv and Henry catching up, Rajiv began to explain the project or projects as there were several. Several central and south African countries had formed a trade group (modeled on the EU) to move the continent towards first world status. They collectively were going to build three to five trade ports. Rajiv and Jeff believed that the location service that Jesse and Henry offered would fit nicely with the project. In fact, it was ideal. Jesse explained that they had the ability to custom design a tracking system that would "ping" devices in the shipments every five minutes to determine location. A lot of problems with shipments in Africa had to deal with corruption and pieces of shipments going missing.

After three hours of discussion and questions, Jesse and Henry were asked to draft a proposal and tentative contract to present the next afternoon at 2 p.m. The meeting broke up and as they were leaving, Rajiv suggested they buy swim trunks for the next day and plan to stay for dinner. When they got to the car, Jesse did a Google search for the closest Target and they proceeded there to buy swim trunks.

On the way back to the hotel, Jesse said, "Let's relax for an hour, have dinner, and then work till about ten on the proposal and then work in the morning to finish the draft."

Chapter 81

Do You Want to
Know a Secret?

S arah was preparing to leave for an appointment with her OB-GYN that Wednesday morning. Mom was staying with them for a few days to help with Emily. Her appointment was at 10 and was a follow up to an appointment she had two weeks before. She had gone to the doctor after she tested positive on one of those home pregnancies tests. Today's appointment would confirm her suspicions.

Driving to the appointment, she couldn't help but think about how happy he would be to be having another child. It would mean they would have to work out a new schedule with the Au Pair to help with the children. After all, she was building a business and Henry was still working, but he would be aging as the kids grew up. He would want to be involved as much as possible in their lives, but as he got older, he would have to conserve and prioritize his energies.

Sarah only had to wait about twenty minutes to see Dr. Brewer, who confirmed that she was in fact pregnant. She would probably have waited until Henry got home to give him the news, but right now Henry needed good news after having to put Betsy to sleep. He was so sad looking the last few days after he lost his best friend. She resolved to call him that evening, mindful of the time difference.

At 6:30 p.m. that evening, Sarah called Henry to give him the good news. Henry answered the phone sounding very tired (9:30 p.m. in LA). Sarah said, "Hello sweetheart, are you working hard?" Henry replied, "As a matter of fact, Jesse and I are still working on a proposal." She apologized for interrupting their work and Henry told her he was going to call her about 8:30 her time. Henry said laughingly, "You are a pleasant diversion honey, considering I've been looking at Jesse all day." She laughed and said that she had some news to share with him. She said, "Are you sitting down?" Henry said, "Are you okay?" (thinking she was ill or had an accident). "I am more than okay Henry, I'm pregnant!" said Sarah. "That's great, you're pregnant! That's great, Emily will have a little brother or sister," replied Henry. "Are you really happy sweetie?" said Sarah. Henry answered that he was over the moon.

Chapter 82
The End

The next morning, Henry was tired and extremely happy. He couldn't sleep for his happiness about having another child. Today, hopefully, he and Jesse could pound out some sort of contract with Rajiv and Jeff. He and Jesse worked for three hours that Thursday morning to wrap up their proposal. They were to meet for lunch and dinner today at Rajiv's house and swim as well today.

Just before noon, they got into the rental car and headed out to Rajiv's house in the Hollywood Hills. As they walked in, they could smell something cooking in the kitchen. Rajiv led them to the dining room where Jeff had prepared a simple lunch of grilled cheese sandwiches and tomato soup. The four of them sat down to lunch and pleasant conversation and then talk about the Africa project.

After a full afternoon of work, drafts of contracts, and agreements, they had dinner (steaks prepared by Jeff) and they hopped in the pool. By 9 p.m., after the swim, Henry went around the dining room table to type out a final contract. The company would receive an initial $100,000 for feasibility work and a $20,000 monthly retainer for their work. This would require Henry and sometimes Jesse to be in Africa a week to ten days every six weeks to manage the project on the ground.

By 11 p.m. after a congratulatory round of drinks, Jesse and Henry headed back to the hotel. They had an 8 a.m. flight back to Louisville in the morning. When they returned to the hotel, they both went to their rooms, packed their bags, and went straight to bed.

Henry arose at 4 a.m. unable to sleep. He felt horrible when he awoke. His body was aching, his joints felt achy, he was tired, and felt like he had the flu. He also had tightness in his chest and arm. As he was up and moving around, he seemed to feel a bit better. Probably just angina he thought to himself, no need to worry Sarah or Jesse. He showered and shaved and then put the last of his things in his bag and headed to the lobby to meet Jesse and then on to the airport. When they reached the American Airlines counter, Henry paid to upgrade their seats to first class. He thought to himself, "If I'm feeling bad, I might as well be as comfortable as I can be."

Henry still had his American Airlines Admirals Club membership up to date, so they could go to the club room and wait comfortably there for their flight. As they were waiting Jesse asked, "Are you feeling okay Henry?" "Sure, why do you ask?" he replied. Jesse told him he looked pale and his forehead had beads of sweat. "No, no, I'm fine, just really tired. This was a quick and intense trip," replied Henry. While they waited, they reviewed their visit, the contract that was agreed upon and the upcoming work to be done here and with the government in Africa (eSwatini).

After about 30 minutes, it was time to get to the gate and board the flight. Jesse noticed that Henry was walking a bit slower and holding his left arm. After they boarded and took their seats, Jesse thanked Henry for paying for the upgrades to first class, it was a pleasant treat. The flight attendant asked if they wanted a drink. Jesse took coffee and Henry ordered a Mimosa before the flight.

As they rolled down the runway, and before liftoff, Jesse noticed that Henry was already asleep. The flight was smooth. Jesse listened to an audiobook on leadership and Henry continued to sleep. About 45 minutes away from landing, Jesse noticed that Henry was awake and noticeably in pain and holding his chest. Jesse hit the flight attendant call button and asked if she could find a doctor on board the flight. There happened to be a doctor three seats away that noticed the commotion and heard the word doctor. The doctor unbuckled his seat belt and moved up to help. It was clear to the doctor that Henry was in cardiac distress. He asked the flight attendant to let the captain know to have an ambulance waiting on the ground when they arrived in Louisville. Jesse knew that Sarah would be waiting at the airport for Henry, so he called her to let her know what was happening. "Sarah, it's Jesse, Henry is having cardiac trouble. There is a doctor on board the plane attending to him and an ambulance will be waiting at the airport," Jesse said. Sarah was upset and in a shaky voice made sure Jesse knew which hospital to take Henry; Norton Brownsboro and she would await them there.

Sarah was at work when Jesse called. She had 30 minutes until the flight landed. She called her mother to let her know the situation and that she would be going to the hospital right away to meet Henry when he came into the emergency room. Sarah gathered her things and rushed to the hospital.

Aboard the plane, the flight was just a few minutes away from landing and an ambulance was waiting on the tarmac to rush Henry to the hospital. Henry was hurting, the doctor on board tried to ease Henry's pain and keep him stable until the plane touched down and the ambulance crew came on board.

The flight landed just a few minutes ahead of schedule. As it taxied to the gate, the passengers notice the flashing lights of the ambulance waiting for the plane to park. The plane taxied short of the jetway and a set of stairs was wheeled to the front cabin door. As the plane rolled to a stop, the captain announced that all passengers should remain seated as there was a medical emergency on board. Shortly after the announcement, the cabin door opened, and the ambulance crew boarded the plane. The crew assessed Henry and removed him on the airline's wheelchair that fit down the aisle. Once off the plane, they transferred Henry to a stretcher and into the ambulance followed by Jesse.

Sarah was waiting at the emergency entrance at the hospital as the ambulance arrived. She tried to grab Henry's hand as the gurney wheeled by. A nurse prevented her from entering the ER suite and said a doctor would be out soon. Jesse came by her side and hugged and said, "Henry will be fine; he's weathered lots of storms and he'll weather this one too," he said. They sat and waited together.

Chapter 83

After 15 minutes, Dr. El-Refai (a cardiologist on call) came out to speak with Sarah. He said to Sarah, "Your husband has had a massive heart attack and we are taking him to the Cath lab to see what has been done to the heart and what we can do." "Oh Jesse, he just got good news and was so happy and now this," said Sarah. Jesse asked, "What was the good news?" Sarah replied, "I'm pregnant."

TO BE CONTINUED....